Sinful Passions

The Anarchy

~Book Three

ANNA MARKLAND

Cover Art by Steven Novak

"There is a charm about the forbidden that makes it unspeakably desirable."
—Mark Twain

Dedicated to my Grace Anne with love

CHAPTER ONE

Ellesmere Castle, Salop, England, July 1153 AD

This argument is a waste of time," Suannoch declared. "Prince Henry Plantagenet will be our next King."

Rodrick de Montbryce bristled, as did most of the men gathered in the gallery of Ellesmere Castle. Even Bronson FitzRam, whose sister had made this shocking pronouncement, seemed outraged.

Rodrick's irritation grew when his twin sister, Grace, smiled broadly, obviously amused by the discomfort of the men. He was compelled to reprimand her. "Suannoch is a mere girl of eight and ten years, a visitor at that, who is not qualified nor entitled to speak in such a manner. Don't encourage her."

"Imagine!" his sister replied gleefully, looking to the rafters. "The stir she's caused in the air has made the banners waft a little."

That Suannoch FitzRam was shrouded from head to toe in the white robes of a novice, her face squeezed into a red ball by the tight coif, only served to compound Rodrick's indignation. "And to stand warming her *derrière* by the hearth as if she were a man—"

"Hush!" Grace admonished. "If the pout she's sending your way is any indication, you spoke too loudly, brother dear."

His visiting Northumbrian relative had raised his hackles, but it was good to be sparring with Grace again. He'd missed her since her marriage. He regretted it was widowhood that had brought her home, but she seemed to have taken the loss of her husband in stride. Rodrick was aware the marriage hadn't been a love match. Victor de Cullène had been more of a father figure than a husband. It saddened him she was now considered too old to marry again. She'd have made a wonderful mother.

Bronson glared at his sister. "Your pardon, uncle," he said to Rodrick's father, Gallien, Earl of Ellesmere. "Suannoch has a habit of not minding her tongue. She takes after our aunt Ragna."

The novice pursed her lips and returned her brother's glare.

Strangely, Bronson's eyes darted to Grace and his face reddened.

Rodrick smirked. "It irks that these northern cousins have been invited to join this family gathering on the eve of one of the most important meetings ever hosted at Ellesmere Castle. They don't belong at an assembly of barons and lords from every part of the country who are coming here to discuss the civil strife tearing England apart."

Grace shrugged. "The FitzRams are cousins, but at least twice removed, and half cousins at that. I assume Bronson addresses Papa as uncle because of the difference in their ages."

Rodrick agreed. "If I recall correctly our red headed cousin is a mere three years older than we are. Strange he shares your hair color. They aren't here to attend the deliberations, although the FitzRams are wealthy Northumbrian landowners and Bronson will doubtless have valuable insights to offer on the situation in the northern reaches."

Grace eyed Bronson. "He says the reason for his presence is twofold. He's journeyed to the Marches to take possession of Shelfhoc Hall, bequeathed to him by his late uncle Edwin, and to deliver his sister to the convent at Whitchurch."

Their father graced Suannoch with a smile Rodrick recognised as one of his indulgent Earl smiles. "Not at all," he replied to Bronson's apology. "I hope you will be at the meetings tomorrow."

To Rodrick's amusement, the girl bristled at the implication she would be not be welcome at the morrow's assembly. Did she imagine her opinion would be consulted? As the conversation turned to Shelfhoc Hall, he studied her. Confinement to a nunnery probably hadn't been her choice. It was the fate of many young women whose husbands-to-be got themselves killed.

Did Suannoch mourn her betrothed, killed in a skirmish with King Stephen's soldiers? The wimple and coif did nothing to enhance her features, but she had good skin—fresh, healthy looking. Her fingers were long, elegant. The robe smothered the remainder of her body, rendering it impossible to tell if she had decent breasts.

Something stirred at his groin when he noticed she was staring back at him. He straightened in the chair, brushing at nonexistent lint on his doublet.

Get your thoughts back on the conversation and the upcoming meeting.

"I was named for Lady Ascha Woolgar."

Again, every eye swivelled to Suannoch who had taken a seat next to Rodrick's mother.

The Countess put her hand on the girl's. "You're right, my dear. Your second Christian name is that of your great grandmother."

Suannoch's eyes widened, their amber brilliance catching him off guard. He noticed for the first time the contrast between her dark eyebrows and the white of her wimple. Perhaps her hair was black. She beamed a smile that transformed her heated face into a thing of beauty, renewing the interest in his *couilles*.

"Yes, she was the lady of Shelfhoc."

Rodrick wavered between scoffing out loud and revisiting his indignation. He threw up his hands. "Is she unaware it was Ascha Woolgar who gave birth to our great grandfather's illegitimate son?"

Now Grace glared at him. "Keep your voice down. Caedmon and his family were welcomed as Montbryces and he accepted the Norman patronymic FitzRam."

Rodrick wrinkled his nose. He was never rude to guests, no matter how tiresome, but this chit of a girl was an irritating cocklebur. He scratched the back of his neck.

Gallien de Montbryce gave the novice another indulgent smile. "It's important to be proud of one's ancestors. My half uncle Caedmon aided in the rescue of *oncle* Robert many years ago, and saved my father's life in Italy. Without his bravery I wouldn't be here today."

Rodrick felt badly. Perhaps he should be more tolerant of these FitzRams. After all, he and Grace and Bronson and Suannoch shared a great grandfather, a hero of the Battle of Hastings, Ram de Montbryce.

Suannoch wished cousin Rodrick would stop staring. Had he never seen a nun before? And what was the reason for his scowl and the rude remarks he'd made to his sister? She'd met Grace earlier in the day when the women of the household had welcomed them with genuine warmth, and liked her immediately. She was relieved Grace wandered over to sit beside her now. She leaned close to her cousin's ear. "I can understand why the older men might object to my asserting my opinions, but your brothers are young men. William and Stephen seemed interested and slightly amused by my comments, but Rodrick simply glared."

Grace put a hand on hers and smiled. "Mayhap being the heir to an Earldom means a man has to affect a serious demeanor."

Suannoch chuckled. Grace had spoken loudly enough for her twin to hear. She decided to compound his obvious discomfort. "If he smiled he might be considered handsome. He's certainly tall, and strong looking."

"Do you think so?" Grace asked, staring at her brother. "I never noticed!"

They laughed out loud, but her body heated. She regretted taking a seat too close to the hearth. Her face was burning. The cursed robes were heavy for summer, and why was a fire necessary anyway? Her gaiety fled. How to bear the coarse fabric against her skin for the rest of her life?

What gave her intended father-by-marriage the right to demand she be shut up in a convent because his son Hiram had been killed?

Poor Hiram—more poet than warrior.

She ached at the terror he must have endured during the brief skirmish he hadn't survived. She wasn't in love with him, but he deserved a better fate than the one imposed upon him by his father.

Now the pompous, overbearing man had sealed her fate too. Her parents had protested, her mother heartbroken, but Cuthbertson had the ear of King David of Scotland. Sir Aidan FitzRam would have a difficult time indeed holding on to Kirkthwaite Hall without the king's benevolence. There was certainly no hope of support from the English monarch, Stephen, a man who had turned out to be a weak king, unable to summon enough support among England's barons to effectively counteract his cousin Maud's invasion fourteen years before.

Now England endured two governments, Stephen's in Westminster and Maud's headquartered in Devizes in the west. Both issued their own coinage and edicts aplenty—none of which were obeyed by the thousands of mainly Flemish mercenaries who had taken advantage of the anarchy to rape and pillage the English countryside, finding refuge in hastily constructed fortifications. The rule of law had dissolved.

Grace's voice jolted her. "Do you believe Maud should have been made queen as her father, King Henry, wished?"

Suannoch snorted. "I do, but the opinions of women counted for even less back then. The English barons were outraged at the notion of a woman being Queen in her own right."

Grace sighed, casting a sideways glance at her mother. "You know my father was one of the leaders of the movement to support Stephen's claim to the throne?"

"Yes, and I'm sure he regrets it. Powerful men such as uncle Gallien have been unable to prevent England sinking into a morass of despair—a broken land."

The Countess leaned closer. "My husband is aware that if it wasn't for the traditional cessation of hostilities during Lent and Advent, the whole country might have gone up in flames. Thousands have already died of starvation, their crops burned, villages destroyed."

Suannoch wondered what the Earl truly thought of his precious Stephen after nearly two decades of civil strife. Would he switch allegiance at the assembly on the morrow? One could only hope. She hesitated to ask Grace, who probably wasn't privy to her father's opinions. Indeed she'd be surprised if the Countess would attend the meeting. At least Bronson would be there. Perhaps her dear brother's keen mind might affect some change. And his participation would give her a day or two's reprieve from the convent. She was grateful he had insisted the Mother Superior allow her to visit their nearby relatives. At least at Shelfhoc he wouldn't be too far away. Would he be permitted to visit her?

These thoughts seethed through her brain as she watched the men talk on and on and the women nod politely. "Am I the only one who sees the injustice and folly?"

Grace shook her head. "No, you're not," she replied quietly.

It was some consolation. "Can they not see Maud's son Henry is destined to be king?"

"Patience," Grace said, taking her hand. "We'll find out on the morrow. I'm for bed. Walk with me."

The men seemed to breathe a collective sigh of relief as they left. When they reached her chamber Grace pecked a kiss on her cheek and bade her goodnight.

She curled up on her bed. Surely Christ and his saints would awaken from their slumber and realize Stephen's son, the brutal and murderous Eustace, was not fit to wear the crown his father seemed determined to pass on to him.

She smiled at the recollection of her prickly cousin's discomfort, suddenly seized by an inexplicable urge to stretch like a languid cat. He might be a typical male, but he was attractive.

What did it matter? Her life was over. No use getting hot and bothered over the likes of Rodrick de Montbryce.

CHAPTER TWO

A s her maidservant assisted with the removal of her gown, Grace de Cullène mused happily that it had been a long time since she'd enjoyed an evening as much.

"It's a relief to be back at Ellesmere," she confided to Lucia, the maidservant who'd been the only bright spark in dark times.

"It was a difficult year of mourning," Lucia replied, unpinning her mistress's hair, "for all of us. What a dreary place. I'm glad to be home too."

Lucia had been born in Ellesmere and had missed her family as much as Grace had missed hers. "I was happy to deed Cullène Hall to my stepson." She shivered. "Godefroy would probably have plotted some way to do away with me had I not satisfied his thirst for the estate."

Lucia pulled the bone comb through her tresses. "I fear you are right, milady. He's a sidekick of the cruel Prince Eustace."

"He's welcome to Cullène, and I'm relieved to be free of him and the house. Papa succeeded in getting my dowry lands back, so he won't get his greedy hands on those. I don't blame him for wanting the estate. He was assured of it until I came along. Do you recall upon first arriving how full of the enthusiasm I was, ready to enliven the manor house with refurbished tapestries, rugs, banners?"

Lucia snorted. "The whole house needed a good scrub."

"But Victor would have none of it, content to wallow in the same dusty dankness he'd apparently enjoyed for years."

Guilt lay heavy in her heart. She had at times wished for his death during the three years of their marriage. To this day she wasn't sure why she had agreed to it. She supposed she'd thought him charming, wise, an older man who would protect her. And why had he married her? Certainly it wasn't for the pleasures of the marriage bed. He lavished more attention on his Steward than on her.

She'd cried on her wedding night, left alone in her bed. She admitted now it wasn't because she'd wanted him to bed her. Indeed she'd feared it. She'd sobbed out her isolation and the dread of long, lonely years ahead.

Godefroy likely labored under the unfounded fear she would get with child and he'd be disinherited.

No one but she was aware she was still a maiden, though Lucia probably suspected. She intended to take the knowledge and her maidenhead to the grave, filled with a strange guilty relief that she had failed to appeal to her husband. Never again would she put herself under a man's thumb. Men were repellent—although Bronson FitzRam had caught her eye this evening. That hair! Redder than her own. She closed her eyes, conjuring a vision of him with war braids framing his strong face.

"Did you happen to see my cousin from Northumbria?" she asked her trusted servant, wondering why it had suddenly grown warm in the chamber.

"The nun?" Lucia replied, her eyes full of mischief.

"No," she exclaimed, swatting Lucia's *derrière*. "You know who I mean."

"You're blushing, milady," her maidservant teased.

Grace rose abruptly. "Fetch my nightgown, bad girl. It's a passing fancy. Seems to me I recall something about him being married."

Lucia slipped the nightgown over her head. "There's no wife with him now."

For some reason she was suddenly lightheaded. "Turn down the linens, then leave me. I was happy this night, and I want to savor being free."

After Lucia left, she sat in the chair by the hearth for a while, wiggling her bare toes. Yes, it was good to be home, and after she had fulfilled her responsibilities to her father's guests on the morrow, she would start to enjoy her freedom. She crawled into bed thinking it was a pity Bronson FitzRam would be occupied in the assembly. They might have gone riding together. He would be a pleasant companion—and safe. After all he was her cousin.

Bronson tossed and turned, sleep eluding him. It had been an unsettling day. He'd disliked the Superior at the convent on sight, which only aggravated the bile in his belly when he thought of his sister incarcerated in the cold place.

The woman wanted to give Swan's clothes to the poor. The idea of his mother's beautiful handiwork being torn to shreds for rags by some impoverished peasant was too much. He'd insisted on taking the garments, suspecting her true plan was to sell the stuff to some local noblewoman.

She'd also balked at the notion of Swan accompanying him to Ellesmere, until he reminded her who their powerful relatives were.

In a day or two he'd have no option but to deliver his spirited sister back into the hands of the crone. He understood Swan's turmoil, but did she have to behave so outrageously, flaunting her opinions, as if they mattered? She was right, of course, and was only repeating discussions they'd had with their father many times, but her demeanor had certainly riled Rodrick de Montbryce.

And meeting Rodrick's sister had been a shock. He'd long since buried his male urges with two wives who hadn't survived bearing his stillborn children. He was determined never to endure such pain again, but Grace's hair, as red as his own, had caught the attention of his shaft. Strange how she had inherited her mother's hair coloring, yet looked exactly like her dark haired twin. It was a potent mix.

But she was a widow, and his cousin. He wouldn't be living too far away at Shelfhoc. It was unlikely she'd marry again. Perhaps they might prove to be good company, one for the other.

CHAPTER THREE

Rodrick entered the crowded Great Hall an hour before midday, apprehensive as to the outcome of the Assembly. His father hadn't confided his decision to him, though as the next Earl he would have to live with the consequences. But he would support his father.

He felt great empathy for the dilemma Gallien de Montbryce faced. It was one understood by every man in the Great Hall. They had declared for Stephen in the year of our Lord Eleven Hundred and Thirty Five, believing he would be as strong a king as Henry Beauclerc. The Montbryce's had even named a son for their king. Time had proven them wrong. Over the last few years he had watched his father's frustration and disillusionment with Stephen intensify.

As luncheon was served, his gaze wandered over the men assembled in his home. Powerful barons, yet they had been powerless to remedy the dire situation in which England floundered. The hubbub caused by their discussions was deafening.

When the luncheon was over, the women left the Hall while the trestle tables were being removed by servants. It suddenly occurred to him the intelligent females of his family had much to contribute to the discussion. However, he was certain his mother would have made her opinions known to her husband, and Grace was never hesitant to inform their father of her thoughts. Aurore was the quiet one in the family. It seemed that was often the way for the middle child.

Suannoch FitzRam bestowed a glowing smile on William and Stephen as she left, but didn't look his way. Strangely disappointed, he was further incensed when several of the belching barons elbowed each other, arching their brows as their eyes trailed after the departing novice. The prospect of any one of them laying a hand on her—

A vision danced behind his eyes—Suannoch, naked except for the cursed wimple. How to discover the color of her hair? Her name sounded like *swan*. Did she have a long graceful neck like the royal bird? What a coincidence she wore white!

A hush had fallen over the assembly. He dragged his thoughts back to the gathering. His father had risen from the lord's chair on the dais.

The presence of many anxious and impatient men, all lavishly dressed and recently fed and watered, had made the Hall intolerably hot and malodorous. He pinched the bridge of his nose in an effort to alleviate the ache in his temples and elsewhere.

His father cleared his throat. "Fellow nobles, my sons and I welcome you to Ellesmere. We recognise the journey has been perilous for many of you."

Robert, Earl of Leicester came to his feet. "Aye! You're lucky here to be somewhat removed from the Midlands where a man cannot walk abroad in the light of day without being accosted by foreign brigands. Peasants are starving, serfs are forced into arms by landowners seeking to protect their estates, leading to a dearth of workers to tend the land."

Gallien raised his hand. "Happy as I am to see you here, Robert, I intend first to make my remarks, then I welcome discussion."

Robert harrumphed but regained his seat.

"All of us face a dilemma of enormous proportions," his father began. "Our great families own lands in England and Normandie, ancestral lands, lands stained with the blood of many of our forebears."

Try as he might, Rodrick couldn't think of a single Montbryce who'd died in defence of any of the castles and manors they controlled in England or Normandie. Cousin Alexandre had successfully repelled Geoffrey's attacks on Montbryce Castle, thanks in large measure to a new rampart built to protect the precious orchards the Angevin had once put to the torch. But the words rang true for many in the Hall who'd lost sons in the struggle for Normandie.

"When our good King Henry died, we believed Stephen was the man born to be king of the English and Duke of Normandie. He was a grandson of the Conqueror, wealthy, charismatic, and capable. He'd grown up at Henry's court, been a favorite of the King. We supported him though King Henry had coerced our forefathers to swear for Maud."

"Aye, but once he had the throne he alienated his supporters," someone shouted.

Hushed murmurs of agreement crept around the Hall. Treason was treason after all.

Gallien didn't continue until silence reigned once more. Pride soared in Rodrick's heart. His noble father had reason to be resentful of Stephen's apparent inability to see that he had over and over again slighted some of his most faithful supporters. Yet he stood now, dignified and seemingly unperturbed by the diplomatic revolution taking place in their midst.

"You all recognise me as an ardent supporter of Stephen. When Maud's half brother, Robert of Gloucester, abandoned our king and declared for Maud, I was outraged."

Rodrick, nine years old at the time, well remembered his father's anger.

"A year later, Ranulf of Chester betrayed Stephen and captured Lincoln. We admired our king's determination to retake the stronghold. Do you recall our anguish when Robert of Gloucester joined the fray and routed our monarch, taking him prisoner?"

Murmured *ayes* did little to break the oppressive silence. Rodrick had wept into his pillow at the thought of his king in chains.

"The imperious Maud then declared she was *Lady of the English*—whatever that meant—and attempted a coronation in Westminster."

Laughter greeted this remembrance. All recognised Maud's abrasive nature had soon alienated the people of London who'd run her out of the city.

"They chased her to Oxford, where she took refuge, but she became a prisoner there, pinned down by Stephen's forces."

"She may have been pinned down but her half brother launched an attack on Winchester."

"And look what that decision got him. Capture by Stephen's army."

Rodrick had long thought that had Stephen's capable wife Matilda not taken charge of her husband's army he might have languished longer in prison instead of gaining his freedom in a prisoner exchange. Gloucester's life for Stephen's.

As the volume of voices grew, Rodrick feared his father had perhaps lost control of the gathering, but a simple gesture brought attentive silence once more.

"Then Maud showed us courage we didn't think she possessed. She escaped from Oxford, alone and on foot, wrapped in a cloth of white that concealed her passage through fields of snow."

"Eight miles to Abingdon she walked," someone observed. "In December."

Gallien continued. "And for ten years now, we have suffered two governments, both equally incapable of enforcing the rule of law, and David holds sway in Northumbria."

He gestured to Bronson who voiced his agreement. "With no English king to stop him, David has claimed Cumbria and Westmoreland too, but the Scottish king believes in order, and from what you're saying, life is more secure there than here."

Rodrick wasn't sure if his father appreciated Bronson's observations. To suggest a barbaric Scottish monarch might be a superior ruler to Stephen would once have bordered on heresy in the Montbryce household.

Gallien assumed control again. "On top of our problems in England, we have the situation in Normandie."

Rodrick's heart ached for his father. This would be the difficult part.

"I have no love in my heart for Maud's late husband, Geoffrey of Anjou and most of you know why."

Wooden benches scraped against stone as men shifted their weight. Some coughed.

"However, I won't dwell on that story now."

A collective sigh of relief soughed through the Hall.

"To my everlasting regret I persuaded my cousin in Normandie, Alexandre, *Comte* de Montbryce to switch his allegiance from Maud to Stephen years ago."

It was likely most of those present at the gathering were aware of the other reason Alexandre had changed sides—to save the lives of the Scottish widow he married and her children.

"After years of valiant opposition to his armies, our homeland fell under the control of the red headed braggart from Anjou. You are all aware my beloved wife came from that cursed land, and therefore I do not subscribe to the legend that all Angevins are descended from Satan's daughter, Melusine, but I have to wonder about Geoffrey."

"Your *beloved wife* would have something to say if you perpetuated the myth that such fiendish blood still bubbles in the veins of her descendants," someone shouted. This remark was followed by loud laughter.

Gallien chuckled, nodding, and was on the point of continuing when a voice declared, "But we don't have to travel far back in time to see the corruption in Geoffrey's bloodline."

"Aye," another said. "His great grandfather had his own wife burned at the stake in her wedding dress on suspicion of adultery with a goatherd."

A dark cloud settled over Gallien de Montbryce's features. Rodrick held his breath. This was too close to the bone. Did men not think before they blurted things out? He watched his father struggle to regain his composure, relieved when he spoke again in a calm voice. "Aye. Fulk the Black's reputation as a perverted rapist and plunderer reached to the Holy Land. But enough of this talk of Anjou. We've had to live with the reality that three years ago Geoffrey declared his son Duke of Normandie, a title Stephen clings to still, though he hasn't visited there in more than a decade. We are in the untenable position of paying homage to two lords for the same land."

If it had occurred to anyone to question Gallien's reference to Normandie as his homeland, there was no sign of it. But all were aware he was the second generation of the Anglo-Norman Montbryces to be born and brought up in England.

"Alexandre, titular head of our family, had to recognize the rule of a man he loathed, until the Good Lord in His infinite wisdom took the Angevin to his eternal rest eighteen months ago."

Robert of Leicester stood again, his impatience evident in his scowling features. "We are well aware of this history, *milord* Earl. Many of us are in the same predicament. We fought Geoffrey for years while he tried to take Normandie, bit by bloody bit, but he was victorious. Normandie is lost to the Plantagenets. The decision we face now is how to solve the failure of either Stephen or Maud to rule successfully here. When Stephen's demoralised forces refused to fight for him at Malmesbury in January, it became evident that he doesn't inspire the confidence of the barons. Maud has more or less given up and gone back to Rouen, leaving her son to fight Stephen. God forbid Eustace take his father's place. Then we'll be in worse straits. I'm for the upstart Prince."

Rodrick's mouth fell open. How had Suannoch known the direction the discussions would take?

The Hall was in an uproar. Gallien called repeatedly for order, and calm was eventually restored.

"Let us take a look at this Prince who would be king," he said calmly. "Is he a prince, or merely the son of a land grabbing *Comte* from Anjou?"

"He's the son of an Empress, grandson and namesake of King Henry," one baron shouted.

Gallien held up one finger. "A true prince then. Has he proven his prowess on the battlefield?"

This was greeted by hoots of laughter. Rodrick wanted to contribute to the discussion. "He was a mere lad when he first came to England, yet he led an attack against Stephen."

His father smiled. "Yes, and it was a complete failure because Henry had no money to pay his mercenaries. Stephen paid them off and sent the boy packing back to Anjou."

Rodrick jumped to Prince Henry's defence. "But the point is he was willing to fight. And King David knighted him."

"David is his grand uncle."

"But later the same year he relieved the town of Devizes after Eustace laid siege."

"A brave soldier then," Gallien confirmed, holding up two fingers.

There was general agreement.

Rodrick took a deep breath. "But we also need to consider the power he now wields. Since his marriage to Eleanor of Aquitaine, he controls vast territories that stretch to Spain and encompass more lands than those of the King of France, though Henry is his vassal— Normandie, Anjou, Maine, Blois, Touraine, Aquitaine."

Gallien narrowed his eyes at his son. "It seems you deem him a fit candidate to be king."

Was his father testing him?

Rodrick clenched his fists. "I do. I have long feared what might happen if Eustace inherits the Crown."

Gallien smiled as he put his hand on Rodrick's shoulder. "Good, I agree."

Robert of Leicester thrust his fist in the air. "As do I."

Pandemonium broke out. Several barons stormed out of the Hall. Others rallied around Gallien and Robert as they clasped arms to seal their new alliance.

CHAPTER FOUR

News of the outcome of the Assembly traveled quickly along the halls and corridors of Ellesmere Castle. It permeated the chapel where Suannoch knelt in silent prayer, her only remaining hope that God would somehow intervene and she'd be spared a life of religious discipline.

Obedience had always come hard. Perhaps it was because of her willfulness that she was being punished. But to never ride a horse again, never to feel the wind on her face as she and her siblings galloped across the moors of Northumbria; never to set eyes on her beloved family, to savor the warmth of her mother's kiss on her cheek; never to know the love of a man, the fulfillment of children. It was unbearable.

For the umpteenth time, she contemplated escape, but where would she run? And Cuthbertson would likely punish her parents if she fled.

Excited whispers among the handful of kneeling servants jolted her from despondency. Ellesmere and Leicester had chosen to support Henry. She smirked, filled with a notion to seek out Rodrick de Montbryce and stick out her tongue at him.

Perhaps the evening meal in the Great Hall might not be the tedious event she had dreaded. The Earl had graciously invited her and Bronson to sit at the head table, an honor considering the illustrious guests who would be present. With any luck she might get to sit beside Rodrick. Then there'd be opportunity to irritate him further with her insights into the wretched state of England. Bronson wouldn't be happy, but she had little time left to speak her mind.

Yes, Rodrick would be a worthy adversary who would likely challenge her solely because she was a woman. But at least it would be conversation, a chance to be herself for perhaps the last time.

It was getting hot in the chapel with all the excitement. She made the sign of the Savior across her body, rose from her knees, and hurried to her chamber. Bronson had balked when the nuns had proposed giving her clothing to the poor. It was difficult to imagine a peasant decked out in her fine wools and silks.

Everything was in his trunk in the chamber next to hers. She doubted he'd locked it. Why not enter the Hall in her own clothes? She wasn't a nun yet. Geography alone had caused her and Bronson to stop at the convent first.

They'd barely exchanged a word in the two hours it had taken them to ride from Whitchurch to Ellesmere. He'd only grunted when she'd thanked him for insisting she be allowed to visit her relatives before entering as a novice. It hadn't hurt that the relatives were a powerful Earl and his family.

It was the first time she'd visited Ellesmere, the castle built by her great grandfather. It was impressive, much bigger and grander than Kirkthwaite Hall, though her home was the largest manor house in the vicinity of the village of Bolton. At the end of the last century, the same great grandfather had seen to the rebuilding after its destruction by marauding Scots.

As she hurried along the corridor, dodging servants lighting torches, she contemplated the strange twists and turns of destiny that had brought her to this place. She wished she'd met the great Ram de Montbryce. Did Rodrick resemble him? According to her father, all Ram's sons had taken after him, including her grandfather Caedmon.

But the present Earl had silver grey hair, perhaps because of his age. Apart from the difference in their hair color, Rodrick did resemble his father.

She'd been told often enough she looked like her aunt Ragna whom she'd met more than once during visits from Denmark where she lived with her husband and family. Suannoch failed to see the physical resemblance, apart from their fair hair, but recognised the same stubborn traits in her aunt that she was often chided for. Ragna had confided gleefully her family had nicknamed her the *Wild Viking Princess* because of their Danish heritage on their mother's side.

What would Rodrick think of her blonde Danish hair when she showed up in the Hall without the cursed wimple and coif? A gurgle of excitement bubbled up in her throat, taking her breath away. She'd obviously hastened too quickly along the corridor in the heavy habit.

She shook off her irritating preoccupation with Rodrick de Montbryce as she tapped lightly on Bronson's door.

From down the corridor, Grace espied Suannoch knock on Bronson's door, then enter. It seemed strange because she was sure he wasn't in his chamber. She tiptoed to the door and put her ear to the wood, then eased it open. She cursed the Steward for not making sure the hinges were oiled. Suannoch, kneeling by her brother's trunk, looked up sharply, her arms full of clothing—women's clothing. For a moment Grace wondered if there was something about Bronson she hadn't suspected, but her fears were quickly allayed when Suannoch scrambled to her feet.

"Please don't raise the alarm. I'm not stealing anything. These are my clothes. I thought to wear them one last time."

A glint of something in her cousin's eyes—despair, mischief, rebellion—touched Grace's heart. Why not? Here was a taste of adventure for them both. She grabbed a pair of shoes from the trunk and relieved her cousin of the chemise. "You'll need help. Come to my chamber."

She scurried back to the door, opened it cautiously, and signalled to Suannoch. Giggling, they ran to Grace's chamber, their arms full. No sooner had she shoved her cousin through the door when Bronson appeared, coming down the corridor. Her throat constricted as her lungs stopped working. She tried to control it, but a loud laugh escaped. She gripped the undergarment and shoes to her breast, sweating with excitement. "Ladies' things," she gurgled. "Just ladies' things."

He looked at her as if she'd lost her wits as she stumbled backwards into her chamber and slammed the door.

Still puzzling over his cousin's strange behavior, Bronson entered his chamber. Women were odd. A man never knew what they might do next. He stripped off the shirt he'd worn all day and decided to rest for a few minutes before dressing for the evening meal. He was on the point of dozing off when a perfume he'd noticed somewhere else wafted into his nostrils. It was the scent of a woman. Grace?

He sat up on the end of the bed, inhaling deeply. Perhaps he'd been mistaken. The Earl's daughter wouldn't set foot in his room. Would she? For what purpose?

Attributing his suspicions to fatigue, he lay back down, putting off getting changed until his unexpected arousal had subsided.

CHAPTER FIVE

A handful of dissenting barons left the castle immediately after the decision, but a greater number rallied to support Ellesmere and Leicester. By the time everyone gathered in the Hall for the evening meal, the two Earls had managed to calm most of the fears of those who remained undecided. Rodrick marvelled at his father's ability to smooth ruffled feathers.

He was confident he could follow in his father's footsteps in that regard. It wasn't only Gallien's physical features he'd inherited, though praise be to the saints his hair hadn't turned white like his father's.

But then Rodrick had never suffered the extreme misadventure that had befallen his father in his younger days. If he ever married and discovered on his wedding night he'd already been cuckolded, his hair might turn white too. Fortunately, the shrew had died and Gallien de Montbryce had been betrothed to Peridotte de Pontrouge.

Rodrick considered he was outgoing, affable, a good conversationalist. People generally seemed to like and respect him. He furrowed his brow, suddenly recalling the scene in the gallery when his Northumbrian cousin had ruffled his feathers. He hadn't handled the situation well. He'd allowed a chit to get under his skin, a girl who might have the body of a boy under the voluminous white material—though he somehow doubted it.

Espying two young noblemen of his acquaintance searching for seats, he hastened over to welcome them, intending once they were settled to speak to Steward Bonhomme. The servants needed to let the fires die down. The stifling heat was making him sweat.

He noticed his brother William and Bronson FitzRam conversing confidently with Robert of Leicester. It was generous of his father to have welcomed the northern cousins to sit at the head table. He hoped Suannoch wouldn't be seated next to him. Where was she anyway? Evidently Bronson hadn't accompanied her to the Hall.

Normally there'd be no danger of getting stuck next to her, but the arrangements had been changed to allow for Robert of Leicester to sit at the head table. Rodrick had ceded his place at his father's right hand.

Of the two, he'd prefer to be paired with Bronson. At least then he might enjoy an intelligent conversation.

His mother entered in the company of Grace and his younger sister, Aurore. He wandered over to join William's little group, watching with pride out of the corner of his eye as the three beautiful women were greeted by visiting barons.

Leicester slapped him on the back. "Well spoken today, young Rodrick. You'll make a fine Earl when the time comes."

William laughed. "Aye, but let's hope that time doesn't come too soon."

Rodrick feigned a blow to his brother's belly. "Right!"

Bronson offered Rodrick his hand. "I agree. It took courage to declare your opinions when you didn't—"

He withdrew his hand quickly, seemingly choking on his words and his face reddened considerably as he stared in the direction of the entry doors. Rodrick frowned, worried his cousin was having an apoplectic fit. He turned to look at what had stunned Bronson into silence.

A young woman had entered the Hall. No wonder his cousin had been struck dumb. She was easily the most alluring blonde he'd ever seen. Her fair hair was covered with a modesty veil, but its transparency revealed luxurious tresses that fell around her shoulders.

She held the copious skirts of her deep red gown in long, delicate fingers. He licked his lips as his hungry gaze traveled to the bodice that clung to perfect breasts then continued to her incredibly long elegant neck. She was a majestic swan, smiling regally at the handful of noblemen who fluttered around her like courtiers wooing a queen. Her smile sent blood rushing to his groin.

Bronson suddenly catapulted himself in the woman's direction. Rodrick would be damned if he was going to let his cousin claim her attentions. He hurried to catch up.

The beauty frowned as they approached. There was something vaguely familiar about the frown, the flashing amber eyes.

"Suannoch, what is the meaning of this?" Bronson spluttered.

Rodrick's feet were suddenly stuck to the stone floor, rendering him immobile. This vision of female beauty was Suannoch?

A maelstrom of conflicting emotions ran rampant through his brain, churning his gut. He wanted to fall to his knees and tell her she was lovely, then pick her up and whisk her off to his bed.

But she was a nun. Wasn't she?

This was a travesty. Here was a woman of great beauty who exuded passion. He would move heaven and earth to spare her imprisonment in a convent.

But then the sky fell in on his head. This incredible creature was his cousin. It was wrong to desire her, a sin in fact.

She stared at him, obviously enjoying his discomfort, while Bronson continued his tirade through gritted teeth. He had to do something. Teetering on the edge of a precipice, he reached for her hand. "Swan," he murmured, brushing his lips across her warm knuckles, inhaling her fresh scent. A jolt of desire turned his already hard shaft to granite. Without thinking, he entwined his fingers with hers and in a raspy voice he barely recognised, said, "It would be my pleasure to sit beside you at table."

When Rodrick whispered *Swan*, his husky voice echoed from her hand into a very private place in her body. It was startling. She'd certainly never experienced such a jolt of desire with Hiram. The servants should douse the fires in the hearths. It was much too warm in the overcrowded Hall. Perhaps the red velvet hadn't been a good idea. Still, it was preferable to the habit.

However, she was confused. "Bronson has obviously revealed the nickname my closest family and friends call me."

He frowned as if she was speaking Greek, so she babbled on. "It's a sobriquet bestowed upon me since childhood because of my long neck and the coincidence of the sound of my name."

His mouth fell open, his gaze fixed on her neck.

"My Scottish mother suggested they baptise me Suannoch because as a newborn I slept a lot. They evidently hadn't enjoyed such good fortune with the rest of their brood."

At last something she had said seemed to penetrate his addled wits and he smiled. Was he making fun of her?

The possibility of sitting with Rodrick had loomed like a jagged rock before a listing ship. Yet it was as if her dearest wish had come true as he escorted her to the dais, his warm fingers entwined with hers. What had happened to the prickly cousin who apparently couldn't stand her when she was shrouded in a nun's habit? Her outspokenness had offended him, but he craved her attention now he'd seen her clad in her favorite gown.

She chuckled inwardly, recalling the expression on his face when he'd first noticed her in the doorway. Had he drooled? Then it was as if he'd been struck by lightning when he realized who she was.

She had to admit to a sense of relief that he hadn't turned away. Ignoring her spluttering brother, he'd shooed away the other noblemen clustered around her like pesky flies.

Poor Bronson followed them to the dais, still scowling. She had put him in an awkward position. But he would forgive her. He always did.

However, his irritation sobered her. Rodrick would probably be like most men, with the exception of her father and brothers, who thought women should be seen and not heard. Well, they'd see.

What was she thinking? This attractive, well-muscled man with the smoldering ice blue eyes was her cousin. It was a sin to feel drawn to him *that* way.

She had no choice now but to sit beside him. This was her last night of freedom and she intended to relish it. Outspokenness would soon curb his interest. This wasn't the time to fall in love with a man, especially one she could never have. Being shut away from her family would be hard enough.

She missed his warmth when he withdrew his hand once she was seated, but was relieved not to be reliant upon her trembling legs when he twirled his finger in a curl at her temple and said, "Your hair is fair."

Given her dark eyebrows, Rodrick had daydreamed of his cousin as a redhead, as a brunette, as a raven haired beauty—never as a blonde. Yet now he couldn't understand why he'd thought she'd be anything other than fair haired. Without the confining coif, her face had transformed into a vision of stunning beauty—high cheekbones, long eyelashes, a perfect nose, and that neck! It begged for his kisses. He would start at the top under her chin and work his way down over her throat to the pulse throbbing—

Bronson's whisper in his ear brought him back to earth. "My sister has appeared dressed this way without my permission or knowledge. I trust your father has guessed this?"

He glanced along the table. His father, seated in the lord's chair, was indeed eyeing them curiously. His mother had a strange smile on her face. It seemed the attention of everyone in the Hall had been drawn to his behavior, including Robert of Leicester. He was drowning in the oppressive heat. He smiled weakly at Swan, cleared his throat loudly, and took his seat, suddenly regretting the impulse to have her sit next to him.

Bronson evidently intended to sit on the other side of his sister, but William appeared from nowhere and elbowed him away with a wink.

"Mind if I sit with Suannoch?" he asked innocently.

Bronson frowned but moved to another seat.

Rodrick was grateful for his brother's quick thinking. Two Montbryces flanking a beautiful woman would seem normal. But woe betide William if he thought to court the lady.

This insane spurt of jealousy convinced him he was losing his mind. Conversation normally came easily. Now not a single word emerged from his parched throat. He took a swig of wine from the goblet a servant had filled, then felt badly; he should have offered it first to Swan.

"My apologies," he stammered, wiping the lip of the goblet with his napkin then holding it out to her.

Instead of taking the goblet, she leaned forward with a smile and sipped, turning her amber orbs on him as she drank. The pleasurable ache at his groin intensified. The slow movement of her throat as she swallowed drew his rapt attention back to her neck. He was doomed.

William coughed.

Swan seemed to become aware of what she was doing and her face reddened.

"Thank you, Rodrick," she whispered, her voice thick with wine.

Was she flirting with him, deliberately trying to make him look foolish in retaliation for his earlier behavior?

He shifted his weight on the bench to ease his discomfort, but she moved restlessly at the same moment. His thigh grazed hers. She looked away quickly as her blush deepened, seemingly as confused at what was happening between them as he was.

"You are very beautiful, Suannoch. I apologise for my rudeness yesterday."

She kept her eyes fixed on the table. "I understand. Sometimes I forget women are not supposed to express opinions to men. You were preoccupied with what might transpire at the meeting."

He suspected her *forgetfulness* was more deliberate than not, but for some reason he didn't fully comprehend, he acknowledged with regret the truth of her words. Men resented women who spoke their mind. Yet Grace had proven on many occasions to have been the one in the right when they'd argued. He was a twin, born minutes after his sister, but he would be the one to inherit the Earldom because he was a male, whereas she'd been obliged to marry a man twice her age.

In hindsight, if Maud had been crowned Queen eighteen years ago, it was improbable she would have made a worse job of it than Stephen had.

"You were right, of course. It's more than likely Henry Plantagenet will be our next king."

She finally looked up, her eyes full of concern. "We cannot overlook Eustace, however. King Stephen has groomed his son to succeed him."

Rodrick leaned back to allow a servant to place a platter of roasted chicken on the table, then sliced off a piece of breast and offered it to Swan. "Saints preserve us if the murderous prince becomes king. He has grown up knowing nothing but division and war. His appetite for blood does not bode well for England. The argument between Stephen and the Pope has resulted in Eustace not yet being anointed as co-king, which is a good omen."

She bit into the meat while it was still in his hand, smiling self consciously as the juices trickled down her chin. He handed her a napkin, his errant tongue slipping between his lips, ready to lick her face clean.

"Grace told me he is pillaging towns and villages near Bury St. Edmunds," she said.

"Yes. He claims he's acting in retaliation for his father's rain-drenched and demoralised army refusing to fight Henry at Malmesbury in January, but it's generally believed he enjoys killing and burning. It's one of the reasons I've leaned towards Henry for a while."

Her eyes widened. "And yet you mocked me when I made my remarks concerning him."

Rodrick chuckled. "I'm a man. What can you expect?"

Her mouth fell open. "I know you are a man, Rodrick."

The heat of her thigh pressed against his, but he caught William's slight shake of the head. He looked around the Hall. They had again attracted attention. "Swan, I'm drawn to you," he whispered. "I've enjoyed our discussion, but we are causing a stir. I don't want people to think—"

A cloud darkened her bright eyes. "We are cousins, Rodrick. Cousins are permitted to be friends, to laugh, to share good times. Nothing can come of our friendship anyway. You are safe. On the morrow I am to be shut away."

Suddenly *safe* was the last thing he wanted to be. Inexplicable anger rose in his throat. "Do you want to go to a nunnery?"

"Of course not," she said through gritted teeth. "I want to live, to ride across the open moor with the wind in my hair, to hug my family, to love a man and bear his children. But such is not my destiny. Hiram sealed my fate when he fell, mortally wounded. This charade tonight was to be my final act of defiance. When the meal is done, I will return to my chamber and don the robes of a novice."

A dangerous idea came to him. "Would you like to ride once more before the dawn?"

Grace had been disappointed not to sit with Bronson. It would have been a chance to get to know him better. After all, they would be neighbors—practically. She could have teased him about assisting Suannoch.

If William hadn't butted in and taken their cousin's place—

Her little brother might want to impress Suannoch, but he'd have a difficult time getting her attention away from Rodrick.

Who knew the novice-to-be was such a beauty! Certainly her brother hadn't guessed until tonight.

Her Northumbrian cousin was destined to be shut away in a nunnery, a worse fate than what she had endured at Cullène Hall. And Suannoch would never be free. They'd had fun together and it had been amusing watching Bronson and Rodrick fall over their tongues. Her cousin would have made a much needed friend.

She poked William. "It's a pity Bronson had to drag his sister away on her last evening of freedom."

Her brother eyed her curiously. "I suppose."

Something in his tone alerted her. "I would think she'd rather be here than tucked up in bed. She and Rodrick seemed to have taken a liking to each other."

William flushed—a sure sign he had a secret to keep.

"Speaking of Rodrick, where has he got to?"

Her brother put a finger to his lips. "Hush. They've gone for a short ride."

Without me?

She struggled to control the rapid beating of her heart. Why hadn't they asked her to go too? She and Rodrick used to ride together all the time. In her absence had he forgotten the good times they had together, what they meant to each other?

She was being silly. They were no longer children. Rodrick was a man, with a man's needs—but with Suannoch? Or had he simply taken two cousins riding to show support? Had Bronson gone along as a chaperone, or was it a friendly threesome? Then why not a foursome?

She came to her feet, then sat down again. She wasn't sure how long they'd been gone. Dangerous to follow alone, in the darkness.

As she sat dithering, she noticed a messenger enter the hall. He'd ridden far by the look of him. He made straight for Robert, Earl of Leicester, bowed, and handed him a parchment.

Robert unfurled it, scanned the contents, then leapt to his feet with a loud "Hah!" that caught everyone's attention. He brandished the document. "Wait till you hear the news from Scotland."

CHAPTER SIX

Swan relished the warm summer wind on her face as they cantered across the plains of Salop, headed west towards Oswestry. Her fine gown would be ruined after this, but she didn't care. Caution tempered her desire to let the horse have its head. Such uncertain terrain was sometimes treacherous in full daylight. She was free, riding by the light of the moon with her dear brother and a man for whom she was developing intense feelings.

Bronson's ready acquiescence in Rodrick's scheme had taken her by surprise, but he had never made any secret of his unhappiness with her fate. William too had wanted to accompany them, but Rodrick had persuaded him to distract their parents' attention.

Bronson and Swan had left first, Rodrick not far behind. They rendezvoused in the stables. The ostler didn't blink an eye when his lord's son picked out three horses to be saddled, hastily rounding up a couple of stable boys to assist.

If the heir to Ellesmere was shocked when she hitched up her skirts and straddled the palfrey, he gave no indication of it other than a slight smile. Bronson rolled his eyes. "That's Swan for you."

She and the horse knew each other well. They'd grown up together and she intended to enjoy this last ride. "Thank you, Rodrick," she said, patting her mount's neck. "You don't know what this means to me. It's an unexpected pleasure to ride Cob one last time."

He laughed. She loved the way he laughed, tossing his head back, a mischievous glint in his eyes. "Your palfrey's name is Cob?"

Bronson joined in the laughter. "What else would a swan name her horse?"

In their youth Rodrick and Grace had often ridden out together. It was always a competition. He loved his sister, and she would have enjoyed this ride, but the idea of letting her lead the way never occurred to him.

Now he was content to watch Swan ride ahead of him and Bronson, her moonlit hair streaming in the wind like a banner, bared legs pressed to the horse's flanks. "She's quite something," he said to himself, blinking when Bronson responded, "Yes, she is."

He cast a sideways glance at his companion. The full moon emphasized the clench of Bronson's jaw. "You're not happy about the nunnery."

"Not happy? I'm furious, livid, resentful. Swan is a woman made for a man. She'll be buried away. It's against nature."

"There's no way to avoid it?"

"Believe me, I have racked my brain for a solution. Cuthbertson has the power to turn King David against my parents in the blink of an eye. It would break my father's heart to lose Kirkthwaite Hall."

Rodrick recognised the implications for all Montbryces of the loss of the FitzRam's ancestral home. Their great grandfather had arranged for it to be rebuilt for Caedmon and his wife, Agneta. He'd never been there, but had heard often enough of its grandeur. "There must be a way to counteract his influence. I'll speak to my father."

Bronson reined in his horse and looked at Rodrick through narrowed eyes. "Why?"

Rodrick halted his mount, his thoughts confused. "I care for her."

Bronson snorted. "You mean you want to take her to your bed. It's a common failing of men who meet Swan."

The pleasant hardening at his groin bore out Bronson's words, but there was more to it. "I can't deny I'm attracted to her, cousin, but I want more. I enjoy her company, her intelligence, her spirit."

Bronson exhaled resignedly. "You've spent exactly four hours in her company. Yesterday you abhorred her."

Rodrick smiled. He appreciated a man who spoke his mind. "Yesterday she was a shrewish nun. Today she's a goddess."

Bronson shook his head. "I won't lie to you. She can sometimes be devilish."

His cousin's warning only intensified his arousal.

Bronson laid a hand on his arm. "If you are serious, I will aid you, but it won't be easy. You and I and Swan—we're half second cousins, only linked by our common great grandfather. But many will cry foul and accuse you of consanguinity if you pursue her. She has been hurt enough. You must be sure."

A strange calm settled in Rodrick's heart as he watched Swan ride back towards them, a happy cherub come down from above. He was sure. He'd never been so drawn to a woman. "I will speak to my father before dawn."

"What are you two plotting back here?" Swan asked breathlessly as she came abreast of them. "I'd have ridden all the way to Wales if I hadn't noticed you weren't still behind me."

The lightheartedness fled when neither of Swan's companions smiled in response to her jest. "What's wrong? I'm sorry I rode off. I thought you were right behind me."

Cob became nervous when Rodrick suddenly dismounted and came to her side. He put one hand over hers, the other on her bare knee. She glanced at Bronson who had definitely seen their cousin's unseemly action yet said nothing. Her heart stopped beating as Rodrick's hand stroked her leg. She managed to squeak, "What's going on?" out of her dry throat.

"Look me in the eye, Swan," Rodrick commanded. "I intend to speak to my father to help me devise a plan to keep you out of the convent."

She stared at him, not comprehending his meaning, but unwilling to douse the spark of hope in her breast. "I don't understand."

"Our cousin fancies he's in love with you," Bronson explained.

She looked into Rodrick's eyes, expecting to see amused denial, but her heart leapt into her throat at the sincerity on his face. It broke her heart. Why now? "This cannot be," she cried. "We are cousins."

Rodrick reached up, put his hands on her waist and lifted her from the horse. The breath wooshed from her lungs when he pulled her body to his. "We are second cousins, Swan, and half second cousins at that. If you tell me you feel for me what burns in my heart for you, I will move heaven and earth to remove any impediments to our union."

Her treacherous hips wanted to press against the evidence of his desire. She'd seen her brothers naked when they were children but didn't recall anything of the size and hardness of the flesh nestled against her mons. Heat flooded her despite the evening chill creeping off the moor. Her knees threatened to buckle. The impulse was to agree, but was it only that Rodrick offered a means of escape, slim though the chances were. Did she yearn for him, or for freedom?

The brush of his warm lips against hers dispelled any doubts. She melted into him, opening readily when his tongue coaxed entry. She savored his taste, drank of his moisture, inhaled his breath as their tongues mated.

Bronson cleared his throat. "I take it that's a yes."

Rodrick cupped her chin. "Good enough for me," he breathed.

Bronson's emotions were confused. A vision of Grace emerged behind his eyes as he watched the smoldering passion erupting between his sister and Rodrick. Why hadn't he told his cousin he suspected she'd been in his chamber and had aided in Swan's game?

His companions were oblivious to his presence. They had set out as a threesome, now he was superfluous. If Grace had accompanied them—

Better not to harbor thoughts that led nowhere. The rapidly developing relationship between Rodrick and Swan would cause enough uproar. Grace was attractive, beautiful, but still she was his cousin. And a widow. Had it even been a year since her husband had died?

This was all moot. He had sworn off marriage. God had taken two wives and two children from him. He was destined to be alone, without a mate.

Besides, he might be drawn to her, but it was unlikely she would care for him, an unsophisticated northern cousin.

CHAPTER SEVEN

Bronson and Swan had suggested it would be better for Rodrick to speak to the Earl alone.

He had never visited his parents' bedchamber at night. It had seemed a good idea, but as he stood outside the heavy oaken door, fists clenched, knees stiff, he questioned the wisdom of it. But the morrow would be filled with departing guests and meetings with Leicester. And Swan would be gone, lost to him forever.

He put his ear to the door. Voices. They were awake. Good! Unless—

His parents were still deeply in love and never made any secret of their physical interest in each other, but—

He wiped the sweat from his brow and tapped on the door, hoping he didn't smell too much of horse—or Swan. What was the scent that clung to her?

The murmurings within ceased.

"Who's there?" his father demanded.

"Rodrick," he replied, hoping he didn't sound like a naughty boy disturbing his parents at night.

"Your father is tired. Can it not wait until the morrow?" his mother said softly.

"*Non, maman.* I must speak with you both now."

The door opened abruptly. His red faced father, clad only in a bedrobe he was cinching at the waist, glared. "This had better be important, Rodrick. Your mother and I were—"

Rodrick struggled successfully to keep his eyes off his father's groin. "I apologise. I wouldn't have disturbed you if it wasn't urgent."

His sire beckoned him impatiently into the chamber. His mother appeared from the *garderobe*. He breathed a sigh of relief that she wasn't still abed and had donned a voluminous nightgown and bedrobe. But her flaming red hair, normally bound up and braided, fell around her shoulders. Its beauty struck him again, despite the steaks of grey. It was odd how Grace had inherited those tresses, and he had not. She motioned him to a chair by the cold hearth.

"I'll stand," he replied. "But you two may want to sit."

His father poked at the ashes. "No use. Gone out completely. Tell us what you want before we all freeze to death."

How could anyone be chilled on this warm summer's night? He was on fire. "It's about our cousins."

Why had he started with that?

His father arched one dark eyebrow. "Cousins?"

"Bronson and Swan."

"Swan?" his mother said, sitting down in one of the chairs.

This wasn't how he'd planned to proceed. "It's a nickname Suannoch was given. Because of her long neck."

The memory of it had him sweating again. This was going from bad to worse. His parents exchanged a strange glance.

"Start at the beginning," his mother suggested.

The beginning? How had it begun? Yesterday he'd been content with his bachelor life, today he was obsessed with a woman he barely knew. Was it because she was being whisked away that he wanted her? He remembered their kiss. There was alchemy between them. He felt the rightness of it in his bones. "I want to marry Swan."

He wished the fire still crackled heartily in the grate if only to alleviate the utter silence that greeted his pronouncement. A nightjar chunnered somewhere in the nearby woods.

"You cannot. She's your cousin," his father finally said, standing with his back to the hearth as if there was still warmth to be found there.

His mother came to her feet and faced her husband. "Only second cousins, and half at that."

His mother's comment seemed to indicate her support. It buoyed his spirits. "Our consanguinity is four generations ago. Surely we can get a dispensation?"

His father scoffed. "From the new Pope? Do you know nothing of Anastasius? You just met the girl, and it seems to me yesterday you indicated you didn't like her much. Mayhap the red gown has you bewitched."

Evidently his father had noticed and paid attention. His mother looked askance at her husband. He understood their skepticism, but it irritated. He wasn't a youth infatuated with his first girl. "I'll admit my first impression of Swan wasn't good, but who can blame me? All the men present reacted negatively to her. But we have to take into account her state of mind. How would you feel and act, *Maman*, if you were condemned to be shut away in a convent against your will?"

His mother looked at her husband. "Resentful, angry."

"But this night I met a different Swan. She's a beautiful, intelligent woman with spirit. If I was being forced into the monastic life, I'd be grovelling on the ground, weeping. You should have seen her tonight, riding—"

Scowling, his father looked him up and down, then raised a hand. "Enough! The less I know the better. I trust you behaved honorably. What of her parents if she disobeys them?"

Rodrick wished he had changed out of his dishevelled tunic and dirty boots before embarking on this interview. "They are not in favor of her exile. The man who was to be her father-by-marriage is insisting on it as penance for the death of her betrothed. He holds the threat of King David over their heads. They might lose their ancestral home."

His father's eyes widened as he came to an abrupt halt. "Not likely to happen."

Rodrick's spirits lifted. "Something can be done?"

His father sat. "Bronson wouldn't have known this when they set out from Kirkthwaite, but we received word earlier this evening of King David's death. The news was brought to Leicester."

Rodrick stared at his father, waiting for his heart to slow. The implications of the death of the Scottish king went far beyond his own problems. "What of the succession. Did he anoint his grandson?"

"It would appear so. He didn't have much choice after his son died. But Malcolm is eleven years old and Donnchad of Fife, Scotland's senior magnate, rules as Regent. David's other grandson, William, younger yet, is Earl of Northumberland. I suspect Donnchad will want to enlist the support of landowners such as the

FitzRams for these young royals. The last thing he'll need is dissension in Northumbria. He's apparently been touring Scotland with Malcolm. It wouldn't surprise me if Aidan has already taken advantage of the situation."

"It's imperative I impart this news to Bronson and Swan at once. We must have already left the Hall when word was brought."

His mother eyed him suspiciously. "We wondered where the three of you had gone."

Rodrick felt a weight lift from his shoulders. "I set out to give Swan one last opportunity to ride, but something happened to me out there on the moors. I don't want to let her go. Now we have hope."

His father came to his feet and put a hand on Rodrick's shoulder. "One obstacle may have been removed, but you must seek the priest's permission next. I'll accompany you when you speak with him."

He embraced his parents then hastened to Bronson's chamber where he hammered loudly. Bronson opened the door wide.

"Good, you're still dressed."

"I wouldn't sleep if I went to bed, so what was the point?"

He clamped a hand on FitzRam's shoulder. "Wake your sister. I have news."

Bronson's eyes widened. "You're smiling. I wasn't expecting that."

Rodrick pulled him towards Swan's chamber. "Hurry."

They both rapped on her door. It opened a crack. Amber eyes peered out cautiously.

"What's happened?"

"Open the door," Bronson said. "Rodrick has news, and he's still smiling."

She allowed them entry. Rodrick wasn't sure whether to be pleased or disappointed she was still dressed in the red gown.

She must have sensed his feelings. "I didn't want to take it off; or rather I didn't want to put the habit back on."

Rodrick took hold of her hands, wondering if she could hear the thudding of his heart. "You won't ever have to don religious garb again."

He tightened his hold on her hands when she swayed.

"How can it be?" she asked.

"King David of Scotland is dead."

Bronson thumped his fist into his palm. "Ha! And Malcolm is anointed king?"

"Yes. With a regent. And don't forget, Montbryces are now supporters of the Plantagenet cause. The Scottish throne is allied to the same cause. The FitzRams are our family. We won't take kindly to mistreatment of our family."

Rodrick had addressed his words to Bronson, all the while keeping his eyes on Swan's face. She had closed her eyes and was breathing deeply, but still gripped his hands. Free of the convent, more or less without his help, would she still be drawn to him, or had he been a means of escape? She might return to Northumbria, or mayhap settle at Shelfhoc with Bronson and marry anyone of her choosing without the issue of consanguinity hanging over them.

Laughing loudly, Bronson put his hands on his sister's waist, picked her up and twirled her around. "This means you can accompany me to Shelfhoc."

"Yes!" she replied, enjoying laughter for the first time in months. Seeing the home of the great grandmother whose name she bore had been one of her deepest desires, but she suddenly became aware of the pained expression on Rodrick's face. She eased out of her brother's grip and turned to the man who drew her like a lodestone. "What's wrong?"

"Nothing. I'm happy you're free now. You can go where you please."

His cool demeanor was perplexing. She had trusted him with her feelings but it was as if he'd become once again the aloof Rodrick of their first meeting. Perhaps his parents had dissuaded him from a relationship with her. "You don't look happy."

He shrugged. "You should go to Shelfhoc. I suppose I assumed you might stay here a few more days."

Her spirits lifted. Maybe he did care for her. "We can, and then you could accompany us to Shelfhoc." She turned to her brother. "If it's agreeable to Bronson."

"Of course. I am anxious to get to Ruyton and see my new home. I have a feeling Edwin may have let things go. He hadn't been well for a year or two before he died."

"You needn't worry. Edwin and my father were friends. We've kept an eye on things there."

Swan's heart raced. "You've been to Shelfhoc?"

Rodrick smiled. "Many times."

She clasped his hands. "I can't wait to see it. But we must send word to my parents. They've probably been frantically worried I've already entered the convent."

"I'm sure my father has it in hand already."

Meeting her Montbryce cousins had filled Swan with apprehension, yet they seemed genuinely concerned for her. "I thank you from the bottom of my heart for my freedom. I can assure you I have a long list of things I want to accomplish I thought I never would."

She had hoped to bring a smile to his face now they had a chance to enjoy her freedom together, but he frowned. "It was none of my doing."

Never one to keep her thoughts to herself, she was about to ask if he had spoken to his father when his sister entered the chamber.

"I heard a commotion," Grace said, unable to take her eyes off the broad smile that lit Bronson's face. He must have learned of King David's death and realized its implications for his sister. The weight of his duty to deliver her to the convent had indeed been heavy if the frowning scowl she'd been used to was any indication.

His hair had come loose from its braid, probably during the ride. It was easily as long as her own. She itched to sift her fingers through the thick copper glory that cloaked his shoulders. His normally pursed lips were full, his green eyes wide.

She wished she hadn't left her chamber clad only in her nightgown and bedrobe.

"Swan is free," he exclaimed. "She can accompany me to Shelfhoc."

She supposed this news must have lightened her brother's heart too, yet he seemed unsure, unusual for the decisive Rodrick. Dragging her eyes away from Bronson, she embraced Swan. "I am relieved for you, cousin. I know what it is to live in a place you hate. Welcome back to your life."

"Thank you, Grace," Swan replied quietly.

Something was amiss. What had happened to her cousin's exuberance?

Bronson swallowed the lump constricting his throat when Grace entered the chamber. Her auburn hair flowed over her shoulders. He wanted to bury his nose in it and inhale her scent. What was this alchemy she seemed to have over him?

Her face reddened when his gaze fell on her. Perhaps she felt something between them, or was she dismayed to have come upon two men while dressed in her night attire?

He didn't welcome the insistent tug in his balls. He'd be glad to leave for Shelfhoc, forget her, and concentrate on settling into his new home.

He deliberately wiped his happiness for Swan from his face, thinking to turn his attention back to his sister, thus demonstrating his lack of interest. His resolve deserted him at the sight of Grace's crestfallen face. "Perhaps you might want to accompany us when we depart."

CHAPTER EIGHT

D id you speak to your father?"
"I did."
"And?"

Most men wouldn't appreciate Swan's forthright insistence, but Rodrick supposed years of tit for tat with his twin who never gave an inch in any argument had prepared him. He actually thought it endearing. Better a woman with spirit. A pleasant tingling in the nether regions followed this notion. "He foresees problems."

"But he didn't dismiss the idea out of hand?"

"Idea?" he teased.

Swan folded her arms. "You know what I mean."

"No. He suggests I consult the priest."

Swan blinked rapidly which did nothing to dissuade the interest of his *couilles*. "When can we go?"

"Not *we*. Papa and I will go."

"He agreed to accompany you?"

"It was his suggestion."

She pouted. He groaned inwardly at the prospect of those full lips on his shaft. He dragged his attention back to the matter at hand. "It's late. Get some sleep. On the morrow we'll discuss what happens next. The important thing is you don't have to go to the convent."

Bronson pecked a kiss on Swan's cheek. "Until the morrow, sister, I must escort our cousin back to her chamber." He sauntered out the door, Grace on his arm.

Rodrick was alone with Swan for the first time.

She stared at him provocatively, the corners of her mouth edging up. "Are you going to kiss me goodnight?"

He moved to stand in front of her, but left a space between them. "If I kiss you, Swan, I won't want to stop there."

She frowned slightly. "Are you certain this is what you want, Rodrick?"

He had to admire her. Women were expected to acquiesce to a man's wishes and wait for him to take the lead. He put his hands on her waist. "If I pressed my body to yours you would see hard evidence this is what I want. You've bewitched me."

She stood on tiptoe and brushed a kiss on his lips, teasing him with her tongue. He gasped when she thrust her hips forward, sending liquid fire flooding through his veins. He cupped her face, deepening the kiss, wanting to savor the warmth of her sweet mouth. Their tongues dueled, parry and thrust, parry and thrust, until it came to him their hips were imitating the movement and she was whimpering. Any more of this and—

He broke them apart.

"I see what you mean," she said with a sly smile.

"You want me as much as I want you," he rasped.

"Mayhap more," she replied in a sultry voice that would echo in his head all night long.

Swan doubted she would get much sleep. Rodrick was gone, but her body still hummed with the pleasant tingling sensations he'd caused with his kisses.

Her mind buzzed too. Life now held promise. Despair had turned to hope for a future filled with love and laughter. She was relieved for Bronson too. She'd seen the anguish on his face when they met the Superior at Whitchurch. He seemed taken with Grace, and she with him. What a coincidence—two redheads! She hoped her cousin wouldn't get too interested in Bronson. He would never marry again after the double tragedies he'd suffered. Her heart ached for her brother. He was a man who doted on children. It seemed unfair. Their brothers Symon and Ingram had both spawned large, boisterous families.

Perhaps Bronson was destined to be alone, like Edwin who had deeded Shelfhoc to him. Edwin had probably deduced their two older brothers would never leave Northumbria, but Bronson was a third son with no ties.

If it wasn't for her feelings for Rodrick, she would have happily been the lady of Shelfhoc, following in the footsteps of her great grandmother. She chided herself. There was no guarantee Rodrick would follow through on his professed sentiments. Perhaps if it became too difficult to secure permission to wed, he'd lose interest.

But the memory of his kisses had her praying fervently such a thing didn't happen.

CHAPTER NINE

After the departure of their guests, Rodrick and his father strolled to the Church built by Ram de Montbryce. They paused for a few moments to watch men at work on the tower. They had sent word of their coming, alerting the priest to be prepared to see them. Brilliant afternoon sunshine warmed their faces. There wasn't a cloud in the sky. "The day augurs well," he remarked.

His father turned to him. "I don't want to sound pessimistic, but our priest is an old man, not renowned for his modern thinking. He's lived a celibate life. Who knows if he's ever had feelings for a woman? It's unlikely he'll be sympathetic."

Rodrick clenched his fists. He had indeed been a babe in arms when Père Rigord had arrived at Ellesmere. "This is ridiculous. He will refuse to marry us because we share a great grandfather?"

His father squinted into the sun. "I agree. Years ago it was common for cousins to marry, particularly in noble families. But intermarriage resulted in problems, so the church went to the other extreme and demanded at least four generations of separation. Some still cling to the rigid rule."

"If I have to crawl on my knees to the Pope, I will marry Swan."

His father put a hand on his shoulder. "Don't be discouraged. If you truly love this woman, I'll not be the one to keep you apart. I spent too much time trying to deny my feelings for your mother. I admire your determination to marry the woman you want."

Rodrick was aware of his father's disastrous first marriage, but it was rare for him to reveal such personal details.

"I don't have much experience of love, Papa, except what you and *Maman* have shared openly, but part of me will cease to exist if I lose Swan."

His father chuckled. "Then you're definitely in love. Let's waste no more time. If we don't get satisfaction from Père Rigord, we'll decide on our next course of action. My concern is that you are my heir. We don't want things to come to a point where your right to inherit might be jeopardised. Much as I love William and Stephen, you're the one who'll make the better Earl."

He had set out on this mission with high hopes. Now his heart was in his boots. He had never imagined pursuit of his happiness with Swan might put his inheritance in doubt.

Never one to sit and wait patiently, Swan paced back and forth in the gallery where she and Rodrick's mother and sisters had gathered to wait.

"Would you care to attempt some embroidery?" the Countess asked. "It helps to pass the time when you're waiting for news."

Swan wanted to scream she hated embroidery—always had, always would—but Rodrick's mother was letting her know she understood.

"No, thank you. I'm not much good at it," she replied.

The Countess held out a hooped linen, complete with needle and threads. "I never was either. My sister, Fermentine, loved embroidery and she and I, well, let's just say anything she liked, I didn't. I've improved with practice. It's taught me patience."

Swan accepted the sampler as Rodrick and the Earl came into the gallery. Their faces betrayed that the interview hadn't gone in their favor. She clutched the embroidery to her breast. "He said no."

"I expected as much," the Earl replied.

His apparent disappointment was heartening, and Rodrick looked positively stricken. She wanted to kiss the frown away from his brow, but touching him in front of his parents would be inappropriate. "I suppose I did too," she replied.

To her relief, Rodrick took her hand and brushed a kiss on her knuckles.

"We'll find a way," he said with such conviction she almost believed it possible.

CHAPTER TEN

Rodrick was filled with an urge to kiss away the tears welling in Swan's eyes, but simply taking her hand had caught his parents' attention. "We will find a way," he repeated, but her frown betrayed her uncertainty.

"Père Rigord is a local priest set in his ways. He is not the Church's highest authority. We'll go to the bishop."

His mother threw her embroidery onto a nearby chair with a skeptical grunt he recognised well. Much as he loved her, he wished she hadn't added to Swan's consternation.

Minutes of silence dragged by.

The normally reticent Aurore came to the rescue. "There's the Pope," she offered.

Her father's reply was interrupted when Steward Bonhomme appeared unexpectedly, accompanied by Robert of Leicester. Everyone came to their feet, surprised by the return of the Earl who had left Ellesmere only two hours before.

"Robert, welcome back," the Countess said, proffering her hand.

Leicester brushed a kiss across her knuckles. "Forgive my abrupt entry. I received a message that prompted my return."

Rodrick's heart plummeted to his boots. He sensed before Leicester revealed his mission it would be a call to arms.

"Stephen has laid siege to Wallingford."

Everyone in the gallery knew Wallingford was loyal to Maud and Prince Henry.

"It's location on the River Thames is apparently too close to Westminster for the king's comfort," Leicester went on. "Henry is marching to relieve the siege. If he succeeds in routing Stephen, an end to the civil war might be at hand."

His father didn't hesitate. "Rodrick, alert our men. Tell them to be ready to march at dawn. It will take at least four days to get there. Seek out William and Stephen—and Bronson. Bring them to the Chart Room."

Leicester clapped a hand on Gallien de Montbryce's shoulder. "Good man. I've sent a message on to my troops. I'll depart with you and meet up with them en route."

The Earls left to discuss strategy. This call to action had fired Rodrick's warrior blood. "At long last we may see an end to the anarchy gripping England."

None of the females replied, but their faces betrayed their anxiety. He supposed that was the way of it for women whose men went off to war. He squeezed Swan's hand, now gone alarmingly cold, and left to organise Ellesmere's fighting men.

Swan's blood had turned to ice. Had she stumbled upon a man who fired her body and her spirit only to lose him in battle? One moment life held promise, the next it was snatched away. And her brother would be expected to join the fray. She shivered, despite the Countess's warm arm around her shoulders.

"This is the way of it, Swan. Every Englishwoman has felt your fear. I can't tell you the number of times I've sent Gallien off to fight, in large conflicts and small, and it never gets any easier."

Swan's palms were sweating. "I suppose I am being selfish. I've come to care for your son."

"What of Bronson?" Grace suddenly blurted out.

Her mother eyed her curiously. "Of course Swan is worried for her dear brother too."

Grace reddened. "I—I'm sorry," she stammered. "It's only, er, well, I had hoped perhaps to accompany the two of you to Shelfhoc."

The reminder that Bronson's claim to his inheritance would now be delayed saddened Swan. She didn't want to wait idly at Ellesmere. Inactivity and endless hours of embroidery and sewing loomed large. An idea occurred to her. "You and I should go. To prepare the hall for Bronson's return."

Grace clapped her hands together. "What a good idea. You don't mind, *maman?*"

The Countess smiled. "If Bronson agrees, I have no objection. I'll instruct Bonhomme to gather a crew of servants to assist you."

Grace had allowed her dismay at Bronson's imminent departure to control her tongue. She must be more careful. There was no point revealing her feelings. Her body heated whenever she set eyes on him. Nay she had only to think of him for strange tinglings to pervade her veins.

It was evident Rodrick and Swan would have difficulty obtaining permission to marry.

Bronson hadn't shown the slightest interest in her.

But ahead lay the promise of at least doing something to prepare his new home for his return. She was certain she and Swan were destined to be good friends.

If the worst happened and the men fell at Wallingford, they would both need a shoulder to weep on. She glanced at her mother. Peri de Montbryce risked the loss of her husband and three sons in the coming conflict, she and Aurore their father and brothers. It would be an intolerable loss, for their family and for the Earldom. But the sharpest ache in her heart was the possibility Bronson might die without knowing of her feelings for him.

"Let's find my brother and explain our plan," Swan urged, jolting Grace out of her reverie.

Bronson was on his way to the Chart Room, having met with Rodrick and William who had imparted the news of the march to Wallingford. Rodrick had been impressed when he'd had no hesitation in committing to the fight. His cousin's apparent surprise was irksome. The FitzRams might be the illegitimate branch of the family, but Ram de Montbryce's blood ran in their veins as hotly as in the Montbryces'.

He was disappointed his possession of Shelfhoc had to be delayed. Swan would be dismayed. She'd never been known for her patience. Waiting at Ellesmere for news from the battlefront would drive her out of her wits.

Why not suggest she go to Shelfhoc without him? Perhaps Grace could accompany her as they'd planned. He rather liked the notion of the auburn haired widow helping to prepare for his eventual homecoming. He'd never had a home of his own.

If he came home. There was the possibility of suffering mortal wounds in any battle. A mere scratch often putrefied. Only the other evening, Uncle Gallien had told the tale of the Conqueror's grandson, William Clito dying a painful death in Flandres when a seemingly harmless hand wound from a lance turned gangrenous. He had been there, had seen the infantryman thrust his lance into Clito's hand.

A warrior acknowledged and accepted the dangers. But for some reason it bothered him that if he didn't return from Wallingford he would never know if Grace cared for him or not.

CHAPTER ELEVEN

Rodrick paced in his chamber, still fully clothed though it was well past midnight. He'd spent an exhausting day supervising preparations for the morrow. Ellesmere's armory was always stockpiled with sharpened swords, lances, arrows, daggers, its soldiers highly trained and battle ready. Damaged shields were either repaired or thrown out. Life in the Welsh Marches was precarious despite that four score and seven years had passed since the Norman Conquest, a reality many Welsh rebels still refused to accept.

Steward Bonhomme's efficiency at ensuring the castle was well provisioned meant Rodrick didn't have to worry about food for the troops on the four day march.

There were good quality tents and pavilions aplenty for the nobles and knights.

The Montbryces who had fought at Hastings were Norman cavalrymen whose lives often depended on their mounts. The stables at Montbryce holdings, from Alensonne, to Domfort, to Belisle, to Montbryce itself in Normandie, and from Ellesmere to the vast Sussex estates they controlled, all were renowned for the care they lavished on their horses.

The Ellesmere army would arrive at Wallingford well fed, well prepared, and immaculately turned out, their armor and surcoats clean and in good repair. Every Earl since Ram de Montbryce had taken pride in their fighting men. A military man who enjoyed the fruits of life fought harder to stay alive.

Emotions had run hot during the evening meal, the people of the castle excited by the looming dawn departure. His father had given an impassioned speech, exhorting his soldiers to help save England from the anarchy tearing it asunder.

Leicester had added to the fervor with rousing words.

Rodrick had been swept up by the prospect of the daunting heroic task ahead of them, yet hadn't been able to take his eyes off Swan. She too was caught up in the spirit of optimism and excitement pervading the Hall, but from time to time she glanced at him, her eyes full of sadness. The longing on her face had sent every drop of blood from his head to his groin.

He was relieved she wasn't seated beside him. He'd have been hard pressed to keep his hands off her. She and Grace and Bronson had chosen to sit at a table below the dais. He understood her need to be with her brother, but why had his twin come between them? It appeared Grace was flirting with their red headed cousin! This was a surprise. He cast his mind back trying to recall if Bronson was married, or had been married. He supposed since no wife had accompanied him to the Marches, she was either still in Northumbria, or nonexistent. Mayhap he wasn't the marrying kind, in which case Grace would get her feelings hurt. And she'd been hurt enough.

Exhausted at the start of the meal, he was a wreck by the time it was over. He'd wanted to carry Swan off to his chamber and devour her, but they'd had to content themselves with perfunctory pecks on the cheek as everyone said their goodnights. His impatience had grown at the sight of Bronson and Grace lingering over their fare-thee-wells.

Was Swan pacing her chamber? What harm in making his way there quietly? It was close by. Everyone would be abed. He wanted one more passionate kiss before he left. Just a kiss to reassure her of his feelings.

He cringed when the door creaked loudly. Strange he'd never noticed the hinges needed oiling. He'd mention it to Bonhomme on the morrow, though chances were he'd have other things on his mind.

He closed the door carefully, but the draught almost blew out the single candle he carried to light his way in the dark corridor. It was good he'd thought to leave his boots behind, although most of the stone floor was covered with rush mats that muffled his footsteps.

He tapped lightly on Swan's door, held his breath, and waited. The hairs on his nape bristled momentarily when he heard another door close quietly further down the hall, near Grace's chamber. He heard footsteps approaching and shoved the door wide when Swan opened it a crack.

Swan stepped back, thrown off guard by Rodrick's hasty entrance. She'd known as soon as she heard the tap at her door that he'd come. She hadn't disrobed, hoping and praying he would, but now her heart skittered around in her rib cage.

"Sorry," he murmured, blowing out his candle as he closed the door quickly and put a finger to his lips. "Someone's coming down the hallway."

"At this time of night?" she whispered.

He chuckled, gazing into her eyes. "Perhaps some other lovesick swain come to kiss his lady love goodbye."

Try as she might, Swan couldn't guess who that might be. "You've come to kiss me?"

He put his hands on her waist. "I have."

His warmth penetrated the thick velvet. Imagine if she'd changed into her nightgown! She pushed away the shameful urge to rip off her clothes and press her naked body to his. Looking up into his darkened eyes she parted her lips and murmured, "I'm glad."

Taking her hand, he led her to the chairs by the hearth. "Sit with me."

He sat down but when she moved to the other chair, he pulled her onto his lap. She squealed as delight ran rampant through her body.

They clung together for long minutes. She stared into the empty grate, her head on his shoulder, listening to the beating of his strong heart. Something hard pressed against her *derrière*.

"You have me bewitched, Swan FitzRam," he rasped, moving his hips. "Just having you on my lap stirs me. If I kiss you—"

"But you must kiss me," she complained. "I want a kiss that will last me until you return."

Swan was a forthright person who spoke her mind, but the brazen words surprised even her. She fiddled with the loosened laces at the neck of his linen shirt. "I am a wanton."

He brushed a curl away from her forehead. "No, Swan, you are a passionate woman, and I cannot tell you how relieved I am you're free of the nunnery."

She sat up to look at him, cradling his face in her hands. "Kiss me."

He smiled. "If you keep moving around I'll do more than kiss you."

"Promises, promises," she teased, sensing she was playing with fire, but not caring. Something was building inside, something that drove her to touch him, savor his scent, share the warmth of his body.

His growl as he took her hands from his face and put them around his neck took her by surprise, but she had no time to think when his lips crushed hers, his tongue demanding entry. She opened her mouth, tasting the sweet wine he'd imbibed at supper, relishing the tingling of her scalp as he ran his fingers through her hair.

Hiram had kissed her, but this was different. She nibbled his lip. "I don't know how to kiss."

"Yes, you do," he rumbled before he delved his tongue in again, teasing hers to follow into his mouth. As far as she recalled, she'd never seen another person's tongue, now hers mated with Rodrick's, sending shards of delicious sensation shooting into very private places. Of its own volition her throat made a mewling sound she'd never made before. There was no fire in the grate, but her body heated. The bodice of her gown was suddenly too tight, her nipples protesting their confinement.

As if sensing their need, Rodrick's hand stroked down her neck and cupped her breast. When he brushed a thumb across the nipple, her body went limp. She stopped breathing, content to let him breathe for her. She put her hand on his face, relishing the velvety softness of his unshaven skin.

"Swan," he rasped, swallowing hard when they broke apart. "Let me touch you."

She wasn't sure what he meant, since they were already touching. He moved his hand over her ribs and her belly until it came to rest on her mons. She opened her legs, seeking release from the throbbing pulse. He moved his hand. She stirred restlessly, torn between propriety and desire.

Her skirts rustled as he gathered the fabric with his hand. "Hush, Swan, let me please you."

"You are pleasing me," she breathed in a voice she barely recognized.

He pecked a kiss on her forehead. "Oh, my Swan, so worldly, yet so innocent."

He came to his feet, sweeping her up and depositing her on the bed. Her heart lurched. She wanted his attentions, but her parents had ingrained in her the importance of a wife coming to her bridal bed a virgin.

As if sensing her reluctance, he touched his forefinger to her lips, then took her hand and placed it on the hard flesh at his groin. "Feel what you do to me. I want you, but I give you my pledge I will return from Wallingford, and we will marry and I will plunge my shaft into your warm sheathe. I am an honorable man and I will take your virginity in our marriage bed. But tonight I want to give you pleasure—something to remember me by."

His words thrilled her, sending her heart soaring, but she was confused. Her married sister, Elayne Agneta, had confided in hushed whispers how husbands inserted their male parts into a woman's body. The size of the shape under her hand made her wonder why her sister had teased her. Such interaction was obviously impossible, though a strange and not unpleasant sensation spiralled up her thighs into her lower belly as the flesh beneath her fingers hardened further.

Rodrick lifted her hand. "Best stop that now, or I may be tempted to foreswear myself. Trust me this night."

She looked into blue eyes full of love and longing and whispered her permission.

He eased off her shoes and stockings. It was the first time since childhood someone else had done so and no man had ever touched her feet. Hiram had not been permitted to see them. Yet she trusted Rodrick, despite the excitement bubbling in her veins like water in a pot on the boil. He put his hands on her ankles. "Open your legs."

She dug her fingers into the damask bedspread and did as he bade her, never taking her eyes off his.

"Good girl."

He feathered his fingers along her shins then grasped her knees, pushing them up as he came to kneel on the bed between her legs,

The fabric of her gown slid to her hips, revealing her to his gaze. She swayed on the edge of a dangerous precipice, yet had never felt safer.

"You are as beautiful as I imagined," he said, his eyes fixed on a part of her body she'd never seen. "So pink, and wet."

She blinked, unable to squeeze words out of her dry throat, filled with a certainty life would never be the same after this night.

"I am honored to be the first man to look at you, Swan."

She was too nervous to tell him she was overjoyed that the first man to look at her did so with love.

But perhaps he didn't love her. Elayne had insisted men were motivated by lust. But she didn't care, increasingly sure she loved him.

He quickly moved his hands to the tops of her thighs, then bent his head. Surely he wasn't going to—

She gasped as he parted her nether lips with his thumbs and put his mouth on her most intimate place. Her hands flew to his head to push him away, but his thick hair felt so soft she raked her fingers through it as rivers of pleasure flowed from where he suckled into her spine, her thighs, her nipples, the soles of her feet.

"Rodrick," she murmured. "I'm sure this is wrong, but don't stop."

He raised his head, his face slick with her juices. "You are warm and wet, and you taste wonderful. I can't wait for us to be wed."

She pushed away the cloud on the horizon of her bliss. They might never be given permission to marry, and here she was allowing him to touch her in places—

"Stop worrying," he whispered.

Then he flicked his tongue over a certain spot—a magical spot—again and again until the low wail emanating from deep within grew into a loud scream when she tumbled off the precipice into an oblivion of pulsating bliss. He lunged forward to press his mouth to hers, stifling her scream as he slid his fingers inside her. She turned her face away, panting breathlessly. "Deeper, deeper," she urged, thrusting her hips towards his hand.

"Not yet, my little bird, you have to be content with only a taste this time."

Her sheath pulsed on his fingers as she returned his kiss, needing his breath to keep her lungs working.

After their mouths parted she clung to him for long minutes, listening to his breathing. Had he fallen asleep? "What happened?" she yawned. "I had to scream."

He withdrew his fingers and smoothed her gown over her legs. "You're supposed to scream."

"I hope it wasn't too loud," she whispered, but exhaustion overwhelmed her and she never heard his answer.

CHAPTER TWELVE

Bronson sat on the edge of his bed, naked, staring at the hard flesh between his legs. The night had been a comedy of errors. He'd gone to Grace's chamber. Why, he wasn't sure. Then he looked again at the persistent erection that he would to have to do something to resolve if he wanted any sleep at all.

My cursed shaft knows why I went.

Frustrated they hadn't been seated together at dinner, he'd tapped on her door.

She'd appeared, floating in a voluminous white bedrobe, her red hair like a blessed aura. For a moment he believed the smiling vision was an angel, seemingly happy at being called upon after midnight.

He'd teetered on the threshold, hesitant to ask permission to enter when she didn't invite him in. But that was a good thing. Respectable noblewomen didn't invite men into their chamber in the dead of night. The flame of his candle had guttered in the draught, filling his nostrils with the acrid smell of smoke. She'd wrinkled her nose.

Confident in what he wanted to say when he'd left his own chamber, he now had no idea why he was there when he'd sworn off marriage. The words that came out of his mouth weren't the ones he'd planned on saying.

Instead of *I'm drawn to you, Grace,* he'd cleared his throat and stammered, "I wanted to tell you I'm glad you're accompanying my sister to Shelfhoc."

He longed to say that her presence at Shelfhoc would be a beacon guiding him home. Into the silence, he spouted, "Swan will appreciate your company. I'm happy you're becoming friends."

He had no recollection of how many times he'd used the word glad, nor of anything else that had come out of his mouth. He prayed fervently he'd said nothing on the subject of never marrying again. Whatever she had whispered in reply was lost to him, his gaze and his thoughts focused on her wide green eyes and her smile.

He did remember kissing her—an awkward, adolescent kiss aimed initially at her lips. It had gone off course, collided with her nose and ended up on her reddened cheek.

Godemite! Had he at least wished her goodnight when he'd fled?

What had happened to the polished, articulate Bronson who'd had no difficulty attracting two beautiful wives? He made the sign of his Savior across his body.

God Rest Their Souls.

It flitted into his confused mind that he shouldn't be calling on the Lord while sitting naked staring at his own rigid manhood, but then he was probably already damned for lusting after his cousin.

Grace had cast a spell on him, turned him into a babbling idiot ruled by impulse, and his cock.

On his way back to his chamber, he thought he'd caught a glimpse of someone entering Swan's chamber, but maybe he'd imagined it, rendered cross-eyed by his errant shaft that even now refused to obey.

Nothing for it but to take matters into his own hands. He rolled his eyes heavenward.

Forgive me, Lord.

After she closed her door, Grace stood for a long while, inhaling deeply, trying to get her lungs to start working again. She touched her palm to the spot where Bronson had kissed her cheek, smiling at the memory. He was like a youth wooing his first girl.

But his nervousness charmed her. It was flattering to have a strikingly handsome nobleman stumbling over his tongue perhaps because she affected him, although he'd mumbled something about not marrying again.

It had been difficult to keep smiling when he'd said that. But his reddened face, his stammer, the bulge in his leggings, his kiss all belied his words. Why else had he come in the middle of the night if he wasn't attracted to her? Mayhap she should have invited him in.

Non! He'd judge her a whore, a lonely widow lusting for a male companion.

Was she lonely? Marriage to Victor had been loneliness, complete isolation. She had determined to enjoy her freedom. Ellesmere was often filled with attractive men whose company she could enjoy without giving control over her life to them, and in any case, Bronson was her cousin. There was no future for their relationship. But she would be his friend, help prepare his new home so he had something to look forward to when he returned from Wallingford.

CHAPTER THIRTEEN

Rodrick brought his horse level with his father's when the narrow, hilly track widened. "Another hour we should make Fernhill Heath," he observed.

His father shifted in the saddle. "We've made good progress. Not as far as yesterday, but acceptable, considering the lay of the land."

After riding for several hours with no conversation, Rodrick needed to fill the silence. His armor had begun to chafe in uncomfortable places. He wasn't looking forward to another night under canvas. "Strange how yesterday the men were full of vim and vigor, and today they're quieter. The infantrymen kept up their ribald songs the whole way to Bridgnorth yesterday."

His father grinned. "The more difficult terrain has a lot to do with it, but on the first day of a march, men are usually fired by the excitement of the expedition and the prospect of the battle. On the second day, they're thinking of the women and children left behind."

The wistful look on his sire's face betrayed exactly where his thoughts lay. Rodrick sought to lighten the mood. "You've most of your children along on this campaign, so it must be *Maman* you're thinking of."

Gallien de Montbryce shifted his weight in the saddle. "I've left your mother many times to go off to fight, but it never gets any easier. In Flandres I carried a sachet of her potpourri next to my heart for months. Same for her. She's strong, but she worries."

Rodrick cast his mind to the future. He wanted with all his heart to wed with Swan and for her to be the one pining for his return. He wished he'd taken a token from her, a lock of hair perhaps. She'd wept when they'd said goodbye in the bailey. But what would happen

60

if they never obtained permission to wed? If he married her without benefit of clergy, he'd lose the earldom.

"A visit to the bishop of Shrewsbury will have to wait until our return."

Had his father read his thoughts?

"Unless we seek out a highly placed cleric in Westminster, once we succeed in lifting the siege of Wallingford."

And how had his father known he'd been contemplating such a possibility?

"Do you believe in love at first sight, Papa?" he asked with some trepidation. These were matters they had never discussed.

"That's the easy part," came the reply. "Yes, I do, but don't be like me and deny you're smitten." He shook his head. "When I think of the time I wasted, and the hurt I inflicted on my wife."

Rodrick had never cared enough for a woman to understand before what his father meant, but now he did. Given the difficulties they faced, and what they stood to lose, he might easily tell himself he didn't love Swan. But he did. "I love Swan, Papa. I'm determined to fight for her."

"Good. I hope you hold onto your determination, because I have a feeling it will be a long fight. However, I've had the good fortune to suffer from the curse of the Montbryces. I hope for the same for you. The love of a good woman makes life infinitely more pleasurable."

Rodrick chuckled, enjoying the reference to the *curse*. Since the time of his great, great grandfather, *Comte* Bernard, the Montbryces had been different from most noblemen—they loved their wives passionately.

As she and Grace approached Ruyton Swan marvelled out loud at the efficiency of Steward Bonhomme. "He'd seen off a huge expeditionary force less than a day before yet managed to provision our escort to Shelfhoc."

Grace concurred. "Indeed, our family has been blessed by the talents of the Bonhomme family, both here and in Normandie. They've served us faithfully for nigh on five score years."

"He didn't blink an eye when I told him we planned to leave the following day. I didn't want to wait any longer to see Shelfhoc."

"I agree. It was good to get underway. The August weather is fair, and we should be there soon. The men who came with you from Northumbria seemed relieved not to be bound for Wallingford and are only too glad to be travelling with us. Two of them have gone ahead to secure our passage past the guards on the rampart ditch. You'll soon espy the little church within the boundaries of Shelfhoc."

The tower appeared shortly thereafter. Swan's head filled with the notion of being wed in the tiny church, though Rodrick would no doubt want to hold the ceremony at Ellesmere in the grander church built by Ram de Montbryce, symbolic for both of them. But she mustn't dwell too long on those thoughts, just in case.

Her first impression of Shelfhoc as they entered the courtyard was of a house not dissimilar to Kirkthwaite Hall, but much older.

A short, balding man clad in the livery of a Steward emerged to greet them. "*Bienvenues, Mesdames*, milady Grace and milady Suannoch."

Stable lads ran forward to assist them as they dismounted. Swan was heartily glad to get off Cob after close to two hours riding side saddle.

"Tybaut is the fourth generation of stewards to serve Shelfhoc," Grace explained.

Swan acknowledged his bow. "On behalf of my brother, I thank you for your service to my uncle Edwin."

"A fine man indeed," Tybaut murmured with obvious reverence. "I miss him. *Milord* Bronson has not accompanied you?"

"No," Swan replied. "He's gone with the Earl to help lift the siege of Wallingford."

Tybaut's eyes widened as if this news surprised him, then he clasped his joined hands to his chest, looking to the sky. "Dangerous times we live in. I thank God daily we have been spared the ravages plaguing other parts of England."

He ushered them into the house.

"Shall I show you everything now," Grace asked enthusiastically, "or do you want to rest first?"

"Time for rest when we retire," Swan replied.

As her cousin led the way she savored every lime-washed panel, every stair, every chamber. "It's a grand house," she remarked to the Steward following attentively behind them.

SINFUL PASSIONS

"Two stories high, as you see," he replied, his chest swelling with pride. "Built from split and planed timbers, fastened together with iron nails."

The interior was elaborately decorated with ornamental wood turnings, the creaking wooden floor softened with wattle mats. The roof was well thatched. The sturdy outbuildings were framed with large timber uprights, filled with wattle and daub and chinked with moss to keep out the winter cold. The stone kitchen was set apart from the wooden house.

"This used to be the weaving shed," Tybaut explained, as they entered a long, narrow building. "Perhaps you ladies might start up the use of it again? It wasn't used during *Milord* Edwin's residence here."

He lifted the end of a heavy canvas covering. "I've kept the old looms covered."

"Perhaps," Grace replied. "I love to weave."

Swan doubted she'd ever set foot in the shed again, but as she touched a hand to the wooden loom beneath the canvas it was pleasing to imagine her namesake great grandmother creating woven goods in the place, and her grandmother Agneta after her. Had her father, Aidan not inherited Kirkthwaite in Northumbria, he might have lived out his life here.

There was a modest Great Hall where she conjured a vision of her grandfather, Caedmon, conducting business, enacting justice and speaking judgments. Had he sat in the massive thane's chair on the dais, his wife Agneta by his side, and signed contracts, praised good deeds, eaten with his men? The Hall was long and narrow and had two doors, one at each tapered end.

"The four windows have wooden shutters for defense and to keep out the cold," Tybaut explained.

She thought of her ancestors here in the days after her grandfather's return from the Crusades, watching the smoke make its lazy way up from the hearth in the middle, out through the hole in the roof.

Shelfhoc was where the FitzRam family had its beginnings on that fateful day so long ago when Ram and Ascha met.

A sense of homecoming washed over her. "I love this place," she whispered to Grace. "And Bronson will love it too."

Her cousin's shoulders drooped. "How far do you think they've traveled?"

63

Swan took her hand, happy not to be the only one missing the men they cared for. "They hoped to reach Fernhill Heath by this evening and on to Chipping Norton on the morrow."

CHAPTER FOURTEEN

Bronson prided himself on being an excellent rider, but was weary of being on a horse. It seemed he'd barely arrived at Ellesmere after a gruelling and unhappy journey with Swan over the Pennines when the call had come to travel to Wallingford. Arriving exhausted didn't bode well for his chances of staying alive if they engaged Stephen's forces.

They'd been on the road three days, this last being the longest, and he was heartily relieved to see the *motte* at Chipping Norton loom out of the late afternoon fog. The only good thing to come from the journey was it had afforded him a chance to get to know his Montbryce cousins. William and Stephen were friendly and outgoing at first meeting, but he was uneasy with Rodrick. However, on the long march he had seen many good qualities in the man who professed to love his sister.

Rodrick would make a good husband for Swan. But the road ahead was murky, filled with ecclesiastical potholes. He and Grace faced the same problems if they—

A commotion up ahead caught his attention. William was slowly riding back towards him, a pained expression on his face. "What ho, cousin?" he asked.

William rolled his eyes, "Seems we're not welcome at *milord* FitzAlan's demesne. His steward told our scouts he doesn't want our men tramping around the area where he's building his castle."

Bronson groaned. "Where will we camp?"

"A place called Hrolla-landriht—Hrolla's land. Don't worry. They say it's only another two miles or so. There's a meadow where we can pitch our tents, and standing stones, apparently."

Wearily, he turned his horse north to follow the others, hoping *or so* meant less rather than more. William rode alongside him. Being a

Northumbrian, Bronson had experience of standing stones and the superstitions they gave rise to. "Ancient monuments speak of fairies and the like. I hope they don't keep us awake this night."

William wiggled his eyebrows. "I wouldn't mind bumping into a winsome fairy who might cast a spell to ease these tired bones."

Bronson laughed, but in his heart he was thinking of a red headed sprite he'd like to be abed with. He straightened his aching spine. It was time to be done with these fantasies that were bound to lead to unhappiness.

After half an hour, the weary army arrived at their destination, a meadow a stone's throw away from an impressive ring of some four score standing stones. They weren't as tall as some he'd seen.

"They look like worm eaten stumps," William remarked with a shiver.

"Limestone, I think," Bronson replied. "The fog's lifted, but this place is eerie."

"And damp, despite the heat of the day," William said resignedly, getting off his horse. "Let's get the men organised to pitch camp."

It didn't take long for the infantrymen to have tents and pavilions pitched, and Bronson wandered off to take a closer look at the circle of stones.

The August evenings were long and the fog had cleared, but mystery and magic hung in the still air. He wasn't afraid of standing stones, but knew enough to be wary. He'd heard tell of strange inexplicable events at some circles. He wondered about the men who'd placed these stones here, long ago. What was their purpose?

"They're the King's Men."

He whirled around, caught off guard by a voice he didn't immediately recognize. Leicester stood behind him, in the company of Rodrick and his father. It was Leicester who had spoken. He supposed the Earl would know the legend behind this local landmark, being from the Midlands.

"And over there, the bigger one, it's the King Stone." He pointed to a taller rock Bronson hadn't noticed before, preoccupied as he was with the circle.

"Underneath the King Stone and the King's Men there are supposed to be caves that are the haunt of faeries. At midnight they come out of a hole in a bank and dance around the Stones by the light of the moon. If the hole is blocked up with a flat stone it will have been turned over by the time the morning sun rises."

An owl hooted, raising the hairs at his nape. He sensed the uneasiness of the other men, all except Leicester who simply laughed.

"There are reports of people disappearing into faerie holes for what seems like many years. When they emerge, however, they discover they have only been gone for a matter of hours."

"Folk tell the same kind of tales in Northumbria," Bronson said.

Leicester played with the lobe of his ear. "Then you likely have the tradition of leaving a token gift for the faeries, for good luck."

Rodrick cleared his throat, grinning at Bronson. "I've heard tell some of these standing stones promote fertility if you touch them."

"Don't mock, young Rodrick," the Earl chided. "Such is true of the King Stone. It's rumored young maidens come here on a certain night to touch their breasts to it, then make merry with cakes and ale."

"Hope it's tonight."

They turned to see William and Stephen. William's red face and Stephen's stern look betrayed who had made the jest.

Leicester walked away. "Further along, you'll see the Whispering Knights."

They followed and came soon to a group of five upright stones.

"Legend has it the Knights are guarding a burial chamber, thousands of years old. They are so named because of the conspiratorial way in which they lean inwards towards each other as if they are plotting against their king."

Heads swivelled to look at him. He grinned back. "Close to the bone, eh lads?"

Their laughter relieved the tension in the air. Gallien slapped Leicester on the back. "I admire a man with a sense of humor."

Leicester put a finger to his lips. "Hush, listen. Young men and women come to hear the Knights whisper the name of their future wives and husbands."

The others listened for a few minutes, then wandered away back to the camp, laughing and jesting. Only Bronson and Rodrick remained, stock still, staring at the silent stones as darkness crept into the meadow.

Grace had often accompanied her father on visits to Uncle Edwin at Shelfhoc. She called Edwin uncle, but he was actually her half cousin once removed. Edwin and her father were great friends, and his dogs were always excited to see her. Today had been no exception and she and Swan had romped with the dogs all afternoon in the field behind the manor house after visiting the church. Prior to that they'd discussed with Tybaut a few changes they thought the new master would require. It was apparent it had been the home of a bachelor, and they'd planned and plotted as to how to introduce feminine touches without offending Swan's brother.

She'd always enjoyed coming to Shelfhoc, but now she saw it through different eyes—as a home. It was presumptuous of her, since Swan had more right to be regarded as lady of the manor than she did. She pouted when Swan suggested things she didn't believe would work, quickly countering them with ideas of her own.

They'd each gone to their chamber after an exhausting day, still friends, but Grace sensed impatience in her cousin. Swan had claimed the master's chamber, which clearly Bronson should have.

She tossed and turned for many hours, wondering how he fared. She presumed all was well. If disaster had befallen her twin she would have known, and she sensed nothing of the sort.

At last she fell into a fitful sleep. And dreamed.

She was standing next to a tall weathered stone. At first she expected to see a vision of her cousin, Adam de Montbryce, who had once saved his lady love Rosamunda from a fall from atop a monolith in Bretagne, but then she was suddenly in the center of a grassy circle of smaller stones.

Hundreds of faeries danced around her, giggling. Uncertain, she glanced back at the tall stone. A man stood beside it. His face was shadowed, but his hair was long—and red.

And he was naked.

The faeries giggled again, and she looked down at her own body. What had happened to her clothes? She looked back at the stone. The red-haired man was striding towards her, his hands held out.

She reached to welcome him, as he pressed his body to hers. Desire blossomed in her woman's place. She moaned and arched her back.

The faeries fell silent and fled. She gasped at the advent of a black-winged angel that flew around the circle then alit on the large stone. The man shook his head and withdrew into the fog. "Don't go," she pleaded. "Please, don't go."

She startled awake, sweating, ashamed to discover her hand in a place it should not have been.

CHAPTER FIFTEEN

While the men were striking camp in the predawn darkness, Rodrick wandered off to find somewhere he might wash his face and hands and see to the call of nature.

Beyond the King's Men he stumbled upon a pond. His mind on his ablutions, he was startled by a movement—something white. He looked across the water as the sun rose, astounded to see a beautiful white swan preening the feathers of its long neck. It stopped when it caught sight of him, and stared for a minute or two. As they gazed at each other, another swan glided towards the first. Riding on its back was a handful of fluffy white cygnets.

He fell to his knees in the marshy ground and thanked God for this sign. Swan would be his.

His heart full, he hastened back to camp, gathered his gear, donned his armor, and mounted in time to join his father, brothers and cousin as they set off for Wallingford.

The trek took the better part of six hours. No one sang. Rodrick assumed the men's thoughts were on the looming battle, as his were. But the sign he'd been granted gave him hope. He would survive and return to wed Swan.

Their father and Leicester spent the better part of the last hour of the journey preparing them for their meeting on the morrow with Prince Henry Plantagenet.

"Remember," Robert reminded them, "Henry was only sixteen when he landed on the shores of Devon and declared himself leader of the Angevin cause after his mother's retirement. She had filled his head with the notion that the throne of England was his birthright and even at such a tender age he burned with the fervor of his mission."

"I was told he doesn't speak English," William said.

Leicester chewed on his lower lip. "*Non*, but he understands our language. I followed him as he traveled throughout the Midlands this past spring campaigning to convince people of his cause. Instead of ravaging lands, he held court and invited nobles to come in peace. Rather than burning crops, he issued charters guaranteeing our land rights in England and Normandie."

Rodrick's father continued. "When he was nine his mother had him brought to England, before her escape from Oxford. He studied in Bristol for fifteen months and met the famous astronomer and mathematician, Adelard of Bath who dedicated a treatise on the astrolabe to him, so impressed was he with the young man's learning."

"But he returned to Normandie," Stephen observed.

"He did," Leicester confirmed. "England was a dangerous place with his mother and King Stephen chasing each other from town to town and from castle to castle. And his father, Geoffrey wanted him back in Normandie to aid in his campaign to claim the duchy.

"He's an odd looking young man, Norman blood from his mother, Saxon from his grandmother and Angevin from his father. But beware of his temper. He can change in seconds from good humor to fierce anger.

"He's a keen rider, often galloping off at breakneck speed. He's been involved in his father's military campaigns and political manoeuvrings since he was eleven. Geoffrey taught him how to conduct business and war in a treacherous land."

"Sounds like the right person for the job of king in this troubled country," Rodrick observed.

Standing in the royal pavilion with the Montbryces and a dozen other barons, Bronson peered over Gallien's shoulder to study Henry FitzEmpress Plantagenet who sat upon a wooden camp stool, meaty legs splayed, hands on hips.

He pressed his knuckles to his mouth as a yawn threatened. They'd been roused at dawn and summoned. Sleep on the road had been fitful at best, especially after a dream of standing naked by the King Stone near Chipping Norton. He'd spent most of the final leg of the journey trying to recall other details of the unsettling dream.

In the camp at Wallingford sleep had been impossible. With a massive force already assembled, they'd had scant space in which to pitch their tents. He and his cousins had been forced to share their accommodations with several other loudly snoring knights. There seemed to be activity of one form or another going on all night. Stephen's army was close at hand outside the walls of the beleaguered town. The reek of smoke from campfires over which game had been roasted earlier filled the air.

Leicester had been right—odd-looking was a good way to describe the Plantagenet prince. He had a large, round head. His ruddy face was covered in freckles. He was broad and square in the chest, his arms strong and powerful. Grey eyes had widened when their party first entered the pavilion. Bronson wasn't certain but he thought the prince nodded at him while tapping his own red hair.

"This land is war-weary," Henry announced to no one in particular in an unexpectedly harsh and strident voice. "*Oncle* Stephen and I have sat here for days on end, facing each other outside Wallingford, neither wanting a clash of arms. What's to be done?"

Leicester and another man stepped forward. Bronson assumed from their resemblance this must be Robert's twin, Waleran.

"My prince, if I may be so bold, there is one thing the people of England resent more than anything else in this senseless conflict. They despise and fear the foreign mercenaries who have torn their land apart. We urge you to send home your foreign soldiers as a sign to your people."

The prince reddened further and he thrust his neck forward from his shoulders. Neither Robert nor Waleran flinched, though Bronson feared one of the famous Plantagenet rages was about to be unleashed on them.

"You are not the first to suggest this, Robert of Leicester, and I have already given orders for five hundred of my hired men to be sent back across the Narrow Sea."

Bronson noticed Gallien's rigid spine relax.

Leicester and Waleran bowed their heads in acknowledgment of the concession.

The prince grinned, slapping his thigh. "Not all the tidings are dire. I have already begun negotiations with Stephen through Archbishop Theobald and Bishop Henry of Winchester. Many barons have come over to our side since my triumphant tour of the Midlands. I am pleased beyond measure to see the Montbryces here."

Gallien and his sons bowed deeply.

"And a cousin from Northumbria, if I'm not mistaken."

Bronson bowed his head. How had the would-be king known that?

"Later, when we are done with this siege, you and I must discuss the situation in the north, Bronson FitzRam."

People turned to see who this unknown person was the prince knew by name. Gallien too looked back over his shoulder, his smile full of pride.

The prince came to his feet. "Good barons of England. I sense the end is near."

Bronson doubted he was the only one who hoped the prince meant the end of the conflict.

CHAPTER SIXTEEN

A fortnight after the men's departure, Grace and Swan were in the weaving shed. Grace was explaining warp and weft and the use of shuttles and heddles. Swan was feigning interest.

Tybaut bustled in, a sweating messenger in tow. Grace's heart stopped for a moment when she recognised him as an Ellesmere man who had obviously ridden hard. He bent the knee before them. She gripped Swan's hand as the color drained from her cousin's face. "What tidings, Rolf de Grise?"

Rolf licked his lips, still panting. "Glad tidings, milady. King Stephen and Prince Henry have settled upon a truce."

Swan's fingernails dug into her flesh. "Without a battle?"

The messenger smiled, handing her a parchment. "Aye, milady. The Earl sent word."

With trembling hands she unfurled the document, recognizing the hand of the scribe who had accompanied her father. She read the message out loud.

"The king marched a splendid army out to meet the prince, but what happened at Malmesbury was repeated. Fellow countrymen shrank from a conflict that would likely mean the complete desolation of our beloved England. Everyone recognised victory for one side or the other would mean massive land confiscations and continued bitter divisions. Stephen's army refused to fight."

Swan swayed, grasping for the wooden loom.

"The king and the prince had a conference alone together, across a small stream, about making a lasting peace."

Grace crumpled the parchment to her breast. "Praise be to the saints. They have woken up at last."

"But did Stephen acknowledge Henry as his heir?" Swan asked, her eyes welling with tears.

Grace scanned the creased parchment once more. "Father writes that the terms of peace are obvious to everyone. Stephen will have to recognize Henry as his heir."

Swan grabbed the parchment. "But what of Eustace?"

Swan had never been a good student. Sitting still while the monkish tutors her father provided for all his children droned on had been torture. As a child she never understood the purpose of learning to read. Now she was elated that she grasped most of the missive as her eyes danced over the symbols. At first she thought she had misunderstood, but then she laughed out loud, gripping the parchment.

"You'll tear it," Grace admonished, frowning sternly. "What is amusing?"

Swan inhaled deeply. "Eustace is dead."

Grace stared.

Relishing the moment of superiority that she knew something Grace didn't, she paused before continuing slowly. *"Angered by his father's truce with Henry, he set about raping and pillaging again. He fell ill one afternoon and was dead by nightfall."*

Only the sound of the jubilant messenger's heavy breathing disturbed the silence as both women stared at the document. There was no mention of the cause of Eustace's death, and Swan wondered if she dared breathe what she supposed many suspected.

Poison?

Grace looked at her. "Rotten food do you suppose?"

"Probably," she murmured.

"You're not setting a good example for our younger brother," Rodrick yelled at William over the din of celebration, wishing they had chosen a seat further away from the musicians playing shawms and hurdy-gurdys.

William tightened his grip on the waist of the village wench on his lap in the overcrowded Hall of Wallingford and laughed. "The people are relieved we're here, especially the women. I am merely taking advantage of their hospitality. Because you've sworn off the fairer sex doesn't mean—"

Rodrick banged the table with his fist, sending ale slopping over the lip of his tankard. "I haven't sworn off women. I consider myself betrothed to Swan and I don't intend to betray her with any of these doxies."

The wench giggled and thrust out her ample bosom as William nuzzled her neck, both apparently oblivious to the insult Rodrick had uttered.

His brother would soon celebrate twenty years, an age when young men's thoughts often turned to matrimony. He supposed he shouldn't judge William too harshly. After all, he hadn't given a thought to marriage, despite the entreaties of his parents, until Swan had come along. And William didn't have the responsibility of the earldom, unless Rodrick fell. Grace would make a better job of running Ellesmere than William, but sadly she would never be given the chance.

He wondered idly what would happen if he and his two brothers fell in battle. Perhaps Ellesmere would devolve to his uncle Étienne, his father's brother. But he had no children of his own and lived with his long time paramour Tandine. Mayhap the head of the family, *Comte* Alexandre, might decide Ellesmere should go to his son, Barr, or to his brother, Romain. Whatever happened in such dire circumstances would lead to dissension within the family, and unity was what had helped the Montbryce family survive and prosper when others had fallen beneath the weight of political intrigue.

Dragging his thoughts back to the present, he eyed Stephen at the other side of the Hall, carousing with a group of rowdy knights, enticing a young lass onto his lap.

"Be careful, William, not to sow any wild oats. Papa won't be happy if you get any of these women with child. It's frustrating being stuck here, but—"

William leaned close to Rodrick's ear, grinning broadly. "Don't worry," he whispered.

Whatever he was about to say next was strangled by a hiccup, followed by a loud belch. Rodrick wrinkled his nose, fanning away the unpleasant stench with his hand.

William laughed then continued, a forefinger pressed to his lips. "I take care to withdraw before—"

He wiggled his eyebrows, as if he'd offered sufficient information for his brother to comprehend.

Rodrick rolled his eyes and decided to move to where Bronson sat alone, nursing a tankard.

"All alone, Bronson?" Rodrick asked as he took a seat across from him. "None of these wenches appeal to you?"

Bronson shrugged off his irritation. "And greetings to you too, cousin."

Rodrick looked sheepish. "Your pardon. I was rude."

He grunted his agreement, unable to look at Rodrick's face without thinking of Grace. Better to establish good relations with his cousin, especially since he would be living close by the castle Rodrick stood to inherit.

To his surprise, Rodrick held out a hand. "We should be friends, you and I, if I'm to marry your sister."

Bronson shifted his weight, suppressing the notion bubbling in his throat to reveal his feelings for Grace. If he admitted them to Rodrick, he'd have to acknowledge he was falling in love with her. But love and marriage led to despair, though he'd never felt for either of his wives what burned in his gut for Grace. "I want my sister to be happy, and it seems she is anxious to wed with you. But you recognize the difficulties ahead."

Rodrick took a swig of his ale. "I do, and I had hoped to speak to Prince Henry about an interview with the Archbishop, but since news came of Eustace's death, he's been involved in negotiations with King Stephen."

"In which Archbishop Theobald is playing a vital role and is likely too busy to deal with a trivial matter such as the marriage of two cousins."

"Aye," Rodrick replied dispiritedly."Especially since I'm the son of a baron who led the fight to have Stephen crowned."

"My hope is you succeed," Bronson said, saddened by the despair on Rodrick's face.

The smile returned. "We will. I was granted a sign."

Bronson's heart thudded, Rodrick's words reminding him of his dream. "Tell me."

"Near the stones. I caught sight of a family of swans. A male and female with a brood of cygnets."

It gladdened Bronson to picture Swan with a brood of children, but he wished the details of his own dream were clearer. Some vital part of it danced around his memory but refused to reveal itself. "I believe I was given a sign at Hrolla-landriht."

Rodrick arched his brows, making him wish he'd guarded his tongue. Now he'd be obliged to explain. Mayhap if he shrugged it off, Rodrick might think he'd misheard amid the din.

"A sign of what?" his cousin insisted, eyeing him curiously.

"It's probably nothing. I had a dream, but I'm sure many others dreamt that night. Standing stones often cause men to believe they have visions."

"But it bothers you."

Bronson had never been a liar and his insightful cousin would recognize a lie if he told one now. "It does. I was standing by the King Stone."

"And?"

He swallowed the lump in his throat, hoping his cousin wouldn't guffaw too loudly. "I was naked."

Rodrick narrowed his eyes, staring at him closely. "Were you alone in the dream?"

Bronson closed his eyes. "No. There was a woman. I walked towards her. She held out her hands in welcome."

"Was it someone you recognised?"

Bronson opened his eyes and his heart leapt into his throat. He was staring at the face he'd seen in his dream, except—

He looked away quickly, a prickly sensation creeping over his already heated skin.

"It was Grace, wasn't it?" Rodrick said.

There was no censure in his cousin's voice, but Bronson put his head in his hands, the dream clear now. "Aye, but it cannot be."

"Why not? It seems Montbryces and FitzRams have a liking for each other."

He raised his head, Rodrick's wry smile lightening his heart for a moment. But then he shuddered at the sudden memory of a part of the dream he'd forgotten—the Dark Angel. "I'll not wed again."

He sensed Rodrick wanted to press him further, but he was spared the interrogation by the arrival of William who staggered to the seat next to him and promptly retched all over the table.

CHAPTER SEVENTEEN

W e're summoned to Winchester at last," Gallien de Montbryce announced to his kinsmen as they gathered around the brazier to break their fast. The chill of the grey November dawn had seeped into Rodrick's bones. He stuck the stale bread and moldy cheese in his mouth while he rubbed his frozen hands together over the glowing embers. "Thanks be to God. I am sick and tired of sleeping in a tent for months on end."

He recognized he was being testy; they were all weary of the long months spent ensuring the security of Wallingford. Some of Stephen's supporters, disgruntled by the turn of events, lingered in the vicinity. Rodrick recognised his sister's stepson, Godefroy, among them.

Tempers had grown short, patience in short supply. His father said nothing, but Rodrick sensed he missed his wife keenly. Despite the warnings, William had impregnated a village wench and the Earl had been obliged to make provision for the girl and her unborn child.

Rodrick hadn't been present, but whatever Gallien de Montbryce had said to William had chastened the young man considerably. Now he behaved like a monk, spending most of his spare time in the nearby monastery. Young Stephen too was rarely seen in the company of women.

"We're to be there by the morrow," his father continued, "which means a long day in the saddle if we want to arrive before nightfall. I've already instructed the men to strike camp. Get your belongings and let's go."

Rodrick threw the remains of his food into the fire. He didn't need to be told twice. The summons to Winchester meant only one thing. The old Minster, resting place of Saint Swithun and legendary Saxon kings, was the place where English kingship was sanctified. A truce was to be signed.

Then they could go home. He longed to see Swan again, worried about how she fared at Shelfhoc, though her missives were full of details of what she and Grace had accomplished. It amused him that there was always a note for Bronson from Grace, ostensibly explaining some change or other she wanted to make, asking his permission. However, the way Bronson salivated when he read the notes confirmed what he suspected—his cousin was pining for his sister.

The journey to Winchester was long, but Rodrick sensed optimism had taken hold. People no longer took flight when they passed. For most of his five and twenty years he had lived in a land filled with fear, and he counted himself lucky to have spent his life in a place isolated from the worst ravages of the civil war. But travel had always been a dangerous pursuit. Hearing the cheers and seeing the relief on the weathered faces of peasants gladdened his heart.

He slept soundly that night, for the first time in a long while, and felt refreshed as he and the rest of his family gathered in the chill of the cathedral to witness the momentous occasion.

Stephen and Henry came to stand in front of the high altar of the Minster.

Rodrick hazarded a glance at his father's stoic face. What must he think now of Stephen, the man in whom he'd placed such faith?

"He's a relic of a departing generation," Gallien de Montbryce murmured.

Rodrick thought he should say something to make his father feel better. "But he is dignified." It sounded weak to his own ears.

"Henry looks like a scruffy imp with his hair all over the place," William whispered.

Stephen's raspy voice broke the utter silence. "Know that I, King Stephen, appoint Henry Duke of Normandie after me as my successor in the kingdom of England and my heir by hereditary right. Thus I give and confirm to him and his heirs the Kingdom of England."

"Eustace must be turning over in his tomb," Rodrick whispered.

His father chuckled. "Best place for him."

Henry more or less repeated the same things, then did homage to Stephen and received the homage of Stephen's younger son, William.

"It appears William is more accepting of the new order of things than his late brother," Rodrick observed.

Bronson shrugged. "No doubt he has been adequately compensated for the loss of a throne."

Gallien inhaled deeply. "Henry has muscled his way into the succession through great military leadership and superb diplomacy. Let's hope it augurs well for the future. Now hopefully we can go home."

A man standing behind them leaned into their conversation. "Not yet. The new king designate will expect us to join the lavish procession of bishops and notable men planned for the streets of Winchester, then we'll proceed to Westminster where the documents will be signed and sealed."

The stranger must have sensed the despondency his words caused. He offered his hand to Gallien. "Henry of Huntingdon, at your service, my lords. Be glad. What inestimable joy! What blessed day! Peace has dawned on the ruined realm, putting an end to its troubled night. We are fortunate to bear witness to this long awaited occasion. I intend to describe it fully in my Chronicles."

CHAPTER EIGHTEEN

Swan and Grace stood together in the windswept bailey of Ellesmere Castle, the Countess and Aurore shivering at their side. Bonhomme had provided the women with woollen blankets, their heavy cloaks insufficient to ward off the bitter cold Advent had brought.

The deep chill and the apprehension of seeing Rodrick again had turned Swan's belly into a writhing mass of adders. She curled her frozen toes inside boots turned to ice, hoping she wouldn't have to flee to the *garderobe* before the men of the family rode into the bailey. They'd been sighted five miles off by expectant outriders.

During Rodrick's prolonged absence, she had begun to wonder if mayhap the night he'd brought her to a pinnacle of ecstasy with his mouth and his fingers had been a figment of her imagination. The muscles of her cleft clenched. Her most intimate place remembered. It had been real. The blanket suddenly seemed too heavy.

Would he taste the same, smell the same? Or had he forgotten her? Perhaps he'd met some winsome noblewoman in Wallingford to whom marriage wasn't laden with the difficulties Swan represented.

Grace's teeth were chattering. Her cousin was as nervous as she. Swan thought she knew the reason. Despite her insistent attempts to hide her feelings for Bronson, it was obvious she pined for him. Swan recognized another woman in love. "You're relieved to see my brother return," she teased.

"Aye, it's been too—"

She glanced sharply at Swan.

"—I mean I'll be glad to see them all return safely, not only your brother."

Swan eyed her skeptically, but all other thoughts fled as her kinsmen trotted into the bailey. She saw only Rodrick. He looked exhausted and in need of a shave, but his eyes lit up when he espied her. He leapt from his horse and strode towards her like a hungry dragon, his breath steaming on the frigid air. He stretched his arms wide, holding open his cloak. She tossed away the blanket and pressed her body to his as he folded the cloak around her.

"Swan," he murmured. "I have missed you."

She swayed against him, unable to speak, warmed by his heat, though his nose was cold. Inhaling the scent of man and leather and horse, she relished the strength of his arms, the power of his thighs, and the potency of the hard maleness pressed against her. Her belly was at peace. All was well.

Grace hugged her father and younger brothers warmly, relieved to see them return safe and sound. William seemed subdued and left quickly to enter the keep with Stephen.

Rodrick and Swan were in a world of their own, cocooned in her brother's cloak.

Her mother and sister continued to cling to her father as she turned to Bronson, feeling like a frozen fool. She'd dreamt of his return, conjured visions of him enfolding her in his cloak as Rodrick had done with Swan, whispering words of love.

Instead he stood before her, kicking a toe into the icy cobblestones, his eyes downcast, an unbroken stallion snorting frigid breath in defiance of anyone who might presume to tame him. He still held the reins of his lathered horse in one hand, ready to flee if need be.

Rodrick and Swan broke apart. He picked up the blanket she'd thrown off and wrapped her in it, never taking his eyes from hers.

She walked over to welcome Bronson, her smiling lips swollen.

Rodrick came to Grace and embraced her. "Sister," he declared. "How good to see your beloved face."

She laughed, hazarding a glance at Bronson, now embracing Swan. If only the words had come from him.

"I am beyond relieved to see you, brother," she murmured.

Rodrick too glanced at Bronson, a strange smile tugging at the corners of his mouth.

"Let's get inside, out of this cold," the Countess urged as everyone made their way to the doors of the Keep.

Only Grace and Bronson remained.

She swallowed the lump in her throat, hoping her words wouldn't emerge as shards of ice. "Welcome back, Bronson."

Finally he looked at her. "May I kiss you, Grace?"

Her heart raced. She parted her lips. He took her hands and pecked a kiss on her cheek. Disappointment flooded her. Anger surged, prompting her to do the unthinkable. As he stepped away, she stood on tiptoe, threw her arms around his neck, and kissed him firmly on the lips.

His eyes went wide. For a moment she feared he might pull away. Had she offended him, or perhaps it was disgust burning in his green eyes.

Suddenly, the blanket was gone, tossed to the ground by Bronson as he groaned, put his arms around her, and thrust his tongue into her mouth. She felt the hard evidence of his arousal. Desire skittered up her thighs and into the most private of places. Oblivious to the howl of the chilly wind and the grinning faces of the ostler and his lads, she clung to him, savoring the warmth of his mouth and the salty taste of him. She pressed her face against the soft stubble of his unshaven face.

As if awakening from a trance, he broke their kiss and stepped backwards, shaking his head. "Forgive me, Grace," he said hoarsely. "I forget myself. It's been a long while since I kissed a woman."

Her heart turned to ice, her knees threatened to buckle. Her reckless act had merely awakened his male lust. "There is nothing to forgive," she said, dismayed her voice trembled. "I kissed you."

He smiled and proffered his hand. "Aye, you did. And a nice welcome home it was. Let's get indoors. It's freezing out here."

Nice?

She had poured her heart into the kiss and he thought it was nice? The unsettling feelings she had for him were obviously not reciprocated.

The weary travellers slept for most of the afternoon, but the family gathered in the gallery before the evening meal. Rodrick chuckled at the sight of Swan in front of the hearth warming her *derrière*. He recalled how outraged he'd been at her behavior when they'd first met, yet now his mind filled with the notion of applying his hands to those warm cheeks.

She beamed a big smile and came to greet him. "My lord Rodrick," she breathed, desire burning her in eyes.

He brushed a chaste kiss on her cheek. "My lady Swan," he replied, his throat suddenly gone dry as the eastern plains the crusaders told of.

His mother beckoned them. "Come, sit while your father tells us of your adventures."

Rodrick shrugged. "There was more tedium than adventure."

Bronson agreed. "You're right, cousin."

William and Stephen mumbled something unintelligible. It suddenly occurred to Rodrick he was more at ease with his cousin than with his own brothers.

"Now," his mother declared, getting comfortable in a chair near the hearth, "explain what kept you in Westminster after the truce was signed. We expected you a fortnight ago, now here it is almost Yuletide."

To Rodrick's surprise, his father proffered his hand, pulled her out of the chair, sat in it and patted his lap. "Sit, lovely wife. I've missed you too."

His mother's face reddened, but she smiled and kissed her husband's lips. Their kiss deepened, only ending when several of those present coughed loudly.

"What?" Gallien de Montbryce declared with a smile. "Am I not entitled to kiss my wife after months apart?"

"Of course you are," his wife replied, her face redder than Rodrick had ever seen it. "Now speak on."

His father sobered. "There was much to be decided, much to be done to repair a broken kingdom. Tell them, Rodrick."

It was a source of pride that his father had chosen to let him continue. "We discussed how to suppress the violence, pillaging and burning. Ejecting the gangs of foreign mercenaries will go a long way toward solving the problem. As a start, the castles they've built will be leveled. The process has already begun. Most of them have recognized their reign of terror is over and have already fled.

"There are still extremist factions dissatisfied with the peace process. Our part will be to assist Robert of Leicester to keep an eye on them and root out any seeds of rebellion."

He looked at Grace. "It probably comes as no surprise to you that Godefroy de Cullène is among them."

His twin shivered, though she stood near the hearth. "But on whose behalf would dissidents rebel? Eustace is dead."

Bronson spoke up, looking directly at Grace. "But his brother William still lives, although I don't see him coveting the throne. Others may push him however."

His sister put her hand on the mantel, as if needing support. Rodrick suspected she was as much in love with Bronson as he was with her. He resolved to discuss the matter with Swan later.

CHAPTER NINETEEN

M ay I ask my brother to escort me into the Hall?" Grace said. "I have missed him terribly."

Swan pouted momentarily, but then smiled. "Of course, and Bronson will escort me. Good idea."

Grace breathed easier; no one seemed to have suspected she wished to avoid walking through the hallways with Bronson. He seemed irritatingly relieved to be accompanying Swan.

The Earl and Countess led the procession along corridors already festooned with boughs of holly.

As usual, Rodrick sensed her mood. "Are you unwell? I understood you were looking forward to Bronson's homecoming, anxious to show him the improvements you and Swan have made to his manor. Yet you've done naught but glare at him since our return."

She studied the stone floor as they walked arm in arm. "I doubt I'll go with them when they go to Shelfhoc."

Rodrick lay a hand on her arm. "I thought you liked him."

Her twin would immediately see through any untruth she might tell. "I do, but he doesn't care for me."

"Why do you think that?"

"It's apparent he isn't interested in women."

As she spoke the words, her body heated at the memory of his kiss in the bailey. He'd enjoyed it.

Rodrick leaned closer. "Bronson guards his emotions," he whispered, "but I have come to know him as an honest man, one I can trust. I believe he has feelings for you, but something holds him back."

She was suddenly breathless, though their pace was slow. "What could it be?"

"I don't know. Mayhap Swan can enlighten us?"

Swan held Bronson's arm tightly. "I'm happy to see you safely returned, brother, but something is bothering you."

Bronson studied the stone floor as they walked. "I'm fine."

"No you're not. What is it? Grace and I have looked forward to showing you our handiwork at Shelfhoc, but now she has intimated she won't be going with us. What did you say to her?"

Bronson furrowed his brow. "Nothing. Mayhap she's offended because I kissed her."

Swan wanted to laugh out loud. "Why would your kiss offend her? She's in love with you."

He flinched, as if he'd been whipped.

"You love her, don't you?" she whispered.

"Aye," he replied sadly, "but it can never be. We're cousins."

Now Swan laughed, drawing William's eye. "I'm the wrong person to use that excuse with."

Bronson gritted his teeth. "I'll not marry again."

Sorrow for her brother's loss swept over her again, as it did whenever she remembered the anguish on his face as he lay first Alys and then Beatrix to rest with his stillborn children. The cold north wind off the North Sea had frozen the tears on his face as he stood in Kirkthwaite's graveyard.

But life was for the living. "You cannot punish yourself for what happened."

"Death stalks me, Swan. I am destined to be alone."

"Rubbish!" she exclaimed.

This time her outburst caught the attention of the Earl who came to a halt several paces ahead of them and turned around. She smiled weakly, and the procession continued.

She glared at Bronson. "Therefore you intend to punish Grace and yourself."

"I love her," he rasped, his jaw clenched. "I will not risk—"

"No, you'll condemn her to a lonely life, when she could have had one filled with love for you and your children. You disappoint me, brother."

She broke away, and strode off to link Rodrick's free arm.

Swan paced in her chamber, rubbing her upper arms, hugging her breasts tightly. She and Rodrick had arranged to meet when everyone was abed. She wanted to discuss their siblings, but feared the moment he arrived she would attack him and insist he touch her again in those special places he'd shown her.

It was growing late. The fire in the grate had burned down, allowing the winter damp to settle on the chamber. Shivering, she climbed into bed and wriggled deep into the heavy linens, one ear exposed, listening for sounds in the corridor.

A warm kiss on her forehead startled her awake. The candle must have burned down, plunging the chamber into darkness. "Rodrick," she whispered.

"Aye, my love. Were you expecting someone else?"

She sensed his grin and sat up. "No. I was cold, so I got into bed. I fell asleep."

He sat beside her. "It's late. Papa talked on and on. He's filled with regret. He's sorry now he named one of his sons after King Stephen."

She leaned into him. "Stephen disappointed many people. It's not your father's fault he was a weak king. Perhaps if he hadn't had to contend with Maud's attacks, he might have made a good monarch."

"You're wise," he said, nibbling her ear, his breath tantalizingly warm.

A warm lethargy crept into her bones. "We need to discuss Grace and Bronson," she said sleepily.

"She loves him," Rodrick declared. "As I love you."

It was the first time he had uttered the words and her heart soared. "I love you too, Rodrick, and Bronson loves Grace."

She sensed his surprise.

"I suspected, but why doesn't he tell her?"

"He's afraid."

"Of what?"

"Of killing her."

"What!"

She gripped his warm hand. "Bronson has been married twice before. Alys and Beatrix both died in childbirth. Neither child survived. He believes he is cursed."

He pressed her hand to his lips. "I had no idea."

"He prefers not to speak of it. Their deaths broke his heart."

"But Grace is strong. She deserves a chance to have children. We must force him to face his fears." He came to his feet beside the bed. "I'll think on it and we'll talk on the morrow."

"Don't go," she sighed as sleep claimed her.

CHAPTER TWENTY

Everyone at Ellesmere was so swept up in the whirlwind of preparations for Yuletide it was more and more difficult to devise a plan to throw Bronson and Grace together. Swan and Rodrick barely had time to see each other, let alone plot a tryst for their siblings.

In addition, the men spent many an hour closeted with the Earl, planning strategy to deal with rumblings of discontent from Godefroy de Cullène and his cronies, though the general opinion was nothing would happen during Advent and rebellious activity was less likely during Yuletide.

By the third week of Advent, Swan had come to the definite conclusion that Ellesmere was not the place to arrange the tryst. As the hour for the evening meal approached, she lingered in the corridor outside the Chart Room and accosted Rodrick when he emerged. "Why not suggest to Bronson he spend Yuletide at Shelfhoc?" she whispered as they walked to the Great Hall. "He is chomping at the bit to go there."

He frowned. "But he wouldn't want to spend Yuletide alone, surely?"

She controlled the temptation to roll her eyes. "No, he wouldn't be alone. I can say I want to go with him. The season of renewal is a marvelous time to begin life in a new home and I wish to accompany my brother."

He pouted. "But I would miss you terribly."

She inhaled deeply. "You wouldn't miss me because you would be there too as a gesture of goodwill towards your Northumbrian cousin. And Grace would have to accompany us, because I cannot go alone with two men."

"Ah!"

At last!

"She might balk."

"Then it's up to her twin brother to convince her."

He rubbed a forefinger across his chin. "*Maman* will be disappointed."

"Not if we let her in on the secret."

"You've thought this through."

Swan wasn't sure what he meant, but decided not to question him. His head was probably still full of weighty matters discussed in the Chart Room. She leaned close to his ear as they entered the noisy Hall. "Are you with me?"

He grinned. "Aye!"

Bronson was surprised to see Rodrick on the threshold when he cautiously opened the door of his chamber. He'd wondered who was knocking late at night. "I was about to retire."

"May I enter? There's something I want to discuss."

His cousin seemed unusually nervous, so he allowed him entry. "What is it?"

Rodrick combed a hand through his hair. "Swan is pestering me. She wants to spend Yuletide at Shelfhoc."

Now here was an interesting turn of events. He'd been trying to come up with excuses for not spending Yuletide at Ellesmere, longing to get to his new home. Grace and Swan had written glowingly of it and he had yet to set foot there. But the Earl and Countess would be offended if he shunned their hospitality for the Yuletide season. He played for time to consider Rodrick's words. "Why didn't she speak directly to me?"

Rodrick hesitated. "She feels you've been avoiding her."

Bronson clenched his jaw. It was Grace he'd steered clear of, but supposed inadvertently he'd also withdrawn from his sister since the two women were often together. "Go on."

"She wants to spend what she sees as her last Yuletide as a single woman with you, her brother, in your new home."

Bronson was taken aback. "You believe you will secure permission to marry?"

If Rodrick and Swan married, then there was a possibility—

Why can I not get the notion of marrying Grace out of my head?

Rodrick braced his legs, arms folded across his chest. "I will marry your sister if I have to go as far as Rome for a dispensation."

Bronson sensed where the conversation was going, but saw no harm in prolonging Rodrick's discomfort. "But if Swan and I go to Shelfhoc, will you not miss her?"

His cousin eyed him suspiciously. "Man to man, cousin, I have more chance of dallying with your sister at Shelfhoc than I do here."

He should have been insulted that Rodrick took it for granted he would allow such dalliance, but in truth he recognised he wouldn't be the one to stand in the way of his sister's contentment. Rodrick was an honorable man whom he trusted. He chuckled. "I suppose it's true. I'm to be the chaperone? But what of your parents? I have no wish to offend them."

Rodrick grinned. "Leave them to me."

Swan's constant chewing of her lower lip and sideways glances were getting on Grace's nerves. Her cousin obviously had something she wanted to say.

"Ouch!" Swan suddenly exclaimed, sticking a finger in her mouth. "I've stabbed myself again with this cursed needle. I hate sewing."

"No wonder," Grace countered. "Your mind is elsewhere, certainly not on the stitches. Careful you don't bleed on the linen."

Swan smiled. "You know me well. I was daydreaming of Rodrick."

And I of Bronson.

"Bronson wants to spend Yuletide at Shelfhoc."

Grace's heart did a somersault. Had Swan read her mind? Or perhaps Bronson had somehow divined her longing to go to Shelfhoc with him. She held her tongue, afraid she might babble like an infant.

"He's asked me to accompany him. I want to go, but not if it means being apart from Rodrick. I cannot go alone with two men."

Swan wanted her along as a chaperone. Or did she? One of the men was her brother—hardly a risky escort. She'd traveled from Northumbria with him as her only companion apart from the men-at-arms who'd accompanied them.

She had to refuse. Celebrating Christ's birth and welcoming the New Year with Bronson in the house she had worked hard to prepare had been her dearest wish and her worst nightmare. Better to be far away from him, enjoying the entertainers at Ellesmere. There would be no such distractions at Shelfhoc, though she guessed the servants would perform some mummery.

"You want me to accompany you?"

Dismayed by her lack of resolve, she poked at an ill-made stitch in her embroidery, intending to unpick it. She cursed under her breath when the needle punctured her flesh. A tiny blob of blood bubbled to the surface of her skin, and sat there like a raindrop on a leaf. She stared at it, close to tears.

"Don't worry," Swan reassured her. "It will soon stop bleeding."

It's not the wound that's painful.

"Will you come with us?"

I cannot.

"Yes. If Bronson allows it."

"Leave him to me," Swan replied.

CHAPTER TWENTY-ONE

Despite the cold weather, Bronson savored the journey to Shelfhoc, his expectations high. A light dusting of snow shone white under the brilliant sunshine. He and Rodrick rode together at the rear, Swan and Grace in the midst of the column of men-at-arms, many of whom had accompanied him from Northumbria. It was reassuring there would be familiar faces among the brigade protecting Shelfhoc.

Village folk they encountered seemed content and unafraid, despite the deep chill. It was a far cry from the journey from the north. Mayhap Advent, traditionally a time of cease-fire, gave folk a chance to get on with their lives again, or perhaps they sensed peace on the horizon at last.

Grace and Swan bubbled with excitement as they crested the rise of the rampart ditch around his new home. He understood why. The house was impressive—smaller than Kirkthwaite, with more wood than stone in its construction, but far more imposing than anything they'd seen since leaving Ellesmere.

Bronson dismounted, his eyes wandering over the façade of his domain. Pride surged through his veins. "Your namesake great grandmother must have married a Saxon with great wealth," he said dryly to Swan.

Swan smiled as a stable lad came to her aid. "Aye. And a good thing for us Thane Woolgar fell at Hastings, one of King Harold's *housecarls* who fought to the death."

Rodrick tsked loudly as he took over from the stable boy, lifting her down from Cob. "Now, now, let's not get into that can of worms."

The lad walked over to assist Grace.

It didn't feel right to Bronson. He quickly motioned the boy away and put his hands on Grace's waist to help her dismount. "I'm lord of this manor now. It's my duty to welcome you, all of you, to my domain."

Blushing, Grace put her hands on his shoulders, but then pouted, her body stiff, back rigid.

Why is it I always say the wrong thing to this woman?

He took his hands off her waist and stepped away.

A man he supposed from his sister's description must be Tybaut the Steward, hurried out of the house, accompanied by two dogs. Apparently Edwin had been very attached to these animals, but Bronson didn't recognise the breed. Compared to his father's mastiffs in Northumbria they were small. They bounded over to Bronson and sniffed him, tails wagging furiously.

Rodrick arched his brows. "I've never received such a welcome from Edwin's dogs. They normally bark their heads off."

"They seem happy to meet you," Grace murmured. "They are hovawarts, descendants of two dogs given to Edwin by his German brother-by-marriage, Dieter von Wolfenberg. They are known as guardians of their masters rather than watchdogs."

Bronson hunkered down, surprised when both dogs allowed him to pet them, then rolled over to have their bellies scratched.

"Welcome back *Mesdames, Milord* Rodrick," Tybaut said effusively, bowing low. Then he turned to Bronson. "*Milord* Bronson FitzRam, welcome to your new home. It appears Bendik and Becca have adopted their new master. It was my privilege to serve your uncle Edwin in the tradition of generations of my family, and it will be an honor to be your Steward. If I may say, I see a resemblance to your uncle, except for—"

He touched a hand to his thinning hair, his eyes darting to Bronson's face, obviously relieved when his new lord laughed as he stood up again. "I'm taller too."

Tybaut smiled broadly. "You are. Come in, come in."

"We had tiles put down in the Hall," Swan gushed as they entered the main part of the lower story, the dogs hard on Bronson's heels.

He wondered who had paid for such a luxurious addition.

"It was Grace's idea," his sister said.

Grace blushed, looking uncharacteristically nervous. "Don't worry, Uncle Edwin left ample funds for such a project. And I did write to ask your permission."

Indeed she had, but at the time he hadn't grasped the scope of the improvement. "I like it," he said lamely.

She pursed her lips, evidently expecting more. "I'm sorry, I thought you would love it."

It was a stunning floor, and he wanted to tell her, but all he managed was. "I do."

"And we'll show you plans for the smoke vent in the roof to be replaced by a chimney," Swan continued. "We didn't have time to start that task."

He looked up. Most of the smoke from the hearty fire in the open hearth did indeed disappear through a hole in the thatched roof, though some of it lingered in the rafters.

"A chimney would be an improvement," he conceded, hoping to make amends to Grace.

"It was my idea," Swan crowed. "Like at Kirkthwaite."

Tybaut ushered them into a passageway. "On the right we have the pantry."

The Steward had to restrain the dogs from following Bronson inside while he inspected the provisions. Ducks, rabbits, pigeons, blackbirds and other game hung from the ceiling beams. Shelves groaned under wheels of cheese. He shivered, missing the warmth of the Hall.

"But no swans," Swan asserted. "I forbade it."

Rodrick laughed loudly and kissed her cheek. "Of course not."

Tybaut cleared his throat. "Yes, well, and here we have the Buttery."

Three barrels of ale and a cask of wine had been crammed into the confined space. "Quite a stock," he observed.

Beaming with pride, Tybaut tapped the side of his nose as if to say, *You've seen nothing yet.* He opened a stout doorway which led to a covered walkway. "*Milord* Edwin had this built to protect people walking back and forth to the kitchens from the elements."

Since it was unlikely Edwin had ever set foot in the kitchens, Bronson deemed this a kindness shown by his uncle to his household staff.

The stone kitchen was large, the spit big enough to roast an ox. He noted the quality of the pewter utensils. Three scullery lads grinned at him and bowed and scraped as if he was the King himself. Tybaut brushed them away as if they were irritating flies, then introduced a rotund, red faced toothless woman named Jolly, the Cook, who was the personification of her name. She offered each of them a pastry, which he ate in two bites. "Delicious, Jolly. I was starving and I love savory pastries. You're going to make me fat."

Her face reddened further as she giggled.

Tybaut seemed impatient to usher them to another room built onto the side of the kitchen. "*Milord* Edwin had this brewhouse added where we produce the finest ale in all Salop. That's what's in the barrels."

Mayhap Edwin *had* ventured to the kitchens.

"I look forward to tasting it."

"Tybaut is right," Rodrick confirmed with a chuckle. "I can attest to its quality."

Returning to the kitchen, Tybaut directed them into another alcove with a large brick oven. "*Milord* Edwin loved fresh breads and pastries, and this bakehouse is the result."

Bronson had expected a fairly comfortable dwelling, but Shelfhoc's amenities were a pleasant surprise.

Upon re-entering the house, Swan pushed him to the private solar on the other side of the Hall. "We had new fabric soaked in resin and tallow added to the latticework in the windows," she explained. "But Grace and I are of the opinion you should replace them with glass, like the ones in the upstairs rooms."

"We have a glazier at the castle," Grace whispered as they climbed the stairs. "And I hope you don't mind that we brought some tapestries from Ellesmere's storage rooms. A place seems warmer with hangings on the walls."

Bronson hated the sound of defeat in her voice. She had put time and effort into making his home comfortable, and he seemed unable to thank her appropriately. But if he softened his demeanor towards her, he was afraid he would babble out his obsession.

Resolved to praise her efforts, his mouth fell open when Tybaut opened the door to the master's chamber. A massive four poster bed dominated the space.

Swan rushed forward and leapt onto the mattress, giggling. "Why do you suppose Uncle Edwin needed such a large bed?" She fluttered her eyelashes at Rodrick. "I slept here—but it will be the Master's bed now. Rodrick can sleep in the smaller chamber at the other end of the landing, and Grace and I will get pallets arranged in the solar downstairs."

Grace blushed and Bronson felt his own face redden. Luxurious as the bed was, it would be a lonely place.

Why not admit he was a man who needed a woman, not only for his physical needs, but as a friend, a companion, a helpmate? He needed Grace.

"Feel the warmth up here too?" Swan asked. "We had the plaster on some parts of the outer wattle and daub renewed where it had deteriorated."

He sat on the edge of the overstuffed mattress. "You ladies have indeed worked hard to make my home comfortable, and it's evident the estate has been well stewarded, Tybaut. I thank you all."

Swan stood directly in front of him, hands on hips. "Grace and I deserve a kiss and a hearty embrace."

His scheming sister was up to something. Coming to his feet, he glanced at Grace as he embraced Swan and kissed her on one cheek, then the other, delaying the moment of truth. Would his body betray him when he touched Grace? Of course it would. The tingling had already begun when he'd lifted her off the horse.

Watching Edwin's dogs delight in Bronson's attention, Grace had been tempted to fall to the frozen ground and beg to be similarly stroked and petted. This man was turning her into a lunatic. As soon as she'd set foot in Shelfhoc again, the familiar warm feeling of homecoming had swept over her.

But she must be rid of these thoughts. Shelfhoc belonged to Bronson, a man who didn't love her. It was obvious from the smoldering look in his half-hooded eyes as he approached to claim his kiss that his thoughts were on carnal matters. How he would laugh if he discovered she was still a maiden. Bronson likely preferred experienced women who knew how to please a man. She'd been a dismal failure in that regard. Victor had never shown the slightest interest in her as a woman. There must be something in her men found repellent.

He loomed over her. "Thank you, Grace. For everything. *Merci*."

She remembered the first time he'd kissed her. It had been awkward for them both, but exhilarating for her at least. Had he felt anything? Then there'd been the kiss in the bailey, which had left little doubt.

He put his hands on her shoulders. She stifled an urge to moan as her knees threatened to buckle. Could he tell she was trembling? He bent to kiss one cheek, then the other. She opened her mouth to tell him he was welcome, but his lips descended on hers. Aware of the presence of her brother and Swan, not to mention Tybaut, she held her body rigid as his tongue explored inside her mouth. She tasted the aromatic spices of the pastry he'd eaten a short time before.

Her heart bounced around inside her ribcage when his arms slid around her. He lifted his head. "Don't worry, they're gone."

Confused, she scanned the chamber. Only Bendik and Becca remained, sitting obediently, watching them. A languid heat stole over her. Mayhap the travelling back and forth had brought on an ague. His body offered strength and comfort. She relaxed against him, feeling the unmistakable hardness of male interest. Perhaps—

The room tilted when he pulled away from her and rasped, "I am drawn to you, Grace, but I will never marry again."

CHAPTER TWENTY-TWO

A s Yuletide progressed Rodrick was enjoying the celebrations more than he ever had at Ellesmere. It had been incumbent upon his parents to sponsor lavish festivities, but there was something to be said for the more intimate surroundings of Shelfhoc.

He'd never paid much mind before to the preparations, but now he savored the delight Swan and his sister took in their handiwork.

They decorated the Hall with ivy, holly, and boughs of evergreens. Tybaut had procured ribbons in Shrewsbury and the women used them to embellish the garlands and wreaths and the Yule Tree.

Swan fashioned a large Yule Wreath from cedar boughs, the scent of the aromatic wood filling the air. Everyone would make a wish on it when they celebrated Epiphany gathered around a bonfire outside the house, then it would be burned. She'd asked him to hold the boughs as she fastened them together.

"Guess what I plan to wish for," he teased.

She fluttered her eyelashes at him, igniting sparks that lit a fire in his *couilles*. "A horse?" she asked innocently.

He smiled indulgently. "No. Guess again."

"Mmmm. Lots of vegetables with your venison on Christmas Day?"

He grimaced, leaning forward to nibble her earlobe. "No!"

She blushed, but didn't shy away. "You're distracting me, Rodrick."

"I have achieved my goal, then," he replied with a grin.

"You seem to be enjoying yourself here at Shelfhoc."

"I am," he admitted. "But I'd enjoy being anywhere with you."

She pouted. "I only wish we had mummers to look forward to. Tybaut has made enquiries in Shrewsbury, but we are late in asking. At home we had Morris dancers, mummers and sword dancers come from the surrounding communities to perform for us."

"Sword dancers? Sounds like a tale my father told me about Izzy de Montbryce, a distant cousin in Normandie."

"Yes, Izzy married Farah who had learned to perform the sword dance during her captivity in Jerusalem."

Rodrick shook his head. "I keep forgetting you and I are related. You know as much of the folklore of this family as I do."

"Probably. We may be FitzRams but we are still part of the Montbryce clan. Anyway, I don't enjoy the sword dances. For Izzy it was a dance of love, but I cover my eyes when the dancers leap over the sharp weapons and twirl intricate patterns in the air with them. The dance inevitably ends with a mock death, but the victim is *revived* by the *physician* who does the same for the dead hero in the Mummer plays."

He feigned a grimace. "Good. We don't want any dead heroes."

Christmas Eve dawned clear and bitterly cold. Tybaut entered the Hall as everyone was enjoying fresh baked black bread with the bacon and leek soup Jolly had prepared. "Your pardon, *milord* Bronson," he said breathlessly, his face flushed, nose red. "A Christmas miracle! I was out looking for the dogs when I was summoned to the gatehouse. A wandering troupe of Morris Dancers has happened by on the way to Shrewsbury. They were promised a night's lodging in Oswestry, but apparently a heavy snowfall has blocked the route. They asked if they can stay in the stables in exchange for a performance this night."

Swan clapped her hands. Her prayers had been answered. "Yes, yes, please say yes, Bronson. It will be more like home if we at least have Morris dancing."

Bronson hesitated. "Oswestry isn't far, is it? Strange no snow fell here."

"True, *milord*," Tybaut replied, rubbing his red hands together. "However, Oswestry is closer to the Welsh mountains. I took the liberty of allowing them into the stables."

"I suppose I should interview them."

Rodrick came to his feet. "I'll accompany you. The women can remain indoors where it's warm."

Bronson waved him back to his seat. "Everyone stay here. Tybaut you look frozen to the bone. Go to the kitchen and get some of this delicious soup. It will take but a few moments to ensure they know what they are doing." He smiled at his sister. "I don't want Swan to be disappointed."

Wrapped in his warm woolen cloak Bronson stepped out into the chill of the morning. The cold never bothered him. Winters in Northumbria were far more severe. He surveyed the courtyard, then lifted his gaze to the stables and thence to the fields beyond his domain, inhaling deeply, relishing the sight of his breath on the frigid air. He wondered idly where the ever-present dogs had gotten to. Probably chasing rabbits.

Swan was right. He loved Shelfhoc already, felt at home here, but Yuletide in the FitzRam household had been memorable, an important family time. Morris Dancers would make it more like home. He closed his eyes, conjuring an image of his father and mother, no doubt celebrating Swan's reprieve from the nunnery. But they'd be missing two of their offspring.

Feeling the chill seeping into his toes, he set off for the stables.

The heavy door was closed, which seemed strange, but he assumed the ostler had granted his lads leave to start the day later given that it was Christmas Eve.

Once inside he shoved the door closed.

During Tybaut's tour, he'd been impressed with the construction of the building which retained the heat of the animals it sheltered. It's warmth was welcome after the chill of the outdoors. But it seemed eerily quiet, as if the horses stood stock still. Even the normally friendly Cob eyed him like a stranger when he walked by his stall. Removing his cloak, he peered into the gloom, seeking the wandering dancers. A troupe usually consisted of at least six men. Where were they?

A young man emerged from the shadows. He looked more like a knight than a mummer. Cob nickered. Warning bells went off in Bronson's head, but it was too late. He cursed when the youth drew a dagger and he realized he'd left his weapons in the house.

Bellowing a war cry, he lunged, but strong hands grabbed him from behind. The armed stranger advanced on him, waving the dagger. Bronson leaned back against his unseen aggressors using them as leverage to kick at his attacker, but they yanked him backwards. The grinning youth took a mighty backhanded swipe at his throat. He jerked aside, but a river of molten lava seared across his chest as the blade ripped open his skin.

Am I to die here?

The answer came as pain exploded in the back of his head.

Swan stared into her empty soup bowl. "What's taking him so long?"

Grace looked anxiously towards the door, chewing on her lower lip. "I have a bad feeling."

On the one hand, Rodrick was tempted to tell them they worried too much, but on the other, Bronson had been gone overlong. He came to his feet. "I'll go out and hurry him along. He's probably required a demonstration of their talents."

He retrieved his cloak from his chamber and left the house. The cold stole away his breath. He drew the cloak up to cover his ears and mouth and set off at a brisk walk to the stables. There was no sign of Bendik and Becca. They must have gone with Bronson.

The door to the stables was closed—strange. He shoved hard, but it refused to budge. An uneasy feeling crept into his gut. If the troupe was demonstrating Morris Dancing they were doing it silently.

He reached without thinking for the dagger he'd left in the house. He decided to check the rear of the stables, or mayhap for some strange reason Bronson had taken the entertainers to the men's barracks near the rampart. Accommodations would be warmer there.

Or perhaps they were in the church, peculiar as the possibility seemed.

Edging cautiously along the back wall of the stable, he put his right eye to a crack between two planks. Nothing—only horses. He went a few paces further and bent his knees to peer through another small space where the moss chinking had fallen away. The breath left his already beleaguered lungs. A man lay face down in a pool of blood—a man with unmistakable red hair. "What the devil?"

Someone tapped him on the shoulder. He whirled around, vaguely aware of a giant standing behind him. A mailed fist connected with his jaw, sending him sprawling backwards, his head smashing into the wooden wall. The sky was suddenly where the earth should be.

Why would a mummer be wearing armor?

He attempted to get up but a booted foot pressed on his chest as the fist landed on his nose. He choked on blood, pain lancing into his head.

"Leave him, Titus. He'll soon freeze to death out here."

He sank into blackness, thinking the sneering voice was somehow familiar.

CHAPTER TWENTY-THREE

Grace jumped up from her seat, sending her bowl clattering to the floor. Her heart was racing; intense pain throbbed in her temples. "Something has happened to Rodrick."

Swan left her place at the table to lift a corner of the window covering. "Where can they be?"

A commotion at the main door of the house caught their attention. Relief flooded Grace. Bronson and Rodrick had returned. But her blood turned to ice when the man who had entered the house removed his cloak. "Godefroy!" she gasped, gripping the edge of the table.

Swan frowned, pressing close to Grace. "Who are you? What are you doing here?"

Grace grasped her hand. "Godefroy is my stepson."

He bowed with a mock flourish. "At your service, step-mama," he said, flicking his still fastened cloak back over his shoulders.

A serpent wriggled in Grace's belly. She had never liked this young man, never trusted him, but she determined not to show her fear. "Where are *milord* Bronson and *milord* Rodrick?"

He sneered. "Safe enough. They won't interfere."

"Interfere in what?" Swan asked, apparently unperturbed though Grace felt her cousin's fingernails pressed into her flesh.

"Don't worry," Godefroy said to Swan. "I'm not interested in you."

"But what do you want with me?" Grace said, deafened by the pulse at her throat. "I have given up any claim on your father's estate."

"That's of no importance now. All is lost if Plantagenet takes what should have gone to Eustace."

He must be mad.

"Eustace is dead."

"But Stephen's second son, William lives. He will be king, not Henry the upstart Angevin."

"William has pledged to Henry," Swan declared.

Grace recognized the malice in Godefroy's gaze. "And what do we have to do with this? Why have you come here?"

"Your cursed father must be persuaded to change sides. He has long been Stephen's man. Now he must support William's claim to the throne."

The serpent bit into the vital part of Grace's body that kept her heart beating. "You believe I can influence my father?"

Godefroy grinned as a burly giant of a man entered the Hall. "No, but if he thinks changing sides will save your life, he will."

Swan thrust her chin in the air, hands on hips. "You can't get away with this. Our Steward will return momentarily, as will my brother and my cousin. There are men in the barracks, dogs—"

She stopped as Godefroy strode toward her, his hand raised.

"Stop!" Grace cried. "Harm a hair on Suannoch's head and I will fight you every step of the way."

Godefroy laughed. "Titus here will tie her up with your puny Steward and your other servants in the Buttery. The dogs have been taken care of, the men-at-arms drugged, your brother and cousin out of the way. Our horses await. Get your cloak."

Rodrick tried unsuccessfully to cover his ears with his hands, desperate to assuage the insistent pounding. He lifted his head, gagging as the world blurred around him. He managed to raise up on one elbow, transfixed by the bright red pool on the white ground. Someone had shoved a knife up his nose. He coughed, spitting up more blood.

No, it hadn't been a knife—a fist. Gingerly he touched a finger to his nose, instantly regretting it as pain flared again. He was *fyking* cold. His teeth were chattering, but at least the pounding had stopped.

Pounding? Sounding like—horses. Galloping away.

He had to get inside, get warm. Had to find out what had happened. Who were these men? The voice—the last thing he recalled hearing—nagged at him.

He scrambled to his knees, resting his forehead against the wood of the stable. The stable—*Dieu*! Bronson was inside.

He put his eye to the crack, careful not to touch his nose to the rough wood. His cousin was still there. Hadn't moved. Was he dead? Rodrick wasn't sure how long he'd lain on the cold hard ground, but for certain he'd be incapable of opening the stable door with his frozen fingers.

He braced himself on all fours, then bent one knee, planting his foot on the ground. He'd lost feeling in his toes and hoped when he tried to stand his legs wouldn't fail him. Bending the other knee, he came slowly to his feet, his fingernails digging into the rough wood.

Panting hard, he levered his body away from the wood, then let go, ridiculously elated when he didn't fall over. As the fog in his head cleared, dread gripped his vitals. Swan and Grace were alone in the house, apart from servants. Someone had made sure of it.

Strangely, his greater fear was for his sister. Her name echoed over and over in his head.

Forcing his frigid body to move, he staggered to the house, pushing the door open with his shoulder, relieved when it gave way, apparently unbarred. He slammed it shut and fell to his knees, hands tucked under his armpits, arms folded across his trembling body.

He scanned the Hall. Empty. But the pounding had begun again. Someone was shouting.

Leaning heavily against the door, he came slowly to his feet and listened.

"Help! Help!"

Swan!

He moved towards the buttery, holding on to the wall. The shouts grew louder. He tried to assure Swan he was there, he was coming to her aid, but sounds refused to emerge from his raw throat.

Someone inside was kicking the door. With trembling fingers, he turned the key in the lock. The banging and shouting ceased.

Not knowing what to expect, he opened the door slowly. Swan and Lucia sat back to back, tied together, the maidservant's feet wedged against a barrel, pushing back against her door-kicking mistress. Swan's knees were bent. Her gown had slipped around her thighs. The abject fear left her face when she saw him, but then her lip trembled as tears welled. "Rodrick, you're alive, but what have they done to your nose? Untie me quickly. They've taken Grace."

He swayed on his feet, unable to take his eyes off Swan's bared legs.

Who? Why? Where have they taken her?

"There's a carving knife in the pantry, *milord*."

Tybaut!

Dragging his gaze away from Swan, trying to make sense of what she'd said, it dawned on him the Steward and Jolly and the scullery lads were bound together, crammed in the tight space amid the barrels. The Cook was sobbing, her face redder than a beetroot.

"A knife, *milord*. In the pantry. You can cut our bonds."

He shook the fog from his head, feeling blessed warmth creep back into his limbs. He crossed the hall, retrieved the knife from the pantry and returned to cut Swan free.

The room tilted when he got up too quickly, so he passed the knife to Lucia. "Cut them loose."

The maid knelt quickly to slice through the men's bonds.

He pulled Swan into his arms, savoring her warmth. "Who has taken Grace?" To his own ears he sounded like a drunkard.

"It was Godefroy de Cullène," Lucia declared. "He wants to force your father to change sides and support William's claim to the throne."

"He is mad," Swan whispered, her voice hoarse. "William doesn't want the throne."

Rodrick's instinct was to leap on his horse and go after Grace, but his cousin—

"Tybaut. *Milord* Bronson is in the stable, badly injured. I need your help to open the door."

He avoided Swan's eyes, unwilling to voice his belief her brother was dead.

"Aye. The lads and I will get it open," the steward reassured him, scrambling to his feet. "I blame myself, *milord*. I should never have allowed them onto the estate."

Rodrick gritted his teeth as the Steward rushed off. "Your nose is broken, my love," Swan murmured. "I don't know how to set it."

"With your permission, *milord*, I do," Lucia said. "I learned from my grandmother, who was taught by your grandmother, Countess Carys."

The maid placed her warm fingers on his nose, barely touching. It was almost pleasant until she suddenly pressed hard. Pain arrowed into his head. But then it was gone. His nose felt better.

"The bruising will take a while to disappear, but it will heal now."

Rodrick thanked the saints for the healing skills passed on since his grandmother's time. If Bronson still lived, he would need this young woman's help.

CHAPTER TWENTY-FOUR

The scullery lads put their shoulders to the stable door and rushed in, led by Tybaut. "There he is," the Steward shouted. "Turn him onto his back."

"No," Lucia yelled as she hurried in with Swan. "Wait. You might injure him further."

Swan fell to her knees at her brother's side, sobbing. "Bronson," she breathed, afraid to touch him. "You cannot die."

Rodrick knelt beside her, his arm around her shoulder.

Bronson's hair was matted with dried blood. Lucia ran her hands over the back of his head. "There is a swelling here," she said. "But he lives. They struck him with a heavy object. We must be careful how we turn him. Judging by the bloodied straw beneath him, he has obviously suffered a grievous wound. If it's his belly—"

Swan shuddered. "Jolly is bringing the *dwale*," she murmured.

Lucia shook her head. "We won't need it until he awakens. Then the drug will calm him and aid his healing."

The men positioned themselves to turn their master onto his back. Only Rodrick's strong hand gripping hers prevented Swan from swooning. His attacker's weapon had sliced through his tunic and penetrated deep into his chest. Blood oozed from the raw flesh.

"Fetch his cloak and wrap it around his lower body while I examine the wound," the maidservant said. "We must warm him up, though the chill may have helped control the bleeding."

She peered at the deep gash that ran from one armpit to the other. "He's lucky it wasn't lower," she observed. "The fabric of his tunic has adhered to the torn skin, and I am afraid to remove it."

"What can I do?" Swan asked, feeling completely useless.

"Put your hands on either side of the wound and slowly press the edges of his tunic together. We'll try to close the wound this way, then pad it with linens."

Tybaut dispatched one of the lads to get cloth from Jolly.

Swan flexed her cold fingers then put her hands on her brother's chest, carefully pushing the edges of the gash together. Bile rose in her throat as more blood oozed from the wound. She uttered a prayer of thanks he hadn't awakened from his stupor.

"Let me," Rodrick whispered.

"No," Swan replied. "I must do this for my brother. Where are the men-at-arms? And the dogs? This was a carefully planned attack. You have to organize a search for Grace."

Rodrick came to his feet. "No need to search. There is only one place Godefroy can have taken her—Cullène Hall. But we'll send one of Edwin's birds to Ellesmere to inform my father. He is closer and can be there before us. At least they didn't hobble our horses."

Swan gagged, sickened by the thought they might have maimed her beloved horse.

Rodrick hurried away, passing the scullery lad returning laden with linens. "Cook says there's more if we need them."

Lucia rummaged through and pulled out an old bedsheet. She folded it into a long pad. "Keep pushing the edges together, milady, then slowly withdraw as I press down harder."

Swan again thanked God for the presence of this servant who might yet save her brother's life. She wished Rodrick still knelt at her side, but was heartsick for him and his fear for his sister. Lucia too must be wretched at the loss of her mistress, yet she tended Bronson calmly and carefully.

The day had begun with great promise. But a dark shadow had been cast over the celebration of the birth of the Light of the World.

Rodrick released the pigeon into the cold air. "Godspeed, little bird." He would have preferred to impart the dire news to his parents in person, but time was of the essence.

Hastening back to the stable, he caught sight of three of Shelfhoc's men-at-arms walking towards the house from the direction of the barracks, one soldier bearing the weight of a dog dangling lifeless in his arms. His heart plummeted. Surely it hadn't been necessary to kill Bendik and Becca.

His spirits lifted when he saw Becca loping behind the men, shaking her head. Beyond her came more soldiers.

He hurried towards the man carrying Bendik. "Is the dog dead?"

The soldier looked half asleep. "Nay, my lord. Drugged. The lot of us. Must have been something in the soup brought from the kitchens."

Rodrick lifted Bendik into his arms. To his relief the hound raised its head, its eyes glazed. "Good dog."

As if understanding his words, Bendik wriggled out of his grip, stood shakily on all four paws and shook himself, yawning widely.

"Aye," the soldier continued. "But how they drugged the dogs is a mystery. What were they after?"

Rodrick gritted his teeth. "They've taken my sister."

The man's jaw dropped as he straightened his shoulders. "We'll find her, *milord*. On my honor, I swear it."

"First we must see to your new Master. He is badly wounded."

The men followed him into the stable where Tybaut and the lads had Bronson propped up, his head drooped forward. Lucia was wrapping linens around his chest while Swan held his long hair out of the way. Her eyes widened with relief when she saw the men-at-arms.

As if sensing their new Master's distress, both dogs lay down alongside him, looking expectantly at those tending him.

"You kept his tunic on," Rodrick said with surprise.

"Lucia thinks it's better to do so until we can stop the bleeding. He is still warm—a good omen. It'll take strength to lift him."

Rodrick knelt beside Bronson. "The men were drugged, but seem to be recovering. The dogs too. At least the blood hasn't seeped through the bandages yet."

"Let's hope moving him doesn't worsen matters," Swan replied.

"Wait!" Tybaut suddenly declared. "I have an idea."

He hurried off in the direction of the house, taking two lads with him.

Minutes later the three trooped back, the boys pulling like a pair of horses between the traces of a low two wheeled cart. "We use this to move barrels and other heavy objects," Tybaut explained, smiling proudly.

"Good thinking," Rodrick said. "It's wide enough, and low enough we won't have to lift him high."

"It's a rustic creation made by one of the tenant farmers and the wheels aren't perfectly round. It won't be comfortable trundling along the frozen ground."

Rodrick refrained from mentioning Bronson hadn't yet awakened from his stupor and likely wouldn't feel anything. "We'll not get him up the stairs to his bed."

Swan came to her feet. "I'll prepare my pallet in the solar."

Hugging her arms, Grace paced in the chilly windowless attic atop Cullène Hall. Her fingers and toes were still frozen from the long ride. For the first few miles she'd tried hard not to lean against Godefroy's giant accomplice, but common sense had forced her to benefit from his warmth. Clinging to his broad back also improved her chances of staying on the galloping horse.

Godefroy had evidently taken over the master's chamber, and the giant had carried her over his shoulder to the top of the house and dumped her unceremoniously onto the pallet bed. It was the first time she had set foot in the cramped room tucked beneath the thatching. There was no fire, not even a grate. The only recourse was to climb under the one meager blanket Godefroy had provided.

She curled up on the musty pallet, drawing the blanket to her chin, determined not to cry. Once she started, she might never stop. Her mind raced through the dire possibilities of what had happened to Bronson and Rodrick. The pain she'd experienced earlier in the day had been a premonition Rodrick had been hurt, but she didn't believe him dead. Her heart and her gut would have sensed if he was no longer of this world.

But Bronson?

She squeezed her eyes tight to shut out the persistent image of the black-winged angel sitting atop a monolith. She'd never had any doubt Bronson was the naked man of her dream. Had the dark angel been the harbinger of his death? Perhaps her sinful longings had brought the wrath of God down on both their heads.

CHAPTER TWENTY-FIVE

Swan clung to Rodrick as they stood gazing at Bronson, hoping for some sign of wakefulness. Her brother had moaned only once while being lifted off the cart onto the pallet earlier in the afternoon. She stared at him, remembering good and bad times growing up. He'd always been her protector.

"He looks helpless," she whispered to Rodrick.

He tightened his grip on her waist. "He's strong, and there is no sign of fever."

As if to confound his words, a flush spread across Bronson's face and beads of sweat broke out on his forehead. Lucia came forward. "I was hoping this wouldn't happen." She looked at Swan nervously. "He's shaking. It's not a good sign."

Rodrick shifted his weight. "I regret having to leave you, Swan, but I must ride on to Cullène Hall. Papa will have received the message by now and is probably ready to get underway. I want to strangle Godefroy with my bare hands for this."

Swan wished with all her heart he didn't have to leave. If her brother died—"You must go. Rescue your sister and bring her back safely. Mayhap if she is here, Bronson might—"

Rodrick kissed her forehead when the words stuck in her throat. "I will take some of the men with me, but you will still be protected. I doubt if the conspirators will return."

Lucia looked up from her task of applying damp linens to Bronson's face. "Perhaps this will help, my lord. When I lived at Cullène Hall, cursed place that it is—"

She made the sign of her Savior across her body.

"—the servants often spoke of a passageway into the house from the surrounding fields. I was never in it, but some boasted of escaping to go to the village without their master's knowledge. A harsh taskmaster was Victor de Cullène, and that Steward of his, well—"

Rodrick held up a hand. "Yes, yes, Lucia. How can I locate the entry to this passageway?"

The maidservant bit her lower lip. "Mostly they were deep into their cups on their return, but I seem to recall something of a big tree growing every which way."

Swan rolled her eyes. "That's not much help."

Rodrick pulled her to his body. "It's better than nothing. Thank you, Lucia."

The maid smiled and Swan regretted having made light of her information. "Yes, thank you, Lucia. What would we have done without your help?"

"Get your cloak, Swan," Rodrick whispered. "Bid me *adieu* in the courtyard."

Lucia touched her hand. "I will watch over him while you go. Godspeed, *milord* Rodrick. Bring my mistress back safely."

Swan retrieved her cloak from the floor where she had hurled it upon first entering the solar and Rodrick draped it over her shoulders, then donned his own. They hurried outside, where the men-at-arms waited with his horse.

He drew her close and folded his cloak around her. "I cannot kiss you as I would wish with the men watching."

She swallowed the lump in her throat as he pecked a kiss on her lips. "Hurry back. Be careful with your nose. It looks painful. I should have taken better care of you."

He smiled, grinding his hips against her. "The cold will numb the discomfort. Besides, you, Suannoch FitzRam, will be taking care of all my wants and needs for the rest of our lives."

She blushed as the hard maleness he pressed against her sent desire skittering up her legs.

He pulled away and mounted his horse. "Go inside."

She shook her head and remained staring at the horizon for long minutes until he had ridden out of sight.

Bronson stood trembling by the monolith, still naked, but some sharp-toothed creature had slithered inside his chest and was eating his flesh. A horse had trampled his head.

The naked woman—he was sure it was Grace—still held out her hands in welcome.

But he shook his head. "I'm too hot," he rasped, his throat parched.

"Drink this."

He sipped liquid, though it wasn't Grace who had spoken. Broth maybe. How can there be broth out here by the Standing Stones?

Grace opened her arms wider, revealing lovely breasts. Mayhap if he suckled, he might feel better. He groaned, reaching to ease the ache at his groin.

I'm still clothed.

But he was naked.

"At least the bleeding has stopped, thank goodness."

Who is bleeding?

"I'm not bleeding, I'm burning."

Grace kept smiling. Why was she smiling when he was being consumed by fire?

"We can consider sewing the wound closed now. I'll get the *dwale* from Jolly and a few men to help."

"Jolly. Jolly. Jolly."

There's nothing jolly about the pain in my chest. Perhaps my heart is broken.

"Dwale?"

"For the pain, brother."

Swan? What's Swan doing at the monolith?

He peeled open one eye. "Swan."

"Hush, Bronson. You've been injured."

He closed his eye. This was too confusing. He wanted Grace, not Swan. But Grace was disappearing, drawn away by—

He struggled to sit up. "The youth with the dagger! Help her."

"Lie down, Bronson. You'll reopen the wound."

As the fires of hell blazed through his body he stared at the faces surrounding him. Grace wasn't among them. He lay down and slipped back into the dream, hoping to find her there.

Jolly bustled in with the *potel* of *dwale*, her face drawn and redder than usual. Swan hoped the strain of the tragedy didn't prove too much for the elderly Cook.

She accepted the drug with trembling hands. "I'm nervous with *dwale*."

"You needn't worry about my *dwale*," Jolly reassured her, somewhat belligerently. "The recipe is one Countess Carys handed down, God Rest Her Soul. The present Countess Peridotte swears by it—saved her life."

"I can attest to it," Lucia confirmed, reaching to take the corked *potel* from Swan. "We've used it at Ellesmere for years. Just the right amount of hemlock. Not enough to be poisonous, but sufficient to induce sleep."

"But he hasn't fully awakened yet," Swan protested. "Only mumbled about being too hot."

"But he sat up, my lady. And he sipped a bit of broth, a sure sign he'll soon be awake. We should embark on the stitching now."

The maidservant looked to the doorway as four burly men-at-arms entered, stamping the snow off their feet. "Good. We'll need them to hold him down if he comes to."

"I've no *kitgut* for sewing," Jolly complained. "You ladies used the last weeks ago for strings on the *rebec*. Tybaut will have to get one of the tenant farmers to slaughter a sheep."

"A sheep?" Swan asked, wishing she'd paid more attention to such matters. She'd left the healing up to her mother and older sisters. She remembered Jolly's disapproving look when she'd insisted on having the *rebec* restrung for Bronson's arrival.

"Aye," Jolly replied. "We make *kitgut* out of a sheep's intestines, but it takes a while."

She thrust a handful of embroidery silks at Lucia, then wiped both pudgy hands on her apron. "I've waxed these. All I've got to offer."

Swan wavered between laughing and screaming hysterically—her well-muscled brother stitched up with embroidery silks. She would never ply a needle again.

Jolly stamped her foot. "Saints preserve me. I forgot the oil of roses and honey."

"What's that for?" Swan asked.

"For the poor man's broken head. We'll need to shave off his hair."

"Absolutely not!" Swan shouted, closer than ever to hysteria. "It's bad enough he has to suffer being sewn up with embroidery silk. We are not cutting off his hair."

Jolly glared, but remained in the solar.

"Me and the lads'll fetch a trestle table from the Hall," one soldier said. "Raise up the pallet from the floor. Make it easier to do the job."

"Of course," Swan replied, nervously wringing her hands. Why hadn't she thought of it? Dread had robbed her of her wits.

CHAPTER TWENTY-SIX

Seated on his horse atop the rampart ditch surrounding Cullène Hall, Gallien de Montbryce, Third Earl of Ellesmere, now understood the anger and dread that must have knotted the belly of his grandfather when he received word his daughter, Rhoni had been taken by brigands.

Fortunately, Rhoni had been rescued by the man she'd eventually married, Ronan MacLachlainn, who'd beheaded the leader of the villains with one swift stroke of his sword. Gallien fully intended to mete out the same punishment to Godefroy de Cullène. He cursed the day he'd ever agreed to Grace's marriage, knowing intimately the pain of a catastrophic union.

Ronan had been in time to save Rhoni from the humiliation of rape. Gallien prayed for the same for his precious daughter. If Godefroy had defiled her, he would choose a slower and more painful death for the wretch.

He pushed aside the dire possibility. Only clear thinking and decisive action would save Grace. "We'd have no difficulty overwhelming them if we attack," he said to Bravecoeur, the captain of his guard mounted beside him. "But that would place my daughter's life in peril."

"But if he kills her, he will have no hold over you," Bravecoeur replied.

Gallien shifted his weight in the saddle, his body tense. "Men such as Godefroy are cut from the same cloth as Eustace. Inflicting pain is what they excel at. If he thinks he cannot persuade me to his cause, he is as likely to kill her for spite."

"And we must bear in mind—"

Bravecoeur stopped abruptly at the sound of horses approaching. He wheeled his mount, stood up in the stirrups and shaded his eyes. "It's *milord* Rodrick and his men."

Gallien was immensely relieved to see his son. His face was bruised and battered, but fury burned in his eyes. They reached over and clasped arms. "Looks like you had an argument with a wall."

Rodrick grimaced, touching his nose carefully. "Aye, but I was the lucky one. Bronson lies near death, his chest slashed open."

Gallien clenched his jaw, bereft that the cousin he barely knew, but who had impressed him as a man of honor and intelligence should lose his life to one such as Godefroy. "We will avenge him, and Grace."

Rodrick nodded. "What's the plan?"

"We were discussing the possibilities," Bravecoeur replied.

"Grace's maidservant told me there is a hidden passageway into the house, but the only detail she recalled was the entry is near a tree that grows every which way."

"An oak," Gallien declared. "An oak grows in every way."

They scanned the surrounding area. Rodrick pointed to a grove of shrubs in a dip not far from the side of house. "There, in the midst of those bushes."

Gallien narrowed his eyes. A lone oak, wider around the gnarled trunk than two men could span, dominated the undergrowth, its bare rugged branches reaching to a large wide-spreading crown, stark against the white sky. "I'd wager it's been there longer than the house," he said.

Rodrick dismounted. "I'll investigate. Lucia believes only the servants are aware of the passage, but it may have been discovered and filled in."

"I'll come with you," Bravecoeur said. "If we stay behind the bushes for as long as possible, we won't be spotted from the house."

Gallien was uneasy. "It's strange they have no guards posted outside as far as I can see."

Rodrick scanned the area again. "There's only the one small window on that side in any case, and Tybaut told of a mere handful in the group posing as mummers."

Men-at-arms came forward to lead their horses back over the rampart. Gallien remained atop the fortification and watched his son and his captain lope across the ridge until they were out of sight of the front of the house. Then they crouched down and disappeared into the ditch.

Grace tightened the blanket around her shoulders and leaned her ear against the door. She'd heard faint voices before, but now it was strangely quiet. Had Godefroy gone off somewhere? She'd not seen him since they arrived and no one had brought her food or drink.

She scurried away from the door when a loud footfall sounded on the stairs below.

The giant?

Wood scraped against metal, followed by a clunk as what she assumed was a bar was dropped to the floor. Her heartbeat thudded in her ears when the door banged open wide. Godefroy stood on the threshold, the giant at his side. Fear closed her throat.

"Don't worry, I'm not interested in having you," Godefroy sneered, his nose in the air. "Titus, however, may be hard to restrain if negotiations don't go our way. He likes a challenge."

"Negotiations?" she murmured, keeping her eyes off the giant, hoping she didn't look as terrified as she felt.

"Your dear Papa is on the rampart."

Papa!

She stiffened her shoulders. "My father will never negotiate with the likes of you, Godefroy."

"Then you will die, *maman* dear."

He strode forward to grasp her arm.

She flinched away.

He held out his hand. "You can come willingly, or I'll have Titus carry you like a sack of grain. Your choice."

"I will go with you, but I won't take your hand," she declared.

His sneering smile sickened her, but he gave a mock bow and ushered her through the doorway. "Let's assure the Earl of your presence. You'll need the blanket. It's cold out."

123

The trapdoor wasn't hard to uncover amid the hawthorn bushes. "The prickly shrubbery has kept even the snow away," Rodrick quipped.

Bravecoeur snickered, braced his legs, looping his hand under the rough rope handle and pulled hard. It creaked open. Bravecoeur pressed two fingers over his nostrils. "What a stench!"

Rodrick shrugged. "Can't smell a thing. One advantage of a broken nose."

They peered into the blackness beyond the two or three worn wooden rungs of a ladder that led into the ground. "Narrow," the soldier remarked, "but we should squeeze through."

"Looks well used," Rodrick remarked. "I hope not by Godefroy."

Bravecoeur shook his head. "Can't see a reason for the master to sneak in and out of the house."

Rodrick unbuckled his scabbard and laid it on the ground. "I hate to leave my sword here, but it will be more of a nuisance." He patted the hilt of the dagger sheathed at his waist.

Ellesmere's Captain hesitated a moment, then removed his sword, and followed Rodrick down the ladder.

They were forced to crouch as they walked in complete darkness, flinching and dodging as they were poked and scratched by the occasional tree root. "If this is a route for servants, I doubt the other end will come out in the main part of the house," Rodrick whispered.

"Right," his companion grunted, sounding out of breath. "I'll be happy to reach the other end. I hate tight spaces."

"Mayhap animals use this too," Rodrick replied, not wanting to dwell on thoughts of what might have lived and died in this tunnel.

He bumped into the ladder in the pitch black, glad he'd held his hands out in front of his body. He looked up. Half a dozen steps loomed in the meager chink of light escaping from the edges of a closed trap door.

He climbed slowly, braced his thighs against the ladder, then pushed the door with both hands. It resisted as though something stood on top of it. Nothing for it but to shove harder and hope whatever it was didn't tip over with a bang.

It opened further when he put his shoulder to it. He peered through the crack into a tiny buttery, lit by a narrow window. Seeing nothing but a few barrels, he shoved the door open a little further, then scrambled out, amused to see a small cask permanently affixed to the door.

Crouching, he beckoned Bravecoeur who also chuckled at the cask lying on its side. "I'd say the servants have gone to a deal of trouble to conceal this," he said.

They crept to the door. "Let's hope it's not locked," Rodrick whispered.

It opened readily into a pantry, but they cringed as the hinges creaked loudly. Suddenly hearing muffled voices, they walked stealthily through the kitchen, surprised it was empty.

"There's been no food prepared here this day," Rodrick said. "Godefroy must have sent the servants away for Christmas."

Bravecoeur looked around. "I'd say this kitchen hasn't been used in a while. The master of the household has been off causing trouble."

They paused at the entryway to the Hall. The sound of voices was coming from outside. Godefroy was shouting. "As you see, my dear Earl, your daughter is safe for the moment. Won't you come inside and together we can formulate a plan to rid our country of Henry Plantagenet?"

"I do not negotiate with men who hold women as hostages."

Rodrick surmised his father had come closer to the house. The strength in his voice was heartening.

"Are you well, daughter?"

Rodrick glanced quickly at Bravecoeur.

My sister is outside with them.

His cohort signalled his understanding.

"I am, *mon père*," Grace replied, her voice clear and calm. "However, I have been kept in an attic with no food or water, watched over by this hulking brute."

Rodrick's heart pounded with fear and pride for his brave sister. He glanced to the stairs, pointing to himself, then motioned for Bravecoeur to remain below.

He ran swiftly to mount the wooden staircase, panting when he arrived at the open door of a tiny attic. He'd been in the house when Victor died and Grace needed company during the long year of obligatory mourning, but never in this chamber.

A wooden bar lay on the floor outside the door. He picked it up, testing its weight as he swung it with both hands.

Perfect.

Grace's fingers and toes were frozen. She desperately wanted to get back indoors, but her father sat atop his horse mere yards away, man and beast snorting icy breaths.

She hoped he'd understood her message—Godefroy and the giant were the only conspirators in the house as far as she knew, though for a moment she sensed movement behind her.

"I will not *parler* with you until my daughter is allowed back in the house. Can you not see she is freezing to death?"

Why does Papa want me back inside?

She stared at him, trying to understand the message in his steely gaze.

"Very well," Godefroy declared, looking nervous. "Titus, take my stepmother back to the attic."

The giant grasped her arm. Should she fight him, try to run to her Papa? Her father inclined his head imperceptibly and she suddenly sensed he had a plan. She had to trust him. She allowed Titus to lead her into the house.

He lumbered up the stairs behind her as she tried to make her numbed feet work. Her racing heart calmed as the certainty her twin was in the house settled in her bones. She walked to the edge of the pallet bed, turning to glare at Titus as he hovered on the threshold, unaware of what she'd seen—her smiling brother hidden behind the open door, a length of wood gripped in both hands.

She had to entice the brute to enter the room. She stuck out her tongue and her breasts. "You'll never have me, Titus. My father will make sure of it."

The pouting giant strode into the chamber and shoved her backwards onto the pallet. He grinned, fiddling with the laces of his leggings. The grin left his face when Rodrick cracked him on the back of the head with the bar from the door. He snarled, whirling around. Rodrick swung with both hands. The wood landed squarely on the giant's bulbous nose. His eyes rolled heavenward and he crashed to the floor, raising a cloud of dust.

Rodrick clenched his jaw as he brought the bar down on the giant's head again. "One more for good measure."

Grace leapt up from the pallet and threw her arms around her panting brother. "Is Bronson with you?" she asked.

126

CHAPTER TWENTY-SEVEN

I t was evident to Gallien when Bravecoeur emerged from the house to stand behind Godefroy that the wretch believed his accomplice had returned.

He smiled inwardly when his son and daughter appeared in the doorway, Rodrick's arm around his sister's shoulders. Still Godefroy did not turn to see who stood behind him.

This nincompoop thinks to govern my country.

As he dismounted, Godefroy strode toward him. "Excellent, my lord Earl. I was confident you would come to see it my way."

Gallien flexed his fingers, drew back his arm and thrust his fist into the grinning face. Godefroy crumpled silently to the ground.

"Where's the giant?" Gallien asked Rodrick.

"Out cold."

He held out his arms as Grace rushed to him, enfolding her shivering body in his cloak. So great was his relief, words refused to come.

Bravecoeur hoisted Godefroy over his shoulder and set off in the direction of the rampart. "I'll get the swords," he shouted.

Rodrick joined his father and sister and the three clung together as Grace sobbed.

"It's over now," Gallien reassured her. "I'm taking you both back to Ellesmere."

Rodrick eyed him strangely. "I cannot, *mon père*. I must return to Shelfhoc. Swan is alone with Bronson—"

Grace turned to Rodrick. "What's wrong with Bronson? Why is he not here?"

Rodrick stepped backwards. "He was wounded. A fever took hold."

"I must go to him," she murmured, swaying against him, her fingernails digging into his hand.

Grace seemed unduly stricken by Bronson's injury. He locked gazes with his son, who nodded in answer to his unspoken question.

It grieved him that both his children had fallen in love with someone they might never be allowed to marry.

Rodrick was impatient to return to Shelfhoc. "What's keeping Bravecoeur?" he muttered. "How long does it take to retrieve two swords?"

"What about Titus?" Grace asked.

Their father had suggested he accompany them to Shelfhoc and insisted Grace ride with him. "He's a follower, not a leader. When he regains his wits and discovers his master gone, he'll go into hiding."

"But he should be punished for what he did to us."

Rodrick dragged his eyes away from watching for Bravecoeur. "He's out cold, and it would take an army to carry him downstairs. His punishment will be the fate of a fugitive, forever looking over his shoulder."

"Look," Grace exclaimed. "Something's on fire."

"*Fyke*," Rodrick exclaimed, spurring his horse towards the oak. The animal shied away from the flames licking at the undergrowth around the mighty tree. He dismounted quickly and slapped the beast on the rump. "Bravecoeur?" he shouted, coughing as smoke drifted into his eyes.

The stiffening breeze would soon fan the flames. He peered into the hawthorn thicket. His captain lay near the base of the oak tree. There was no sign of Godefroy.

Covering his mouth with his cloak, he strode into the prickly bushes. He knelt beside Bravecoeur and shook his shoulder. The man coughed, trying to sit up. "Your pardon, *milord*. They got away."

"Let's get out of here," Rodrick shouted, urging the well muscled captain to his feet, thankful he wouldn't have to carry him.

They stumbled away from the burning bushes as the fire took hold with a vengeance. They fell to their knees, watching as flames crept up the trunk of the mighty oak.

"What happened?" he asked.

Bravecoeur swiped his hand across his forehead. "I was stupid. I tossed Cullène to the ground while I buckled on my sword. Next thing he'd leapt on my back, his arms clamped around my neck."

Smoke swirled in the shifting wind, choking them. They moved further away from the now burning tree that hissed and crackled as it gave up its long life to the flames.

"He hung on like a limpet I couldn't shake off. Then to my surprise, the giant lumbered out of the trap door."

"They must have been aware of the tunnel."

Bravecoeur shook his head. "Mayhap, but he looked around uncertainly as if he'd never been there before, and he'd brought a torch from the house. When he saw me struggling with his master, he thrust it in my face. I stumbled and fell. Last thing I recall is him tossing the torch into the trees as he lunged at me. Godefroy must have hit me on the head with something."

"They escaped."

"To my everlasting shame," the soldier replied. "Or the flames have consumed them."

They stood for long minutes watching the tree burn, then Rodrick slapped Bravecoeur on the back. "Now comes the hard part, my friend—explaining this to my father, and to Grace."

CHAPTER TWENTY-EIGHT

As she'd tossed and turned on the meager pallet in the cold attic of her former home, one thing had become clear to Grace. She loved Bronson FitzRam. The possibility of never seeing him again had pained her the most as she contemplated the terrifying likelihood Godefroy intended to take her life.

She didn't know why he was determined not to remarry, unless he was still in love with his first wife, but she was certain he felt something for her. She was ready to accept whatever he had to offer.

Rodrick had held nothing back about Bronson's injuries, and she was grateful. They'd always been honest with each other.

As Shelfhoc came in sight, the familiar sense of homecoming swept over her. She suspected her father had sensed her feelings. He'd barely spoken a word, obviously furious with Bravecoeur. At the risk of infuriating him further she had to speak. "I belong here," she told him with conviction as they entered the courtyard.

He dismounted and lifted her down. "With Bronson, I suppose."

"I love him, Papa."

Her father winced. "As I told your brother, it will be difficult, but your mother and I want you and Rodrick to be as happy as we have been."

She looked her father in the eye. "And you experienced difficulties at first."

He chuckled. "We did, saucy chit. Now go in and see if he still lives."

Tybaut rushed out, bowing briefly to the Earl, then addressing Grace. "*Milady*. Saints be praised you're safe."

She swallowed hard as he ushered her into the warmth of the house, glancing up the stairs. "How fares your master?"

He touched her elbow, moving her towards the solar. "His sister tends him. He is still feverish, but everyone is praying hard."

She breathed again that he was still alive, but the news was nevertheless not good.

Swan dozed in a chair, head thrown back, mouth open. She looked exhausted. Rodrick picked her up and cradled her in his arms. She blinked awake and smiled, then saw Grace. "Thank God," she murmured. "He will get well now you've returned."

Rodrick carried his beloved out of the solar.

Fearing the worst, Grace turned her gaze to Bronson. He dwarfed the raised pallet on which he lay. The golden stubble of his beard already darkened his face. Lucia stood at his side, tears streaming down her cheeks. She came willingly into Grace's outstretched arms.

"God be praised," the girl sobbed into her mistress's bosom.

"You need sleep," Grace whispered into the girl's hair. "Tell me what to do. I will tend him."

Lucia wiped her eyes with the back of her sleeve. "He hasn't wakened, though he thrashed around when we had to cut away his tunic and sew him up. It's a deep wound, and the vinegar I poured on it must have stung like the devil. But it's the blow to his head that has stolen his wits."

Carefully she folded the linen away from Bronson's chest. Grace winced at the thick wad of padding caked with dried blood.

"It bled for a long time, but has stopped now," the servant explained as she lifted the pad.

Grace wrinkled her nose. "What smells?"

Lucia poked at the poultice, and then peeled it back, rolling it up from one end. "Used everything available, mint, yarrow, onions, garlic. There's a poultice of onions under each armpit too. I've been burning rosemary in the fumitory, but it doesn't seem to help."

Grace clamped her hand to her mouth to stifle a strange sound threatening to emerge from her throat as Bronson's chest was revealed. She'd seen soldiers stripped to the waist in the training yards and peasants laboring in the fields in the hot sun, but she had never set eyes on a male chest of chiseled rock. She wanted to run her fingertips over the golden hair dusting his chest that wandered in an intriguing line down his belly.

But his incredible beauty was marred by a neat line of bizarre stitches stretching the breadth of his chest, above his dark nipples— nipples she had a sudden urge to lick, a notion she hadn't known she was capable of.

Stitches of blue, of red, of green held onto the jagged edges of a ghastly wound like shipwreck survivors clinging to driftwood. The juices of the poultice seemed to have rendered the colors more vivid.

Lucia cleared her throat. "I did my best, milady. It was all we had."

"Thank you," Grace managed from her parched throat. "Your needlework has always been the finest."

Lucia put back the poultice and the pad, pulled the linen back over Bronson's chest, bobbed a curtsey then left.

He lay like a stone statue atop a tomb, needing only a kiss to breathe life into him. She stroked his matted hair off his forehead, leaned forward and kissed his fevered brow, savoring the salty taste of his sweat. "Come back to me, Bronson."

Then she pressed her lips to his, delighting in the swans' down softness of his beard. Pangs of desire skittered into her womb, despite the sharp taste of henbane that told her they'd drugged him with *dwale*. "I love you," she murmured.

She startled when he inhaled sharply then slowly touched his fingertips to his lips. She clasped his warm hand and held it to her breast. "Bronson," she whispered.

His hand tightened on hers. "Grace," he rasped, licking his lips. "You taste salty."

A kiss awoke Bronson from a dream. He was lying atop a sarcophagus, a tiny winged cherubim hovering by each shoulder. He didn't want to open his eyes, fearful he'd been kissed by the Angel of Death.

He risked touching his fingertips to his parched lips.

He'd heard whispered words of love, tasted salt. Surely harbingers of death breathed fire and brimstone?

He inhaled deeply to reassure himself of his mortality. Someone took hold of his hand and pressed it to something soft and warm. As his palm absorbed the warmth, his heart filled with the certainty he was going to survive whatever ailed him. Pungent aromas assailed his nostrils, but overriding all was a scent he recognised immediately. "Grace," he rasped. "You taste salty."

The cherubim giggled like naughty children and disappeared into the fog clouding his wits. "They're gone," he said, thinking suddenly of his unborn babes. He peeled open his eyes, elated to see Grace's lovely face, but saddened by her tears.

"You're awake," she sobbed.

His throat produced a grunt of confirmation as he scanned the space around him. "Why am I in the solar and why do I smell like I've bathed in onions?"

She smoothed a hand over his brow. "Rodrick was afraid carrying you upstairs would worsen your wound."

Wound?

He furrowed his brow, trying to recall—

It came to him then, the grinning face of the man who had slashed him. Now he understood the army of tiny creatures marching across his chest in boots spiked with nails. He raised his free hand to touch the wound, reluctant to remove the one cupped under Grace's breast.

Breast?

Embarrassment washed over him. "Forgive me," he drawled, making a half hearted attempt to remove his hand. "I'm in a stupor."

She resisted his efforts and grasped his free hand. "It's the *dwale*, but you mustn't touch the stitches. Lucia did a—"

She hesitated.

"—remarkable job."

It occurred to him he should ask what she meant but a dull ache throbbed at his temples and a pleasant one was stirring in his loins. "I'm hungry," he managed, suddenly realizing he was, though he doubted she understood he thirsted for her.

She laughed. "It's a good sign."

Her bright smile filled him with contentment, though he missed the warmth and the weight of her breast when she removed his hand and stepped back.

"I'll fetch some broth."

He made an attempt to sit up, but she put a hand on his shoulder. "Lie still. He hit you hard, and you lost a lot of blood."

He lay back, enjoying her coddling as the warmth of her hand heated his bare skin. "Who did this? What did they want? Did they harm anyone else?"

"Too many questions," she said, obviously avoiding answering. "All will be revealed after you have eaten."

He watched her go, knowing deep in his heart she was made for him. But what did his dreams of angels portend? Were they to remind him life was fleeting and the risks of losing another wife in childbirth too great? Or did they signify something else?

Rodrick carried Swan into the Great Hall, where his father was in discussion with Bravecoeur, though it seemed a one-sided conversation.

The soldier studied his feet when his Earl abruptly stopped talking and hurried over to his son. "Suannoch, I regret the attack on you and your brother in my territory. Godefroy will be punished, if he still lives."

Swan furrowed her brow and looked at Rodrick. "He isn't in custody?"

Bravecoeur coughed as he bent the knee before her. "Forgive me, milady, he is still at large because of my failure."

Rodrick set her on her feet as the soldier explained. She offered her hand to the captain. "You're excused, Captain Bravecoeur. I don't fault you."

The soldier rose. "I swear I will do everything in my power to recapture him, if he survived the fire."

Swan suppressed a yawn.

Jolly bustled in with a large tureen of broth and a ladle, setting them down on a trestle table. The lads brought wooden bowls. The cook filled one and offered it to the Earl. "My lord, please take sustenance before you depart, and milady Swan, you must eat before you rest."

"You're leaving, Papa?" Rodrick asked.

"*Oui*," his father replied, sipping the broth. "I must get back to Ellesmere for Christmas Day, or your mother will never forgive me."

Swan sighed. "I had forgotten the morrow is Christmas Day with this upset."

Swan and Grace's carefully planned celebrations had been ruined, but Jolly came to the rescue. "This horrible day is nearly over, and God willing our Master is on the way to recovery, but on the morrow you will have your Christmas feast if the lads and I have to toil through the night to assure it."

The grinning scullery boys nodded in unison like puppets on strings.

Grace came into the Hall. Rodrick was relieved to see a smile on her face. "How does Bronson fare?" he asked.

His sister embraced Swan. "Thanks to you, I believe he will recover. He's hungry."

"I am beyond relieved to see you safely returned, Grace. It was more thanks to Lucia that my brother is still alive, but I was confident your presence would work miracles," Swan replied as the two women clung together.

Rodrick's father came to his feet. "Delicious broth. I must be off before it gets dark."

He embraced his daughter. "Mayhap Jolly's suggestion of a Christmas celebration might help Bronson on the road to recovery."

Her eyes brimmed with tears. "Thank you, Papa. Give my love to *Maman*."

The Earl next kissed Swan's hand. "It seems I am to be blessed with another beautiful daughter. I will petition Archbishop Theobald."

She blushed and threw her arms around him. "Thank you, my lord Earl."

He patted her softly on the back, then released her and turned to Rodrick. "Take care of your nose, *mon fils*. It looks painful."

"In truth, I'd forgotten it," he replied, touching his nose gingerly.

Grace scooped a bowl of broth. "This is for Bronson, Papa. Come with me to say goodbye."

When they were finally alone Rodrick cupped Swan's face in his hands. "Now, Swan FitzRam, it's my bed for you."

Her eyes filled with uncertainty, and a hint of desire.

He laughed. "Don't worry. You can sleep in my room upstairs. I'll be honorable, much as I want to make you mine. I'll bed down in the Hall with Tybaut and the lads."

CHAPTER TWENTY-NINE

R odrick vaguely heard the scullery boys scurrying off to the kitchens in the early hours of the morning to wake Jolly who slumbered in her cot behind the brick chimney. Tybaut snored on not too far away.

He fell back to sleep and wasn't sure how much time had passed before his nostrils twitched—roasting venison. It evoked a memory of happy Yuletides at Ellesmere. But he had a sense this was a day of new traditions for him and Swan.

He turned over onto his side on the uncomfortable stone floor.

The Earldom of Ellesmere was his birthright. When he and Swan were granted permission to marry, she would be his Countess. His father had promised to petition the Archbishop of Canterbury. Surely his support carried weight?

Could he forsake her if permission was denied? To marry without the blessing of the Church meant abdicating the Earldom to his brother William—not a comforting thought. What would his great grandfather Ram have thought of such circumstances?

But being the Earl would mean nothing without Swan at his side.

Thoughts of the woman he loved, who was sleeping upstairs in the same house caused his manhood to stir. He intended to honor Swan by granting her what every maiden desired—to surrender their virginity on their wedding night. It was a gift he wanted for himself.

But it would be a simple matter to sneak quietly up the stairs and bring her pleasure—a Christmas gift if you will.

Unless Grace had decided to leave Bronson's side and share Swan's bed.

Rubbing her full belly, replete after eating too much of Jolly's cooking, Swan thought she understood why Rodrick seemed to be in an ill humor. Sleeping on the stone floor would make any nobleman irritable, especially with a broken nose. She'd tossed and turned all night with worry for him. The aroma of roasted venison drifting up from the kitchen meant the lads had left the Hall, and she'd been tempted to sneak down the stairs, to check on how he fared. But the wooden steps creaked—something must be done to solve the noise—and Tybaut might still be abed.

But everyone should be joyful. It was Christmas Day after all!

Jolly had produced a mouth watering feast, filling platters with leeks, onions, carrots, winter chard and parsnips to accompany the venison. Swan wondered if there was anything left in the root cellar.

They'd been elated Bronson had been hale enough to be assisted to walk to the Hall by Rodrick and Tybaut. He'd relied heavily on their support, but it was a major step forward.

He looked exhausted now, sitting propped up by cushions in the master's chair, dressed in a nightshirt and bedrobe, but he'd enjoyed himself and eaten heartily. She was glad Lucia had insisted on binding his wound. If he saw the stitches—

Grace had never stopped fussing over him, which Swan inwardly admitted made her jealous. It dismayed her.

"Did you not enjoy your meal?" she asked Rodrick seated beside her.

He shrugged, belching into his fist. "It was delicious. I ate too much."

"Is your nose painful?"

"No."

She squirmed in her seat, bothered by his sullen demeanor. "Do you wish you were at Ellesmere?"

He arched his brows, pressing his thigh against hers. "Why would you think that?"

She hated pouting. "You seem preoccupied."

He exhaled deeply and took her hands in his. "The thoughts preoccupying me are to do with how much I love you and how desperately I want to make you mine. I'm sorry if I've been morose. Christmas is a special day for you."

She giggled, feeling better. "It will be special for you too when I tell you what Tybaut has procured for dessert."

His eyes widened. "Something I'm fond of?"

"Something you love."

He nibbled her ear. "You?"

She shrugged her shoulder, pretending to be annoyed. "No. Marzipan and custard."

The corners of his mouth lifted. "I do like marzipan, but I wouldn't say—"

The secret burst forth. "With cobnuts!"

He frowned. "What?"

She feared perhaps Grace had got it wrong. "Cobnuts. Tybaut had them brought specially from Farnham in Surrey."

An expression of pure delight crossed his features. "You mean hazelnuts."

What a relief!

"Yes. In Northumbria we call them cobnuts."

He came to his feet, tapping his goblet. Every eye turned to him. "Swan FitzRam," he declared, "a man must declare his love when a woman procures hazelnuts for him."

He bent to her ear. "Are they roasted?" he whispered loudly enough for everyone to hear.

She felt her face redden as his audience chuckled.

He picked up his goblet. "With your permission, Lord Bronson, I propose a toast to your sister."

Bronson raised his goblet. "Only if we include your sister, Grace, who I suspect had much to do with fulfilling your desire for hazelnuts."

Clearing his throat, Rodrick wiggled both eyebrows at Swan. "I drink to the health and long life of women who fulfill our desires. To Lady Swan and Lady Grace."

Men-at-arms, tenant farmers, and servants raised their tankards and goblets and joined the toast.

Swan's heart threatened to burst out of her chest.

Chin and nose in the air, shoulders squarely braced, Tybaut signaled for the dessert to be served. Rodrick devoured the roasted hazelnuts before he touched the marzipan. To her surprise he suddenly came to his feet and hurried out of the Hall, returning a few moments later with one hand behind his back.

Instead of returning to his seat, he stood in the middle of the Hall, crooked his finger and beckoned Swan.

Curious and not a little nervous, she joined him.

He took her hand. "As everyone knows, one of my great grandfathers was a Welshman."

Evidently some in the room hadn't been aware of it if their murmurs of surprise were any indication. Rodrick ignored them. "I was named for Rhodri ap Owain who believed in many of the ancient Celtic traditions.

"I am a proud Norman, but cannot deny the Celtic blood flowing in my veins," he continued, producing from behind his back a twig with green leaves and white berries which he held up for all to see.

Some laughed and cheered, apparently knowing what it was. From the glint in his eyes, Swan suspected she would soon learn the significance of the twig.

"Before the birth of Our Lord that we celebrate today," Rodrick droned on with mock seriousness, "pagan peoples regarded *Mistiltan* as a representation of divine male essence."

He winked at her.

The men in the hall *oohed* loudly, some elbowing their neighbors.

Rodrick raised his hand for calm. "The Celts used it as a remedy for barrenness in animals and a cure for poison."

Silence suddenly ensued, all eyes on the heir of Ellesmere.

Rodrick waited, plainly relishing his control over the assembly. Her heart fluttered proudly in her chest.

"More importantly, when you have male essence, you have fertility and vitality."

Loud guffaws broke the silence, accompanied by banging of tankards on tables.

"But!"

Everyone quieted as he raised the twig over Swan's head.

"It only works if you kiss a maiden beneath it."

Without warning he bent his head and took possession of her mouth with his warm lips. She tasted the fruit of the hazel tree, and knew in her heart it would forever evoke this Christmas memory. He kissed deeply, twirling his tongue with hers, all the while holding the sprig over their heads.

The loud cheering came to an abrupt end when one goblet banged more loudly than any other. Her brother's voice caused her to pull away, afraid their public display had angered or offended him.

"Fetch that twig over here," Bronson demanded, his voice slurred, "and hold it over me and Grace. I've a mind to kiss my most excellent nurse."

Rodrick did as he bade. Swan watched Bronson lean his head back and accept a blushing Grace's kiss. Perhaps the mingling of *dwale* and wine hadn't been such a good idea. Would he recall the kiss on the morrow?

CHAPTER THIRTY

Twelve days after the Christmas celebrations, Grace was in two minds about the burning of the Yule Wreath. This would be the finale of Yuletide, and her last chance to force Bronson into admitting he loved her.

The day after Christmas, he'd lain in a stupor, complaining of a pounding headache.

Grace had fumed. Obviously the kiss beneath the *mistiltan* had happened as a result of imbibing wine on top of *dwale*.

For a few wild moments during the feast she had been a tavern wench lured into a kiss by a lusty warrior. And a rousing kiss it had been, firing her blood. Yet he seemed to barely recall anything of the celebrations.

Her fuming turned to worry when he lapsed into another bout of fever that lasted over the New Year and resulted in a subdued marking of the dawning of the year of Our Lord One Thousand One Hundred and Fifty-four.

As Master, Bronson should have been the first to enter the household at midnight with bread, and wood for burning, symbols of warmth and plenty for the coming year. Rodrick had taken his place. Grace thought her brother a more suitable person because of his dark hair, but she kept it to herself.

During Bronson's relapse Lucia had been able to remove the bandages to check on the stitches. Everyone dreaded Bronson's reaction if he saw them. His constant complaints about the itching was their justification for keeping them bound.

Swan was proud of the large wreath she'd fashioned and heartened when Bronson rallied the previous day and expressed a wish to attend the ceremonial burning.

The weather had turned mild and Grace's heart skipped a beat as she watched Bronson walk outside slowly but unassisted and take his place on the bench in front of the already burning bonfire. Tybaut had lectured the stable boys endlessly about making the pile of wood big enough, but not too big, and had supervised the lighting as soon as the sun went down.

Bronson stretched out his long legs and held his hands to the fire, then rubbed them together, his red hair aglow in the light of the flames. He put his arm around Swan. "That's a marvelous wreath you've made, sister. It's a pity we have to burn it."

She laughed, fluttering her eyelashes at Rodrick. "No, I'm looking forward to it. I'll go first."

She plucked a branch from the wreath, then closed her eyes and tossed it into the flames. "I wish to be married to Rodrick de Montbryce."

Grace's brother laughed as he selected his own branch. "Well, that's no surprise!" He threw his cedar frond into the fire. "I wish to be married to Suannoch FitzRam."

Grace's heart filled with joy for her brother and Swan as they held hands, gazing at the brief flicker as the fire carried their wishes heavenward. But nervous apprehension crept in closely behind. Bronson had said nothing, his facial expression blank as he too peered into the flames, stroking his beard.

It was now or never. "My turn," she said as she pulled at a frond with trembling hands. It resisted until Rodrick came to her rescue. She held the cedar out towards the fire. "I wish—"

She risked a glance at Bronson who still gazed into the flames. "I wish to be Mistress of Shelfhoc," came out in a rush as she threw the cedar, missing the fire completely.

Her brother kicked her offering into the flames. "Has to burn or your wish won't come true," he said, looking at Bronson.

Some creature gnawed at her innards as Swan held the remnants of the wreath in front of Bronson. "Your turn, Master of Shelfhoc."

He accepted the garland and gripped it in both hands before throwing it to the center of the fire. "I wish to be rid of the ghosts of the past," he declared.

No one spoke. At first the wreath threatened to smother the fire. Smoke filled the air. Then the cedar boughs crackled and hissed in protest as the flames again took hold. Bronson raised his head to look at Grace, fire dancing in his eyes. He scratched his chest. "And for this infernal itching to cease."

Bronson was on fire. The flames heated his face. His chest prickled with the stings of a thousand barbed insects. He hated the itchy beard and moustache and longed for a shave. But it was his burning passion for Grace that would no longer be denied. He was grateful when Swan and Rodrick slipped away, leaving him alone with the woman he loved. "I told you once I will never marry again," he said.

She kept her gaze fixed on the fire, hands clasped in her lap.

"You never asked me why."

Her knuckles turned white. "I assumed you are still in love with your first wife."

Had he loved either of his wives? Certainly he'd liked them, been comfortable with them, and enjoyed making love to their bodies. But he'd never been consumed with wanting as he was with Grace. "No, that's not it."

She glanced up at him, then looked back at the dying fire.

"I was married twice."

Now she stared at him, open mouthed.

"Both died."

Strangely, he was calm now when he spoke of their deaths. The next part would be difficult. He swallowed the hard lump in his throat, but Grace guessed his torment.

"They died in childbirth," she murmured hoarsely.

He clamped his hands on his knees.

"You lost both babes."

Only glowing embers remained of the fire. If he stared hard enough mayhap the pain would go away. "I couldn't bear it if the same thing happened to you, Grace."

To his surprise, she leapt from the bench and came to stand between him and the fire, hands on hips.

The fire no longer warmed him, but he suddenly felt hotter when he looked up at her face.

"Foolish man. Every woman fears death in childbirth, but we accept the possibility because children bring joy, and love. No one would make a better father than you, Bronson. And I will be an excellent mother. Give me the chance. Don't deny what we might have because you are afraid. I love you, and you love me."

She moved to sit beside him on the bench. He turned to look at her, warmed by the love burning in her eyes. "I do love you, Grace, more than you can imagine. I've tried to deny it, fearful of facing the pain again. If I lost you—"

"—you would condemn us both to a lonely life of frustrated love."

He looked back at the embers. Perhaps they did hold the answer. Grace's words made sense. A leaden weight lifted from his heart. "I want to scoop you up in my arms and carry you to my bed, Grace de Montbryce, but—"

She leaned her head against his arm. "I know. You'd break open your stitches."

He chuckled. "You mean the ones on my embroidered chest?"

She looked at him in alarm. "You knew?"

He arched his brows. "I'm good at feigning sleep."

Tybaut appeared out of nowhere. "May I douse the fire now, my lord?"

Bronson came slowly to his feet. "Yes, faithful Steward. Thank you." He proffered his elbow to Grace. "The future mistress of Shelfhoc will see me safely into the house."

Tybaut grinned, beckoning to the shivering stable lads who appeared with buckets of water.

CHAPTER THIRTY-ONE

Rodrick rode away from Shelfhoc with a heavy heart and tired limbs. After the wreath ceremony he'd dozed all night in a chair in front of the hearth in the Hall, Swan on his lap. Sweet torture it had been!

Bronson had insisted he was well enough to be left during the night and Grace had been convinced to take Swan's place in the bed in the upstairs chamber.

This morning he'd voiced the desire to move back into the master's chamber, and Rodrick had helped Tybaut and the lads move pallets and rearrange sleeping accommodations.

Swan insisted she understood why he had to return to Ellesmere, but he recognised she was bereft at his leaving. At first she'd whined. "Why can I not accompany you?"

"What's the point? I have to leave with father on the expedition to aid Robert of Leicester in closing two mercenary castles. And in any case, Grace and Bronson cannot be left alone here together. They'll be good company for you."

She sulked, studying her feet. "They only have eyes for each other."

He tilted her chin to his gaze, wishing to carry the memory of her lovely face with him. "Like you and me."

Hoping to erase the pout, he added. "And Papa is talking of going personally to see Archbishop Theobald, in which case I'll go with him."

Bringing his thoughts back to the track, muddy now after the mild weather, he touched his fingers to his lips, savoring the taste of their farewell kiss in the courtyard. He offered a silent prayer that the Archbishop would grant the dispensation on which much depended.

Bronson had mixed feelings as he watched Rodrick disappear over the horizon, and suspected he wasn't the only one. He put an arm around his sister's shoulder. "You're sad to see him go, Swan, but his mission is an important one."

Swan sighed. "Yes. England needs to be rid of the mercenaries."

"True, but I meant the petition to the Archbishop."

She smiled wistfully. "Yes, that's important to both of us now, brother."

He scratched the irritating whiskers under his chin, stretching his arm around Grace's shoulders when she took over the job. Somehow her touch was more effective. "Indeed, and with the men he's left here and the ones we brought from Northumbria, we are well protected."

It didn't ring completely true. They'd been protected before and succumbed to treachery. He would feel vulnerable until Godefroy was captured or confirmed dead.

Grace's scratching wasn't helping any longer. "I have to get rid of this beard. Today!"

"I can do it," Swan volunteered. "We had planned to have Lucia take out your stitches too."

His sister had shaved him before, but it was the touch of another female he craved. "I was going to ask Grace to do it."

Swan's lip quivered. She darted a jealous glance at Grace. Perhaps this hadn't been the best time to mention it. He opened his mouth to soothe her hurt feelings but she scurried off towards the stables, leaving them to enter the house without her.

Grace hesitated on the threshold. "I should go after her."

"No. She'll spend some time with Cob and be over it soon. She has to get used to sharing me with another woman. She's taken care of me since—"

The dark memories threatened to surface.

Grace turned to face him and stood on tiptoe to kiss him. The darkness lifted as she thrust her tongue into his mouth. When they broke apart, she smiled mischievously. "A bath is in order once we get those stitches out. You still reek of onions."

He wiggled his eyebrows. "I can hardly wait."

Watching nervously as Bronson sharpened his razor on the leather strop, Grace wished she'd spoken up. Swan may have shaved her brother, but Grace's brothers had valets to take care of such things. An Earl's daughter was never called upon to groom males, even when the men in question were her brothers.

Jolly bustled in with a bowl of hot water and linens, followed by Tybaut with a bar of what appeared to be soap held aloft in both hands as if it were a Mass offering. "Here we are. My finest hard shaving soap, handmade from beeswax and lard and my special secret ingredient."

He placed the bar next to the bowl of water on a small table Jolly had provided near the hearth in the solar.

With a flourish, he produced a furry object from the pocket of his tunic. "There aren't many of these around, my lord Bronson. Please accept it as my humble gift."

Bronson furrowed his brow as he examined his gift. "Boar's hair?"

Tybaut grinned gleefully. "I sensed you were a perceptive man of good taste."

Grace, who'd believed the boar's hair object had been a lucky rabbit's foot, wiped her sweaty hands on the apron Jolly had provided. The Steward stared at her for long moments. She eyed the table on which the brush, the razor, the hot water, and the soap had been lovingly placed. "All is in readiness?" she ventured.

Tybaut looked down his nose. "One more thing." He opened his palm to reveal a tiny jar, big enough for only a fingertip to be dipped inside. "Just in case."

Frowning, she sniffed the contents. "What is it?"

"A perfumed ointment of my own creation, with the added luxury of spider webs soaked in oil and vinegar."

She stifled a giggle at the thought of the portly Tybaut harvesting spider webs. "What on earth is it for?"

He laid it on the table that now looked like a sacrificial altar. "In case of accidents."

As Lucia prepared to remove Bronson's stitches, Swan refrained from commenting on the nicks and scratches on her brother's face. Served him right for not letting her shave him, though she had to admit Grace had done a creditable job, considering it was likely the first time she'd ever shaved a man.

It was curious. Grace was a widow, yet she was reluctant to speak of her husband, and seemed to know nothing about him. Lucia also avoided answering questions concerning life at Cullène Hall.

Poor Grace. She was trembling like an aspen tree and looked exhausted.

Bronson gazed down at the scar on his chest. "Looks good, Lucia. Fine needlework."

The maidservant blushed. "Thank you, my lord. You have healed well."

"Too bad the colorful stitches have turned black," Swan teased. "You looked pretty when they were a rainbow."

Bronson laughed.

Grace tsked. "You must keep still. Lucia is using the smallest pair of *cisoires* in this masculine household. These are pivoted and are normally used for—"

Her face reddened considerably. "What I mean is—"

Swan had to rub salt in the wound. "What she means is they are from her sewing supplies and are normally used for embroidery."

There was an uncomfortable silence. Grace glared at Swan. Lucia's eyes darted from one face to another. Tybaut coughed.

Bronson leaned back in the chair, staring into the rafters. "I suppose I'll have to get used to you two sparring like fighting cocks. Snip away, Lucia."

Swan felt badly. She loved her brother. She was elated he seemed ready at last to put the past behind him. There was no better sister-by-marriage than Grace. But she missed Rodrick terribly, and he'd been gone less than a day.

"I apologize, Grace. I don't understand why I am being mean spirited. My brother looks much better without his beard. You did a fine job."

Grace took her hand. "You miss Rodrick. I understand."

"At last!" Bronson exclaimed, startling them both. He came to his feet, scratching his chest. "I am no longer a tapestry."

Swan clapped her hands together, gladdened by the return of her brother's good humor. He had grieved for too long.

"Now for my bath. Which one of you lovely ladies will scrub my back?"

CHAPTER THIRTY-TWO

Tucking the eating dagger he'd wiped clean into his belt, Rodrick grinned at Bronson. "There you were, alone at Shelfhoc with two lovely women doting over you, yet you chose to join the fray."

Bronson scratched his chest. The scar no longer itched, but the scratching had turned into a habit. He wondered if coming to Ellesmere to join Gallien and his sons in the ongoing fight against the Flemish mercenaries was indeed the decision of a madman. How to explain? "Grace and Swan may be lovely, but—"

Swan narrowed her eyes and stuck out her lower lip.

Grace glared at him.

Careful!

Rodrick chuckled, stretching his arm around his betrothed seated next to him in the Hall. "I understand. I see my Swan's ruffled feathers."

She shrugged away from him, but he held tight. "Let's not fight. We haven't seen each other for sennights. Spring is already upon us."

Bronson was happy to see the pout leave his sister's face as she nestled into Rodrick. He glanced up at the head table, relieved to see his future father-by-marriage nod imperceptibly when he put his arm around Grace.

The Earl had proposed they take the opportunity of everyone's presence at Ellesmere to formally sign betrothal documents. He hadn't yet been able to procure an appointment with Archbishop Theobald and believed signed documents would help the cause once an audience was granted.

It was a source of pride for Bronson to represent his father in signing the documents pledging Swan to Rodrick, but he hoped Grace hadn't noticed the tremor in his hand as he'd signed his own betrothal document in the Chart Room. He had no doubt he loved her, but this was a momentous step he'd sworn he would never take.

He wondered why she seemed as apprehensive as he. Perhaps all brides-to-be were nervous at their betrothal ceremony, although Grace had been married before. She knew what to expect. But she'd never borne a child of Victor de Cullène. Perhaps she was barren. Strangely, the possibility depressed him. She was a woman born to be a mother.

Swan's voice broke into his reverie as he sifted his fingers through Grace's hair, conjuring images behind his eyes of a child born of two redheaded parents. "Seriously, you're not going off to fight simply to get away from me and Grace?"

"No," he replied truthfully. "I am recovered from my injuries and anxious to join the battle to restore peace to England. I was a boy when King Henry died, but I remember life being more secure than it has been under Stephen's rule. If it wasn't for the Scottish king's intervention in Northumbria, we'd have descended into the same anarchy.

"Besides, the news of a plot to assassinate Henry Plantagenet brings to mind a certain young man who I would dearly love to come face to face with."

"You believe Godefroy still lives?" Rodrick asked.

"My bones tell me he does, and I would have vengeance for what he did to Grace—to all of us."

Rodrick fingered his nose. "Yes, I remember it well, and I too would love nothing better than to despatch the wretch to his Maker. We leave on the morrow to rejoin Robert of Leicester who reportedly has spies among the conspirators. There are rumors Stephen's son William is involved."

Grace snuggled into him, the swell of her warm breast against his arm stirring the interest of his shaft. "I wish you didn't have to leave."

Bronson wanted nothing more than to whisk her to her chamber and lie abed there for sennights, but revealing his thoughts would be deemed inappropriate with others present, although Rodrick probably wanted to say the same to Swan.

At least he and Grace had been able to spend time together at Shelfhoc, whereas Rodrick and Swan had been parted for sennights, and on the morrow would have to say farewell once more.

"We'll have many happy years to enjoy together in peace and prosperity once we rid our country of troublemakers," he said.

Rodrick arched a brow. "And if Henry Plantagenet lives up to expectations as our king."

Swan sighed. "He has to be crowned first."

Strolling through the ornamental garden at Ellesmere, Swan fanned her face with the parchment Steward Bonhomme had handed her. "Is it usually so hot here at this time of year?"

"This is a very hot summer," Grace replied trying to wrest the message from her hand. "But I've heard it said the weather is normally warmer here than in Northumbria."

Swan stepped away, unfurling the long awaited missive. "It's from Rodrick."

Grace pouted.

"But Bronson has added a note at the end."

Grace put her hands on her hips. "Have you noticed, sister, we are the best of friends until our men intrude?"

Swan had indeed remarked on it, but was too intent on reading Rodrick's letter to respond. Her eyes widened at the news he'd imparted.

"What is it?" Grace asked impatiently.

"The conspirators in the assassination plot have been arrested. Godefroy languishes in the Tower with his confederates, awaiting Prince Henry's wish and pleasure. Prince William has been exonerated of any complicity."

Grace gasped and threw herself into Swan's arms. They both laughed and sobbed and laughed again.

When they broke apart, Swan handed the missive to Grace. "My brother misses you."

Grace read Bronson's note, then clasped the parchment to her breast. "Perhaps now they will come home."

Grace tugged her cloak more snugly around her shoulders as she watched the leaves fall from the oaks in the ornamental garden. "It reminds me of the splendid oak that burned the day I was rescued," she told Swan as they huddled together on a bench. "It seems a lifetime ago and yet it hasn't been a year."

"Time crawls by when you're waiting for someone to come home," Swan replied.

Grace agreed. "Thank goodness you are here. I would have lost my wits without your friendship to see me through these long separations. I had hoped after Godefroy's capture and execution our men would return for good, but they've only been home three times since then."

Swan shivered in the chilly breeze. "I suppose as long as Stephen lives, there will be factions who will oppose Henry. Once Plantagenet is king—"

She jumped to her feet as Rodrick sauntered into the garden, followed by Bronson. Grace's heart turned over as she ran through the crackling leaves into his arms, savoring his warmth. "We didn't expect you."

"Come inside," Rodrick said as he and Swan broke apart. "There is much to tell you."

"Tell us now," Swan demanded impatiently. "Is it good news?"

"Some good, some bad," Bronson replied.

A shiver of apprehension danced up Grace's spine. Bad news meant—

"Stephen is dead," Rodrick declared.

But this is good news.

Swan laughed. "I suppose one shouldn't rejoice at the death of a king, but—"

Rodrick put a finger to his lips. "No, but you're right. Henry can now be crowned and we can hope England will be a safer place with a strong king."

"What happened?" Grace asked. "We didn't hear of his illness."

Rodrick scratched his scalp. "Apparently he was meeting with the *Comte* of Flandres when he was suddenly seized with a violent pain in his gut, accompanied by a flow of blood. He took to his bed in Dover Priory and died."

Grace glanced from her brother to Bronson to Swan. Were they thinking the same thing she was? "Like his son. A sudden death."

"He'll be buried with Eustace, and his wife Matilda at the Cluniac monastery in Faversham," Bronson said.

By now they had reached the warmth of the Great Hall, where Grace's father and mother stood warming themselves by the fire. Grace embraced her parents. "We are at long last to have a new king."

Her father clenched his jaw. "But Henry is in Normandie, which means a coronation will have to be postponed until he returns. Have they told you the other news yet?"

Bronson put his arm around her waist, preparing her for the worst.

"Archbishop Theobald denied our request, didn't he?" she murmured.

"No!" Swan shrieked.

Rodrick stroked her hair as she sobbed into his shoulder. "He has been named Regent until Henry is crowned and claims to be much too busy with his new responsibilities. He has recommended we petition the Pope."

"That will take months, years," Grace said, clinging to Bronson, feeling she should sit down before she fell over.

"Perhaps not, if you go in person," her mother said.

To her surprise, her father seemed to agree. "*Oui*, Theobald insists you make a pilgrimage, only then will you prove yourselves worthy. He wants you to go to Rome and speak directly to Anastasius."

CHAPTER THIRTY-THREE

Preparations took a sennight. Grace's father set about informing a wealthy family in Rome that Ellesmere had traded with for many years. Ram de Montbryce had met with the influential Italians on the return journey from Constantinople. A reliable system of pigeon relays had been established linking Ellesmere, the Montbryce holdings in Normandie, and the Frangipanes. "Oddone Frangipane will be only too happy to take care of you once you arrive in Rome," her father assured them.

Bonhomme organised a contingent to accompany them—three cooks, two monks, a blacksmith, four ostlers, several archers and huntsmen, two falconers, squires to pitch, strike and repair tents, and a brigade of handpicked men-at-arms.

Swan and Grace would share Lucia's services as their lady's maid. To everyone's surprise, William and Stephen de Montbryce volunteered to act as valets for Rodrick and Bronson.

"I wonder if my father suggested it as a penance for my wayward brothers?" Grace mused as they sat in the chapel, listening yet again to Père Rigord's explanation of the pilgrimage route they would take.

"I never heard of Archbishop Sigeric before now," Swan whispered as the elderly priest droned on.

"Neither have I," Grace whispered back, "But it is more than a hundred and fifty years since he wrote of his trek from Canterbury to Rome."

Père Rigord suddenly stopped talking and glared at Grace. She felt her face redden as Bronson and Rodrick grinned at her discomfort.

"Did you have a question, milady Grace?" the priest asked. "Something you wished to say?"

She searched her memory, trying to recall what he'd been saying a few moments ago. "I've never heard of most of the places you mention, Father."

He steepled his fingers under his nose, evidently seeking divine guidance. "Mayhap it's because you never paid much attention in my Latin classes and I am giving you the Latin names. Atherats is Arras, Bysiceon is Besançon. It's simple. Everyone knows the stages of the Via Francigena."

Bronson stared at the ceiling, his fist planted firmly over his mouth. She'd wager there'd be teeth marks in his flesh from stifling his amusement.

"Your pardon, Father," she said, avoiding Swan's gaze less she burst out laughing. "As you say, Latin was never my strong point, and I'm confident Rodrick and Bronson will ensure we follow the route."

The cleric sighed resignedly. "But I want you to recognise the historic places you will pass through, so you'll appreciate them more. I wish I was young enough to accompany you."

It came to her then that the inconvenient and daunting journey ahead of them was an adventure few women ever got the chance to experience.

Swan must have been thinking the same thing. "It's a happy coincidence," she said as Père Rigord took his leave. "Our common ancestor, Ram de Montbryce travelled through Rome on his way back from Constantinople."

"Yes," Grace replied, "in the company of your grandfather, Caedmon, and my grandfather, Baudoin."

Bronson came to stand behind Grace and put his hands on her shoulders. "Our grandfather wrote of his travels in a codex. My father still has it, though the ink has deteriorated over the years and most of it is barely legible."

Rodrick came to his feet. "We should keep a journal of our travels as we journey to Rome. Then we can pass it on to our children."

The notion pleased Grace. "Good idea. Mayhap we'll be as famous as Sigeric."

Archbishop Theobald du Bec sliced the air one way then the other as he made the sign of the Crucifixion over the codices Rodrick had procured for the journey. The cleric had been impressed with the journals during the audience he'd granted them in his apartments at Canterbury, especially when it had been explained how the priest at Ellesmere had personally sewn together the quire of blank manuscript pages. Rodrick chuckled inwardly. The old priest had been overjoyed at the idea when they'd suggested it.

He wondered why the Archbishop had insisted they begin their trek in Canterbury and follow Sigeric's route exactly. In normal circumstances, they'd have crossed the Narrow Sea to Normandie further south and been able to visit their kin at Montbryce, Alensonne and Belisle en route.

From Canterbury they would have to cross from Dover to Calais and thence journey south east, and would be mostly reliant on abbeys for hospitality.

He brought his mind back to the interview. Theobald had opened the Codices and was preparing to read Père Rigord's Latin inscription. *"Rodrick Rambaud de Montbryce et Bronson FitzRam et Suannoch Ascha FitzRam et Grace Mabelle Carys de Cullène peregrinati sunt,"* he intoned. "Good, good, yes, indeed, you are pilgrims."

To Rodrick's surprise he beckoned his secretary and dictated a benediction. The monk dipped a quill and scratched the blessing into each codex. *"Benedicti ab Theobaldo Archiepiscopo Cantuariensis sunt."*

"A high honor, your Excellency," he said. "We thank you."

Under his breath he whispered what each of them was no doubt thinking.

Why can't he simply give us the dispensation?

"Go now," Archbishop Theobald commanded, waving at them as if they were troublesome gnats, "I'm told the winds are favorable for your crossing to Calais."

They bowed their way out of his presence and mounted their horses for the short ride to Dover and the longboats ready to take them and their entourage across the Narrow Sea.

Despite the calm waters, Rodrick started to retch as soon as the boat left shore. "This is something else I've inherited from our great grandfather," he lamented. "Ram de Montbryce suffered terribly from seasickness! He apparently struggled to keep the bile from rising in his throat when he was crossing from Normandie to England with William the Conqueror at the outset of the invasion."

Swan shivered. She had dreaded this voyage, but not because Rodrick had forewarned her of his malady.

He looked forlorn. She wasn't used to seeing weakness in him. He was her strength. If he faltered on this journey—

"I'm aware you'd rather be tending Cob than looking after me."

"No. I was thinking of the wreck of *La Blanche Nef.*"

He put his hands over hers on the side of the boat. "Whenever I make this crossing, I think of that fateful night and the horror of it for your grandparents."

She huddled deeper into her cloak. "It happened before I was born, and I regret I never met them. It's four and thirty years ago, and I shudder at the terror they endured in the dark, cold waters, the desperate screams of hundreds in their ears."

Rodrick indicated Bronson and Grace standing together near the prow. "He's thinking of it too."

It wasn't a good beginning to their odyssey. By the time they arrived in Calais, Rodrick was pale and weak, Bronson morose, and Grace short-tempered. Swan was relieved they planned to spend the night at Witsant, a Flemish fishing village south west of Calais. However, there was nowhere to lodge and they continued on to Guînes where they were welcomed at the Abbey of Saint Léonard.

Swan and Grace shared a musty pallet in a nun's cell; Lucia slept on the floor. Rodrick and Bronson camped in the abbey grounds with their entourage. Swan fretted all night because Rodrick was sleeping outdoors after the terrible day at sea.

CHAPTER THIRTY-FOUR

*G*uînes, Flandres,
    *November, One Thousand Eleven Hundred And Fifty
    Four, Anno Domini.*

*Nigh on three score years have passed since my grandfather,
Caedmon Brice FitzRam, traveled through France and Italy on his way
back from the First Crusade. He wrote a detailed account of his travels in
a codex which is now in my father's hands. I never met my grandfather,
but I learned a great deal about him from his journal, timeworn as it is.*

*The journey changed him, as I expect this pilgrimage will change
me. From my cold and damp tent outside the Abbey of Saint Léonard near
Guînes, I dedicate my journey to my grandfather's memory.*

*My fervent hope is that Grace and I will receive the dispensation to
marry and for a sign the Angel of Death no longer stalks me and mine.*

Written by my own hand, Bronson FitzRam.

*Guînes, Flandres,
November in the Year of Our Lord One Thousand Eleven Hundred And
Fifty Four.*

*Be it known that I, Rodrick Rambaud de Montbryce, am embarking on
a pilgrimage to Rome, following the Via Francigena. I do this to obtain a
dispensation to marry Suannoch Ascha FitzRam, my second cousin.*

I dedicate this journey to my great grandfather, Rambaud de Montbryce, from whom Suannoch and I are both descended. I feel in my bones he would have approved of our marriage.

Pope Anastasius is reputed to be a difficult man. In the event he refuses to grant us permission to wed, I herein declare I will marry her anyway, though it means the loss of my earldom.

I do so swear.

Rodrick de M.

Post Scriptum. I am recovered from mal-de-mer.

Doingt, Flandres

The first three days have gone well.

There is a monolith here known as the Stone of Gargantua. Legend tells of the giant halting his stroll through this grassy meadow bothered by a stone in his shoe. He shook his foot and the stone flew out.

It's at least twice as tall as I am.

They say the fairies in the woods of Recogne dance around the stone by the light of the full moon. I was reminded of the King Stone. I mentioned it to Grace and told her of my dream. She in turn revealed to me she had dreamt of seeing me by a giant monolith. It took her a while but she admitted when I coaxed her that I was naked in her dream.

Last evening I dreamt of fairies dancing around Gargantua's Stone. One of them had dark wings.

Bronson FitzRam

Reims,

We have reached the ancient town of Reims and walked in the footsteps of Charlemagne. Swan was fascinated by the tale of the Holy Ampulla told to us by one of the monks at the Saint Remi Basilica. She almost had him convinced to open it up and show us the Saint Chrême brought by the white dove at the baptism of Clovis more than five hundred years ago. At the last he seemed to recollect his wits and remember the sacred oil is used to anoint the kings of France.

She is one persuasive woman. Anastasius beware!

We walked beneath the Porte de Mars. Inspiring to think of Romans building these structures hundreds of years ago.
Rodrick de M.

Besançon

The four of us looked out today at the Alps to the south of this town, much as Julius Caesar must have done hundreds of years ago. They are a daunting sight. We've been on the road ten days since landing in Calais.

Travelling is never easy for women. Despite Lucia's best efforts, both Suannoch and Grace are feeling the effects of a lack of the comforts they are used to. Neither has complained, but they are short tempered with one another. Rodrick and I try to keep them apart as much as possible.

I have great admiration for the scores of fellow pilgrims who don't have horses and servants to take care of their needs. Many of them barely have decent covering for their feet. This experience has been a good lesson for William and Stephen.

If we maintain our pace we should be in Rome for yuletide.

May God be with us as we venture into the mountains. It already feels colder than it did traveling south through France.
Bronson FitzRam

Saint-Rhémy-en-Bosses

We gave heartfelt thanks at Mass today. We have reached the safety of the Saint Bernard Hospice. A hundred years ago Bernard of Menthon, the archdeacon of Aosta, determined to put an end to the dangers posed by brigands harassing travelers in the mountains. This place is a safe haven, well guarded by huge dogs, and we have no fear of being attacked by bandits. The cold is enough to contend with. It will be heaven to sleep indoors this night.

We are only half way to our destination, but I am more convinced than ever that Swan is the woman I am meant to marry. The journey hasn't been easy, particularly in this season of the year. There were times I feared we might freeze in the mountains. But Swan seems excited by change, adventure, and excitement. She has never lost her optimism and has kept everyone's spirits up.

She and Grace have both willingly helped many of the pilgrims who are forced to walk, sharing food, clothing, blankets, recruiting some of them to travel with us as servants.

They have wept over those who died en route, offering consolation, as we all did. Young and old, rich and poor, we have become one family. Swan has helped me see things from different points of view. I never gave much thought before to the plight of the poor.

There is no one more suited to be my Countess.

Pray God Anastasius sees it the same way.

Rodrick de M.

CHAPTER THIRTY-FIVE

Bronson scratched his bushy beard, complaining loudly about the itching. Grace was grateful she and Swan didn't have to contend with facial hair on the road.

She eyed the threatening clouds. "Thank the saints the interminable drizzle has stopped. Mayhap in Pavia we might find somewhere to shave off nigh on three sennights of hair from your face. I've forgotten what you look like."

He grimaced. "Me too. Hopefully you are right, though I don't trust young William's hand with a razor."

She fluttered her eyelashes at him. "Mayhap I can do it for you?"

He looked askance, but smiled. "Perhaps."

"When Père Rigord was droning on about these faraway places, I barely paid attention, but now we're here, I'm glad he gave us some of the history. I particularly want to see the Basilica of San Michele Maggiore. According to him the reconstruction should be nearing completion. It was destroyed by fire one hundred and fifty years ago."

He winced.

She was contrite. "Forgive me. I'm like a tutor. You were there when the priest lectured us. Imagine this is where Louis the Third was crowned."

He rolled his eyes, but they reined their horses to a halt as the Basilica came into view. "It's not what I expected," she said. "Very different from Norman architecture. The façade is flat."

Bronson cleared his throat as he came to assist her to dismount. "According to Père Rigord this is Romanesque architecture."

She glanced at him sharply.

He winked. "See. I was listening."

This was the best part of the day. The comforting pressure of Bronson's hands at her waist renewed her spirit no matter how tired she was from the day's travel. He lifted her as if she were weightless, pulling her to his body as he set her on her feet. The kiss they shared had become part of the ritual—chaste, yet sensuous, innocent yet full of promise. She would never admit it to him, but she loved the softness of his beard on her face.

"Truly?" Swan asked incredulously.

"Truly," Rodrick replied.

"This is the place?" she asked again.

"I wouldn't lie to you," he reiterated.

They stood together on the ferry crossing the river Po, gazing through the rain at the town of Piacenza.

"It's hard to believe," she murmured, leaning into him, held in history's grip.

He confirmed what he had told her minutes ago. "The Council of Piacenza was where Pope Urban proclaimed the call for the First Crusade in response to the Byzantine Emperor's pleas for help. More than thirty thousand religious and lay attended the Council—so many they had to hold it outside the town."

"And my grandfather answered the call," she murmured.

He nibbled her ear. "Perhaps it was your destiny to come here," he whispered.

"Perhaps," she said hoarsely, lost in thoughts of what she knew of her grandparents. "I don't believe it was a call to fight the Turks my grandfather answered. He was lost, and hoped the Crusade would be a way to come to terms with his bastardy."

"And he was right. You are a perceptive woman," he replied.

The northern part of Italy is different from England. Most of the towns are communes and the people band together to defend and govern

themselves within fortified walls. In some of them, however, the defensive towers of different families suggest there is conflict within the walls.

In Borgo San Donnino we saw an interesting sight at the front of the cathedral—a statue of Saint Peter pointing in the direction of Rome. There is an inscription. "I show you the way to Rome."

Pilgrims are welcome in this region, especially now when only the foolhardy like the four of us attempt this journey. We are tired of being cold and wet. But Rodrick and I have chosen well—Swan and Grace are both strong women. It's fortunate we brought a large contingent of guards. There are few women among the pilgrims, and the best of men can be driven to depravity by the lack of female companionship. There have been times I've wanted to take Grace down from her horse and make love to her there and then. My grandfather wrote of his longing for his wife. I have my love with me as my constant companion, and sometimes I think it is worse than being apart. I want her but cannot touch her.

I will forever cherish the memory of standing with Grace on a hillside in Pietrasanta looking out over the Mediterranean Sea. Even in winter it is strikingly beautiful. My grandfather remarked it was unlike any body of water he'd seen before.

I told her the Romans arrogantly called it Mare Nostrum, 'Our Sea'. We talked of empires. The mighty Roman Empire crumbled in this very region hundreds of years ago with the overthrow of the last Emperor. The Norman Conqueror must be twisting in his tomb now the empire he won for his people will soon pass into the hands of the Angevins with the crowning of Henry Plantagenet.

I fear we will miss that historic ceremony.

Bronson

I would love to revisit this region in summer. Surprisingly, we have encountered many Normans who came here generations ago. In Gimignano we sampled Vernaccia wine, an excellent vintage from ancient vines growing on the fertile hills. We drank too much, but it was good to relax and enjoy ourselves. Swan became very amorous and I was tempted to whisk her away to some secluded spot and make love to her. It is difficult to spend every day with the woman I love and not touch her intimately, but our monks are ever vigilant.

They grow saffron here too and Swan insisted we take a supply with us. She guards it like gold.

Gimignano was called Silvia in Roman times but the name was changed after Saint Geminianus saved the town from Attila the Hun.

Attila the Hun! I have much to learn about history.

We are nearing the end of our journey. There are reports from pilgrims leaving Rome of great unrest in the city. King William of Sicily is openly hostile to the Pope. Frederick Barbarossa stirs up trouble. The barons fight with each other and with the Pope and raid the countryside, even robbing pilgrims on their way to the tombs of the Apostles.

The people of Rome are in open revolt under the leadership of Arnold of Brescia.

Anastasius is apparently ill.

None of this news bodes well and has dampened our spirits.

Rodrick

CHAPTER THIRTY-SIX

L *a Storta*
Fourth Day of December

     Much has happened since our arrival yesterday at this last station outside Rome. We sent our monks ahead to inform Oddone Frangipane we were nearing the city. He has returned with them and a large armed brigade to accompany us to his home.

     The flamboyant Roman has brought the astounding news of Anastasius' death only yesterday. Another Pope has been elected in his place who has taken the name Adrian, the fourth Pope to do so.

     According to Oddone, this Pope has long insisted serfs be allowed to marry lawfully without the consent of their lords.

     This alone would seem to augur well for us.

     Another surprising thing is he's an Englishman, Nicolas Breakspear, born in Abbots Langley.

     What's more, Oddone knows this Pope. Adrian has asked him to assist in negotiations with Barbarossa in the conflict over the powers of the Holy Roman Emperor.

     He has arranged an audience for us, insisting Adrian will be happy to receive fellow Englishmen who will convey our new Sovereign's congratulations.

     These developments have lifted our spirits.

     We must hope it doesn't come up in the conversation that Henry has yet to be crowned less than three sennights from now.

     Rodrick

Grace and Swan rode in the midst of the men-at-arms. Rodrick and Bronson had reminded them over and over to keep their mounts close together and to stay within the protection of Oddone's guards. Their English entourage had remained in La Storta. Only Lucia, William and Stephen rode with them.

Grace suspected everyone thought Swan would disobey their command, but as the narrow streets of Rome became more and more clogged with excited people, Swan seemed determined to obey the directive not to look at the frenzied crowd.

The men-at-arms had been instructed to force their way through if necessary, but not with belligerence. *Slow and steady* was how Oddone had put it.

"I hope we have managed to look important enough," she murmured to Swan. "And not the ragamuffins we've turned into on this journey."

Swan nodded, but she looked uncharacteristically nervous as their cavalcade came to a halt. Even the normally placid Cob was being difficult.

Bronson made his way to them from the front of the column. "There's been an assassination on the Via Sacra. A cardinal apparently. People are in uproar."

Grace took several deep breaths, hope slipping away. "We'll never get an audience now."

Bronson reached over and put a hand on hers. "Don't give up. We will see this Pope. I believe him being an Englishman is a good omen."

They made their slow way to the Palazzo Laterano, the main papal residence. Oddone was allowed inside the gates, but they had to remain outside.

After an interminable wait, during which they were warned more than once not to dismount, admittance was granted. "We must look the part," she remarked to Swan.

Swan smiled for the first time, nodding towards a statue of a man on horseback. "Marcus Aurelius," she said. "Exactly as Père Rigord described it."

They left their horses with the guards and were led inside along endless corridors before entering a magnificent hall. "*Aula Concilii*," Oddone explained. "In English, Hall of the Council."

They craned their necks as he pointed upwards. "Eleven apses. Here are held the councils of the Lateran. His Holiness awaits you in his private apartments. Follow me please."

As soon as Rodrick laid eyes on Adrian he recognised they were dealing with an intelligent and determined man. He swallowed his nervousness. They had come a long way and endured much in seeking this audience. He didn't intend to squander the opportunity. "Your Holiness," he said after Oddone had introduced them, bowing low, as did the other three, "you honor us."

Adrian waved a dismissive hand. "You honor me by bringing greetings from Henry Plantagenet. However, I am curious. You must have set off from England sennights ago. How did Henry know I would be elected Pope? I myself was unaware of it until a few days ago."

Bronson stepped forward. "You have seen through us, Your Holiness. We have been presumptuous in claiming to represent our new King, though you can be assured of his good wishes."

"But he isn't king yet. However, I understand Westminster is preparing for the ceremony on the nineteenth day of this month."

Rodrick decided to get straight to the point. "Your Holiness, I am Rodrick de Montbryce, the eldest son of an English Earl. I wish to marry Suannoch FitzRam, but she and I share a great grandfather—"

"Rambaud de Montbryce," Adrian said softly.

Rodrick wasn't sure if this development was a good thing or not.

"You see, I am well acquainted with your family," the Pope said, "and Oddone has told me something of your purpose here." He gestured towards Grace. "This young lady is your twin sister, if I'm not mistaken, and she wishes to marry the other young man, who is also a distant cousin."

Rodrick had rehearsed over and over what he would say to the Pope, but now his mind refused to work. "I am overwhelmed you are aware of our family."

"Do you know where I was born?" Adrian asked.

What that had to do with anything, Rodrick didn't understand, but—"Abbots Langley."

"Which is near a sacred shrine."

A bubble of hope prompted by a memory from the past gurgled up in Rodrick's throat. "To Saint Alban."

"Exactly. I received my early education in the Abbey school there, and anyone who has benefitted thus knows the name Montbryce."

He glanced away from Rodrick to look at the other three. Only Grace looked as though she understood. "You are puzzled," he said to Swan and Bronson. "Perhaps the young lady can enlighten you."

Grace flushed, obviously not having expected to be called upon to speak. Rodrick smiled his encouragement.

Her eyes darted to the Pope. "Adam de Montbryce was our cousin, twice removed I think."

Adrian's nod confirmed it.

Grace swallowed hard. "He was a patron of the Abbey dedicated to Saint Alban."

"The first English martyr," Adrian added, his voice edged with pride. "But calling your late cousin a patron doesn't do him justice. Adam de Montbryce was exceedingly generous and his sons continue to support the Abbey to this day, despite that they live in Normandie."

A long silence ensued, during which Rodrick thanked God over and over for the circumstances which had led Adam to donate to the Abbey at Saint Albans. He wondered if Adrian was aware Adam believed Alban had worked a miracle in curing him of a malady every virile male dreads.

Adrian seemed to be pondering, tapping his fingertips together. Rodrick hoped it was their dispensations he was considering. They hadn't been invited to sit, though there were several upholstered chairs in the opulent apartment.

Suddenly, the Pontiff's demeanour became stern. "I must endeavor to bring down Arnold of Brescia, the leader of the anti-papal faction here in Rome. The king of Sicily is openly hostile. Disorder has led to the murder of a cardinal. If things do not improve quickly, I will have to consider the previously unheard-of step of putting Rome under interdict."

The Pope seemed suddenly to have forgotten their request, but Rodrick strove to keep his anxiety in check. He clasped his nervous hands together behind his back. "Such a move would seriously affect the number of pilgrims," he offered nervously.

Adrian grinned. "And thereby the local economy. Without the Easter services the pilgrims will not come. The City Council of Rome will then exile Arnold." He rubbed his hands together. "Barbarossa thirsts to be crowned Emperor by my hand. He will help Rome rid itself of Brescia. Oddone will be instrumental in this."

Rodrick glanced at Swan who had suddenly grasped hold of Bronson's arm. He feared the excitement of the day and this sudden turn of the discussion away from their plight may have been too much. He hoped she would keep her mouth closed.

Too late!

"What of our request, Your Holiness?" she asked hoarsely.

Adrian chuckled. "I plan to withdraw to Viterbo where I will ponder the matter. Oddone will take you to his home."

Frangipane bowed to the Pope then indicated the door.

"And thank Henry Plantagenet for the good wishes," the Pope said as they exited. "He will be a great king."

CHAPTER THIRTY-SEVEN

Grace had grown up in the comfort of a well provisioned and comfortable castle, but the chamber she and Swan shared at Frangipane's villa was breathtakingly opulent. "I've never seen so much marble," she exclaimed, sprawled fully clothed on the enormous bed.

Swan winced as Lucia pulled a bone comb through her tangled hair. "Decadent. But welcome after sennights on horseback and in tents."

Grace sat up. "It has been wonderful, seven days of being treated like long lost friends by Odonne and his brother Cencio—feasting, dancing, Advent observances, and preparations for Yuletide."

Swan turned away from the mirror, her face somber. "Remember last Yuletide?"

Grace shivered. "Indeed. A lot has happened since then, and thanks be to God we survived Godefroy's madness."

"But a dispensation would be a nice Yuletide gift. I cannot bear the prospect of the return journey if I cannot marry Rodrick."

Grace hesitated, but then decided to share her thoughts. "Rodrick will wed you if the dispensation isn't granted."

"But that would mean—"

"William would become Earl of Ellesmere."

"Rodrick has confided this to you?"

"We are twins. I know my brother as well as he knows himself."

"But I cannot allow it. The Earldom is his birthright."

"Not to mention William is not a good candidate. I love my younger brother but he isn't the man Rodrick is. However, without you as his wife, Rodrick's life will be miserable."

"As will mine," Swam murmured.

There was a long silence, then Swan asked, "What's it like to be married, Grace?"

Cold dread blossomed in Grace's belly. Swan was her dear friend, indeed more the sister she'd never had, who must be understandably nervous about what happens between a man and a woman in marriage. And she had only Grace to turn to for advice—the one person who could tell her nothing.

"It requires patience."

Swan eyed her curiously. "Yes, but I mean—"

Lucia coughed, dropping the comb.

Grace narrowed her eyes as they watched Lucia pick up the comb, hoping Swan would interpret it as meaning they shouldn't discuss such things in front of servants. She sought to change the subject. "We must continue to pray—"

An insistent rapping at the door intruded on their conversation. Lucia opened it to admit Rodrick and Bronson. Both men looked too serious for Grace's comfort. She suspected instantly that word had come from Viterbo. Out of the frying pan—

Bronson held out a hand. "Come, my lady, our fate awaits us in Oddone's salon."

Oddone brandished an envelope. A priest stood at his side. "*Amici*," he shouted, "an emissary from *Il Papa*."

Rodrick's lungs refused to fill with air. This was the moment of no return. Life would never be the same again, no matter what was contained in the envelope the Italian handed to him with a flourish.

He stared at the elaborate insignia. "It's from the Pope," was all he could stammer.

"Open it," Swan murmured.

He pulled out the parchment that had been folded in three, the bottom edge folded up and secured with a lead seal.

"Attached with twine," Oddone pointed out. "For a document of lesser importance."

Rodrick was relieved Swan didn't scream out loud.

He desperately wanted to sit down, afraid his knees might buckle. He unfolded the parchment. "Adrianus, Roman numeral IV, Papa—"

He scanned the ornate script. "It's in Latin."

"Of course it's in Latin," Grace snorted. "*Padre*, please."

Rodrick gave the missive to the smiling priest who coughed into his fist then began.

"*Licet enim conjugium Rodrick de Montbryce et Suannoch Ascha FitzRam. Quattuor generationes impedimentum consanguinitatis a nulla.*"

The silence was deafening. Rodrick tried desperately to recall anything of his Latin primer. "What does it mean?"

The young priest smiled. "He has granted your dispensation. You can marry Suannoch, the consanguinity of four generations has no bearing."

Swan looked ready to launch at Rodrick, but she hesitated. "What of Bronson and Grace?"

The priest looked back at the document. "*Licet enim conjugium Bronson FitzRam et Grace Mabelle Carys de Montbryce. Quattuor generationes impedimentum consanguinitatis a nulla.*"

Bronson let out a whooping sound. "It's the same. We too can marry." He scooped Grace up in his arms and twirled her around.

Rodrick was about to embrace Swan when the priest coughed, handing him a smaller envelope. "There is another missive."

With trembling hands, he ripped it open. It contained an unsealed note, written in English.

He scanned it then read the contents out loud.

"*To Rodrick de Montbryce.*

In remembrance of your cousin Adam, it would bring me great pleasure in these troubled times to hear my native language during Yuletide. I have taken the liberty of proclaiming banns for your marriages in the church of San Giovanni di Laterano. Christmas Day is an excellent opportunity for a double wedding of four of my countrymen.

Nicolas Breakspear, Adrian IV"

CHAPTER THIRTY-EIGHT

R oma
    Palaccio Frangipane

     Twenty-Fifth Day of December, One Thousand One Hundred and Fifty-Four Anno Domini

    Bronson and I concur that these journals should contain an account of our weddings. Our brides are of the same mind, but correctly assume neither of us is likely to render a description of events that will satisfy them. Grace is therefore assisting me and Swan is helping her brother. We won't be missed in the Grand Sala for a while as servants prepare for the second banquet of the day. Most people seem to have disappeared, I suspect for a nap.

    In telling of my nuptials, I would simply say my dearest wish came true when Pope Adrian explained that in the eyes of the Roman church, Swan and I had been married since the day we were betrothed. If I'd known—

    Grace has elbowed me in the ribs, and therefore I cannot continue with my train of thought.

    Only the Pope's blessing was required, which he gave with due ceremony. Not many in England can claim to have been married by a Pope—an English one at that! After the blessing in Latin, he repeated the words in our language and seemed genuinely happy for us.

    Oddone's tailors and seamstresses fashioned wonderful garments for the occasion. Swan's gown of burgundy velvet took my breath away. It was laced at the sides and back with golden ribbon. Its narrow shape showed off her lovely figure. If Grace were not censoring what I write I might include my thoughts about those laces.

The same ribbon had been fashioned like a halo into a circlet atop her golden hair. She is my angel.

My sister is smiling and hugging my arm. It is a source of great joy to me that I was able to share my wedding day with my twin and see her happily wed also.

Rodrick de M.

Roma
Palaccio Frangipane

Twenty-Fifth Day of December, One Thousand One Hundred and Fifty-Four Anno Domini

My sister Swan is keeping an eye on me as I write this account of my wedding to Grace de Cullène.

She will be surprised by what I have to say as a preface. Neither she nor Grace are aware that yesterday I went to the church to speak to the priest.

(Imagine! I have managed to keep a secret from the two of them. Swan's glaring pout is evidence of her annoyance!)

I went because I was still plagued by my dreams of dark angels. I had some difficulty communicating with my limited Italian and the priest's nonexistent knowledge of my language. I tried in Latin, which was worse. As I was attempting to explain my concerns, an enormous sculpted frieze on the wall behind him caught my eye. I took him by surprise when I ran over to it. Chiselled into the stone was a life size figure with black wings. I don't believe the sculptor intended them to be black, but over the years, the stone has turned dark.

This was the angel of my dreams.

I gestured like a madman, feeling the weight lifting from my shoulders. The Lord God Almighty knew Grace and I would come to Rome. The angel wasn't meant to be a harbinger of death, but a sign of things to come. I have married the woman who was my destiny. My fear has turned to optimism for the future—mine, Grace's and our children's.

All that remains is to inadequately record another vision I will never forget: my beautiful bride in a dark green velvet gown that emphasized her tempting curves, a simple circlet of ivy atop her head. In the years ahead I will fondly recall the look of surprise on her face when Adrian informed us we'd been married since the day of our betrothal.

Now Swan is crying and hugging my arm. It has been a joy beyond measure to share this day with my sister and to see her happily wed to Rodrick de Montbryce.
Deo gratias,
Bronson F.

Addendum
Swan and Grace insist we record the details of the wedding banquets. While it seems enough food to feed an army, rather than a score, it should be borne in mind the feasting will go on for two more days, and we haven't yet eaten everything listed here.

Today we enjoyed pastries with pine nuts and almonds, and something similar to marzipan. Everyone expressed amazement at the sweetness of the asparagus, especially since it's out of season.

The tiny sausages and meatballs were spicier than we normally would eat in England, but the roasted partridge and sauce was delicious, as were the capons and pigeons, hams and wild boar.

For the morrow's festivities the Frangipanes have planned a whole roast sheep with a sour cherry sauce, and a great variety of roast birds—turtledoves, partridges, pheasants, quail, and olives—the last a novelty for us.

The Frangipanes eventually understood why we preferred no swan be served.

On the final day we'll be fed chicken cooked in rosewater, a whole roast suckling pig, roast peacock with artichokes, and sweets of quinces cooked with cinnamon.

Bear in mind this is Yuletide, a time of year Italians seem to celebrate to excess.

However, Bronson and I both have an appetite for something other than food this night.
Rodrick de M.

CHAPTER THIRTY-NINE

As Swan and the women of the Frangipane family assisted in the removal of her velvet wedding gown, Grace was suddenly filled with misgivings. She was so preoccupied with memories of the night she'd wed Victor, her arms became stuck in the tight long sleeves.

Oddone's wife smiled at her stuttered apologies. "A bride is forgiven for being nervous on her wedding night."

How to tell the dignified Italian woman of the shame of Victor's rejection?

Would Bronson be disappointed? Would he also turn away?

She fumbled with the laces at the neck of the elegant silk nightgown the women pulled over her head. This time Cencio's wife came to her rescue with an indulgent smile. "*Tutto bene.*"

Grace prayed fervently all would indeed be well.

Male voices emanated from the other side of the screen where Oddone and his brother and Rodrick were stripping Bronson. The raucous laughter was something she didn't recall from the night Victor's steward had prepared him for bed. When she thought back to that night, she wasn't sure where Godefroy had got to either.

She'd lain on her back beside Victor, staring into blackness, not sure what to expect, assuming he would take the lead. Instead he'd snored loudly for a while, then got up and left in the middle of the night.

Her reverie was interrupted when Richalda Frangipane took her by the hand and led her out from behind the screen to the bed. She kept her eyes averted from the rambunctious men.

Swan pecked a kiss on her cheek. "Good night, sister," she said with a wink. "Don't be afraid to confide in Bronson."

She looked at her sister-by-marriage in alarm. "Confide what?"

Swan opened her mouth, but Rodrick came to claim her. "Good night, sister dear. I would stay and taunt Bronson further, but I have more pressing things to do."

He scooped up his giggling bride and carried her from the chamber.

The Frangipane brothers linked arms with Bronson and led him to the end of the bed. "Here is your groom, *bella*," Oddone declared. "Now we go to prepare Rodrick and his bride."

The exuberant Italians left, the skirts of the women swishing on the pink marble tiles.

Deafened by the beating of her heart, Grace looked up at her husband. Her eyes barely had time to travel from his hair, still bound in a queue, to his grin, to the silk nightshirt before it was pulled over his head and a naked Bronson was prowling across the bed towards her like a hungry lynx.

Taken unawares, she scrambled backwards away from him, unable to take her eyes off the evidence of his arousal.

The smile left his face. He knelt in front of her, arms held open. "What's wrong, Grace? Do you not like what you see?"

She stared at the scar meandering across his chest. It reminded her sharply of the despair she'd known when she believed him dead.

But, how to tell him she had never seen a man completely naked? She grabbed the bolster and clasped it to her breast.

Bronson furrowed his brow. "Did Victor hurt you? Is that why you're afraid? I know I am big, but—"

Grace shook her head vigorously. Swan was right, but she hoped what she had to say didn't disgust him. "I've never seen a man naked," she blurted out, fearful of looking him in the eye. "Victor didn't find me pleasing."

Bronson's eyes widened. "You never saw your husband naked? For the love of God, Grace, if I'd known I wouldn't have stripped so quickly. I didn't mean to startle you."

He rubbed his chin. "What do you mean he didn't find you pleasing? Was he mad?"

Despite her best efforts, a tear trickled down her cheek, then another. Words died in her constricted throat.

The truth struck Bronson like a bolt of lightning. He sat back on his haunches and carefully eased the bolster out of his wife's arms, holding it across his thighs. He'd assumed Grace was a woman with experience of intimate relations. If he'd known he'd have shown more finesse. "Look at me, Grace. Are you trying to say your first husband never made love to you?"

She shook her head, still refusing to look at him.

"You're telling me you are still a virgin."

In the silent seconds before she responded, confusion reigned in his heart. That his new bride might be a maiden elated him, but it would mean a completely different kind of lovemaking than what he'd had in mind.

"Yes," she whispered. "I'm sorry."

Sorry?

He wanted to fall to his knees in thanksgiving for this unexpected gift—one for which his still covered shaft was showing its appreciation. Then it came to him he was already on his knees. Here he was, a man twice married, afraid to reveal his manhood in case he alarmed the skittish woman in his bed—a desirable creature who'd been married to a fool. He had a growing suspicion what Victor's problem had been.

The urge to laugh bubbled up in his throat, but that wouldn't help matters. "Look at me."

He waited until she raised her eyes.

"I am the one who should be sorry. Ever since we met, I've been preoccupied with memories of my past marriages, and never given a thought to what you might have endured. After tangling with Godefroy, I should have deduced what kind of man his father was. Forgive me. I never want you to be hurt in any way, Grace. I love you."

She stopped fiddling with the laces of her nightgown. "I love you, Bronson, but my marriage to Victor was a dismal failure. I don't know how to please a man."

Thank you, God.

He prayed he would do this right as he moved the bolster aside, rising up on his knees. "It will be my great honor to show you."

Grace had often felt Bronson's arousal pressed against her, and during his illness when he'd lain naked beneath the linens, she'd had wicked notions of cupping him in her hands, of feeling the weight, the warmth.

However, none of her imaginings of his male part came close to the reality of the proud lance jutting from its nest of chestnut curls.

She clenched her inner muscles, filled with a sudden inexplicable urge to have the hard flesh thrust into her fevered body, knowing instinctively nothing else would assuage the throbbing need pulsing inside. She ached to be a woman.

Bronson took hold of her hands. "You do like what you see."

She licked her lips, dragging her eyes to his. His teasing smile made her giddy. "I do," she purred, astonished at the wantonness in her voice.

He leaned towards her. "Then let me help you remove your lovely nightrail."

She came up on her knees, raised her arms and arched her back, wanting Bronson to see her breasts and yet shy and nervous.

He peeled the garment over her head and stared. "You are exquisite," he rasped. "Any man who finds you unattractive isn't interested in women."

An inkling of understanding permeated her desire-fogged brain.

Of course! The odious steward!

The bonds of guilt slipped away. Without a second thought she reached for Bronson's shaft, tracing a fingertip from base to swollen tip.

He lifted his chin, stretching the muscles of his neck, and growled. "Believe me, Grace, your touch is more than pleasing."

He kissed her then, swirling his tongue around and around the inside of her lips, sucking her tongue into his mouth, gently, seductively. She loved it.

He ran his hands across the top of her shoulders, then cupped the sides of her breasts, pushing them together. When he brushed his thumbs across her nipples she had to break the kiss, gasping for breath, consumed by the fire of desire building in her lower belly.

He leaned back slightly to look at her, still caressing the hardened nipples. "Beautiful," he breathed. "I want to suckle."

Their eyes locked for a moment. Her longing for him to put his mouth on her must have been evident. His smile sent winged creatures fluttering in her belly. He bent his head and suckled, drawing hard on the nipple. She wove the fingertips of one hand into his hair, and cupped her breast closer to his mouth with the other. Her existence suddenly had meaning. It was for this man she'd been born. She purred her contentment. The wait had been worth it.

The smoothness of Grace's skin, her scent, her taste, everything about her intoxicated Bronson. He swirled his tongue around the rigid nipple then moved to the other breast, savoring her purring moans. He'd never been a man to take his pleasure and leave his wives wanting, but he was consumed with a need to bring Grace to ecstasy. However, if he didn't slow down he'd be spilling his seed like a green lad with his first tumble.

He eased away from her, and braced one foot on the floor. "Turn over," he whispered. "On your belly."

She frowned momentarily, then did as he bade, one arm dangling over the edge of the bed. He moved her hair off the nape of her neck and kissed her there, once, twice. She scrunched her neck, giggling into the linens. "I'm ticklish."

He traced a fingertip down her spine, but his eyes were on her *derrière*. At her waist he spread his hands and stroked her hips.

Child-bearing hips.

He kneaded her cheeks, spreading them apart with his thumbs, the breath catching in his throat at first sight of her perfect pink rosette.

His tarse bucked when she moaned. He sent his thumbs deeper, opening her more to his gaze, caressing her outer lips, hoping he wasn't going too fast.

She pushed out her bottom when he opened her legs wider. Taking it as a good omen, he slid a finger inside. She was ready.

She ran her dangling fingers up the side of his leg then gripped his ankle, squealing with surprise when he grasped her hips, flipped her over, and planted his mouth firmly on the intimate place he had to taste.

He rejoiced in the touch of her fingers in his hair, the deep longing in her voice when she whispered his name, the moans of pleasure.

He savored the taste and smell of her arousal. Her skin was sheened with sweat, her cleft hot and wet. He gripped her quivering hips as she dug her heels into the mattress. He licked and suckled and licked again the hardening nub of her arousal, faster and faster until she screamed loudly, her words strangled by breathless ecstasy, but he understood, and it humbled him.

Never before had a woman's pleasure ignited him to such a degree. He had to be inside her. He clamped his mouth on hers, positioned his shaft at her opening, and plunged, breathing for her when she stopped.

Her inner muscles pulsated on his rigid flesh and soon he joined her in a euphoric fall into the abyss, pumping his essence into her body, determined to give her a child.

CHAPTER FORTY

R odrick and Swan lay side by side in the bed, only their fingertips touching, the linens tucked up to their necks. He hoped his bride would contain her giggles until the Frangipanes had exited their chamber, but as the ornately carved door clicked shut, she took him completely by surprise.

In the blink of an eye, she was out of bed, and out of the nightgown. The fancy creation flew through the air like the dove freed from the Ark.

If the touch of her fingertips had roused the interest of his shaft, the sight of her ripe breasts and perfect body sent desire roaring through him like a herd of rutting boar.

"I want to see your body, Rodrick," she teased, frustrating his attempts to make his suddenly clumsy hands grasp the fabric of his long nightshirt from beneath him. At last he got it off over his head and tossed it in the same general direction she'd thrown hers.

"Minx!" he shouted, lunging at her as she leapt from the bed and backed away from him, beckoning.

By the time he caught her only minutes later, they were both giddy with laughter. He ensnared her in his arms, feeling her breasts rise and fall against his chest as she tried to regain her breath. "I can feel your nipples," he rasped, looking down at the enticing cleavage pressed against him. "Let me see them."

She thrust back her head. Her nipples peeked at him. "I love your breasts," he growled. He licked her long neck then bent to suckle, drawing the rigid flesh into his mouth.

Home.

She kneaded her fingertips into his shoulders. "I've longed for you to do this," she said hoarsely.

He took his mouth off her nipple long enough to make a noise of agreement and grin at her, then moved to the other nipple.

A tremor shivered through her body.

"You're cold," he said, scooping her up.

"I'm on fire," she replied, shaking her head, but he carried her to the bed anyway and laid her on her back.

She spread her legs and put a hand on her mons, staring at him seductively through half closed eyelids. "Lick me there again."

He didn't need to be asked twice. Kneeling between her bent legs, he curled his arms around her thighs and buried his face in her juices, relishing her scent, her taste, her heat.

An image of their first meeting rose up behind his eyes— Suannoch FitzRam in a nun's habit, warming her backside in front of the fire. He'd an urge to laugh out loud. Who would have thought what lay beneath that habit?

And soon he'd plunge his rampant cock into the wet warmth of her sheath. Now the urge was to beat his chest and give vent to the savage maleness surging through his veins.

But Swan had turned out to be more than a beautiful female who excited him beyond measure. She was intelligent, courageous—and she loved him!

He looked up from his task. "I love you, my Swan," roared up from the center of his being.

She parted her lips as her eyes rolled back. She keened out her release, calling his name over and over.

Swan stopped breathing, willing time to stand still so the intensely pleasurable sensations pulsing through her body would go on and on and on. Though a single candle cast its meager glow in the chamber, sunlight shone behind her eyes.

A thought intruded that there should be more. "I need—"

But Rodrick knew her needs. His hard male member penetrated her body, heightening the euphoria as he thrust in and out, in and out.

"I—love—you, Rodrick," she stammered as he took possession of her body and her soul, filling her with contentment and love.

And to think I didn't like him when we first met.

Having pumped the last drop of his essence into Swan, Rodrick collapsed on top of her, blinded by the light of the most intense sexual experience he'd ever had. Possessing Swan had exceeded expectations, and they'd been considerable.

He lay still, willing his softening cock to remain in the warmth of her newly breached sheath as long as possible.

She was panting as hard as he was. Perhaps he was too heavy, but he didn't want to move, didn't have the strength to move.

Gradually his happy shaft curled up in the sticky wetness at her opening. He tried to summon his arms to lift his weight.

"Don't move," she murmured.

But a little voice in his head urged him to seek the evidence of his conquest on the linens. "They'll come early for the sheets," he rasped, filled with satisfaction at the sight of blood on his tarse and on the linens.

"Sheets?" she said hoarsely, lifting up on her elbows.

The sight of her ripe breasts, the still hard nipples pouting provocatively, stirred renewed interest in his *couilles*. "They'll want to run the bloodied sheets up the flagpole."

She covered a yawn with the back of her hand. "They'll need two poles."

He looked at the sheets again. "Two?"

She collapsed back onto the mattress. "Two marriages, two wedding nights, two sets of sheets."

Rodrick furrowed his brow. Evidently her first intimate experience had stolen his wife's wits. "No. You don't get my meaning. It's the bloodied sheets. To prove the bride was—"

She raised up on her elbows again and stared at him with those big amber eyes, and the truth hit him as hard as Titus had punched him in the nose. "Grace?"

She said nothing.

Anger surged into his throat. "You mean Victor—Grace—their marriage—"

He came to his feet, filled at once with fury for his sister's torment that he'd failed miserably to even guess, and elation for

Bronson. He raked a hand through his hair. "If Victor wasn't already dead, I'd kill him myself. Did she tell you of this?"

"No, but I've suspected for a while. Things she said, and a reluctance to venture into topics young women who are about to be wed usually discuss. She evaded my curious questions."

His male pride reasserted itself. He lay back down, gathering her warm body into his arms. "And have I answered the questions to your satisfaction?"

She sighed deeply, snuggling into him, pulling the top sheet over them. "I am more than satisfied. But I have a feeling there is still a lot to learn."

She reached down to cup him in her hand. "For example, Grace wouldn't say whether women are allowed to put their mouths on a man's part."

She pulled back to look at him, a wicked glint in her eye. "Oh! It got bigger!"

"We'll have to change your name, milady Swan," he growled. "Minx is more appropriate."

EPILOGUE

April 1155 Anno Domini, Ellesmere, Salop, England

The babe in my belly seems determined to make me cast up my accounts this morning," Swan lamented. "However, I am just as resolved not to retch over our new King."

Standing beside her in the bailey as they anxiously awaited King Henry's cavalcade, Grace patted her hand reassuringly. "You'll be fine."

"Easy for you to say," Swan retorted. "You haven't been bothered by morning sickness. It's unfair."

Rodrick tightened his arm around her shoulder. "Lean on me. You'll feel better."

She snorted, regretting it instantly as bile surged up her throat. "Tell that to your son."

Bronson chuckled. "You look pale, sister dear, whereas my bride is the picture of health."

She stuck out her tongue, but in her heart she was happy for him. Both his wives had struggled with pregnancy, whereas Grace had blossomed. It boded well for the birth of their child. She'd been heard to express an intuition she was carrying twins. Swan wouldn't be surprised since Grace was a twin and Bronson and Swan's father had a twin sister, their aunt Blythe in Germany.

At the insistent invitation of their jovial hosts in Italy, they'd remained in Rome until the end of February. It had given them a chance to rest, recuperate and spend time together before undertaking the long journey home. Swan liked Italy and would have stayed longer, but King Henry needed loyal young noblemen like Rodrick and Bronson in England.

En route, Swan had been the one indisposed in the mornings. She'd begun to doubt Grace was *enceinte*.

To get her mind off her roiling belly, she thought back over the almost two years since her first visit to Ellesmere. She'd arrived in a state of despair, angry at a social system that had condemned her to life in a nunnery. Now she was Countess-in-waiting of a powerful Earldom, in a kingdom with renewed hope for peace, married to a man she adored and whose child she carried.

She thanked God and his saints that she and her dear brother had both found happiness, despite the best efforts of the Church to censure their love.

She closed her eyes, chuckling at the vision she conjured of Bronson chasing red headed twins around the grounds at Shelfhoc.

Indeed, many things had turned out differently from her expectations. But she'd been right about one thing. Henry Plantagenet was King of England.

FAMILY TREE

Aidan FitzRam — Nolana Kyncade

Gallien de Montbryce — Peridotte de Pontrouge

Suannoch Ascha FitzRam ══ Rodrick de Montbryce

Bronson FitzRam ══ Grace de Montbryce

MARKLAND'S MEDIEVAL WORLD

Cast of Characters

CP=*Conquering Passion*
AMOV=*A Man of Value*
ILDE=*If Love Dares Enough*
PIB=*Passion in the Blood*
DP=*Defiant Passion*
DB=*Dark and Bright*
WTH=*The Winds of the Heavens*
CA=*Carried Away*
STL=*Sweet Taste of Love*
WVP=*Wild Viking Princess*
DOL=*Dance of Love*
DIK=*Dark Irish Knight*
HK=*Haunted Knights*
HC=*Hearts and Crowns*
FT=*Fatal Truths*
SP=*Sinful Passions*

Aediva Melton—Sister of the Saxon heroine of ILDE
Agnes—Norman scullery maid at Domfort Castle ILDE
Agnès—maidservant of Maudine in HK
Agneta Kirkthwaite—English heroine of Danish and Saxon descent in AMOV
Aidan Branton FitzRam—Son of Caedmon and Agneta, twin of Blythe; named for Agneta's brothers slain at Bolton. AMOV, CA; hero of STL
Aiweeda—elderly nun in DIK
Alain Cormant—steward at East Preston HK
Alexandre de Montbryce—Eldest son of Robert and Dorianne. Heir to the title Comte de Montbryce. Born in Caen during his father's incarceration PIB; appears in HC; hero of FT
Alphonse Revandel—father of Letyce HK
Alys—maidservant of Peridotte HC
Amadour de Vignoles—Norman comrade of Caedmon during Crusade; hero of Civitote AMOV; DOL
Andras ap Rhys—Welshman—Friend and comrade of Rhodri ap Owain in CP and DP
Aneurin ap Norweg—Welshman—Friend and comrade of Rhodri ap Owain in CP and DP
Angeline Hugo—Norman peasant, rape victim of Arnulf de Valtesse CP
Anna—Dieter's housekeeper, CA

Annalise de Vymont—Heroine of DB. Niece of the Earl of Chester.
Antoine de Montbryce—Norman hero of ILDE; brother of Rambaud and Hugh
ap Owain—Welsh patronymic—son of Owain
Arnulf de Valtesse—Norman half brother of Mabelle de Montbryce, heroine of CP. Bastard son of Guillaume de Valtesse. Murdered in CP by Simon Hugo
Artus Aubin—Norman steward of Giroux Castle DOL
Ascha (Bronson) Woolgar—Saxon mother of Caedmon; in CP and AMOV
Aurore de Pontrouge—mother of Peridotte HC
Barat Cormant—Norman steward brought to England by the Montbryces for Sussex properties; ILDE; son of Michel, brother of Théo.
Baudoin de Montbryce—Norman born in England; second son of Ram and Mabelle de Montbryce; becomes 2nd Earl of Ellesmere; marries Carys verch Rhodri; appears in CP, AMOV, DP and PIB.
Beathan—Elayne's brother FT
Bemia Melton—Saxon sister of heroine of ILDE
Bernard Chauvelin—Norman soldier at Montbryce Castle PIB
Bernard de Montbryce—Father of Ram, Antoine and Hugh. Dies in 1066 while his sons are fighting in England.
Bernadine de Montbryce—daughter of Antoine and Sybilla
Bernhardt—Dieter's valet, CA
Berthold de Quincy—Hospitaller Knight DOL
Bertrand de Poitou—herald of King Henry HK
Bianca—camp follower and cook from Genoa FT
Bileaud—Norman steward at Domfort Castle ILDE
Blythe Lacey FitzRam—Daughter of Caedmon and Agneta, twin of Aidan. Born in AMOV. Heroine of CA
Bonhomme—Normans; family name of the stewards of Montbryce and Ellesmere.
Bradick Ronan MacLaichlainn—name handed down through generations of descendants of Ronan, hero of DIK; FT
Bravecoeur—Gallien's captain SP
Brémonde—Norman; one of Ram's commanders at Ellesmere CP
Brodeur—Captain of the guard at Montbryce FT
Bronson FitzRam—son of Aidan, hero of SP
Brother Christian—religious name given to Aidan when he enters the monastery STL
Brother Tristan—Cellarer in charge of mead making at Lindisfarne STL
Caedmon Brice (Woolgar) FitzRam—Illegitimate son of Ram de Montbryce and Ascha Woolgar. Appears in CP, PIB, CA & STL; hero of AMOV
Caryl Penarth—Welsh healer; appears in CP and DP

Carys verch Rhodri—Welsh; healer; daughter of Rhodri and wife of Baudoin de Montbryce. Becomes 2nd Countess of Ellesmere. Appears in PIB, DP and DB

Catherine de Montbryce—Daughter of Robert and Dorianne PIB

Claricia Dunkeld—daughter of heroine of FT

Conall MacCathail—steward's son DIK; helps Ronan escape

Cormant—Normans; family name of stewards at Alensonne in CP and at East Preston in ILDE

Coventina Brightmore—Saxon; friend of hero and heroine in AMOV; marries Leofric Deacon

Daegal—Saxon brigand DIK

Dagfinn Alfredsen—Dane; ally of Reider in WVP

Dagfrid—Dane; cousin of Kjartan in WVP

Dareau Revandel—brother of Letyce HK

Dda—Welsh surname of Rhonwen and Myfanwy; CP and DP and DB

de Valtesse—Maiden surname of heroine of CP

Denis de Sancerre—Angevin; son of Sybilla and adopted son of Antoine de Montbryce; dwarf ILDE & PIB; hero of HK

Devlin de Villiers—villain of HC

Devona Melton—Saxon; heroine of ILDE; marries Hugh de Montbryce

Dieter Von Wolfenberg—German hero of CA; marries Blythe FitzRam; appears in WVP

Dominguez—Aragonese; King Alfonso's lieutenant DOL

Dorianne de Giroux—Norman heroine of PIB; marries Robert de Montbryce

Dugald Dunkeld—illegitimate son of King David of Scotland; 1st husband of heroine of FT

Edwin FitzRam—English; brother of Blythe, Aidan and Ragna; son of Caedmon and Agneta STL

Elayne Douenald—Scottish noblemwoman, heroine of FT

Eldwyn—Saxon brigand DIK

Elenor de Giroux—Norman; mother of Dorianne de Giroux; wife of Francois. PIB

Emrys—Cook at llys Powwydd. DB

Emyle Bossuet—Norman commander of mercenaries in Ireland DIK

Enid—Saxon maid of Ascha Woolgar. CP & AMOV

Ermintrude de Calumette—Empress Maud's confidant HC

Étienne Robert de Montbryce—Second son of Baudoin and Carys; DB,STL; HC

Farah—Aragonese; heroine (María Sancha Tarazona) Arabic word meaning 'joy'DOL

Felicité—Gallien's treacherous first wife HC

Fernand Bonhomme—Norman; second generation of his family to be steward of Montbryce Castle. Father of Mathieu and Honore. Married to

Vangeline.

FitzRam—Norman patronymic surname bestowed on Caedmon by Ram. AMOV

Fleurie Mabelle de Montbryce—Daughter of Baudoin & Carys. Her mother almost dies giving birth to her. DB

Florymonde de Montbryce—daughter of Antoine and Sybilla

Fothud MacFintain—villain DIK

Francine Beaujoie—lady-in-waiting to Empress Maud; friend of heroine HC

François de Giroux—Norman father of Dorianne and Pierre PIB; sworn enemy of the Montbryces ILDE

Frederika—Dieter's first wife, CA

Gabriel Duquesne—Norman Captain of Rhoni's bodyguard DIK

Gallien Rambaud de Montbryce—Eldest son of Baudoin and Carys DB, STL; hero of HC; FT; SP

Gareth Bronson—Saxon brother of Ascha Woolgar; takes Ascha to Scotland. CP & AMOV

Gawain Bronson—Saxon nephew of Ascha Woolgar; CP & AMOV

Georges de Giroux—Norman, Crusader. Reappears in DOL

Gervais—Norman soldier; Ram's second in command; CP & DP

Gerwint Isembart de Montbryce (Izzy)—Second son of Hugh and Devona. Named for his grandfather and great grandfather, and the rat catcher, Jubert. Prefers to be called Izzy.PIB; Hero of DOL

Gerwint Melton—ILDE Saxon grandfather of heroine

Gicotte—Norman soldier at Montbryce Castle; PIB

Giroux—Norman surname of the family sworn to avenge Valtesse's cruelty to their ancestor; CP, ILDE & PIB

Giselle—Norman maidservant who accompanies Mabelle to England and becomes chatelaine of Ellesmere; kidnapped with Mabelle; CP

Glain verch Llewelyn—Welsh bonesetter in DB

Godefroy de Cullène—villain of SP

Gorm—villain of WVP; step brother of Reider

Grace Mabelle Carys de Montbryce—daughter of Gallien and Peridotte; twin of Rodrick HC; heroine of SP

Grouchet—Anglo-Norman baron, villain of STL

Guillaume de Terrence—champion supposed to guard heroines in HK

Guillaume de Valtesse—Norman father of Mabelle; his cruelty begins the feud between the Valtesses and the Giroux family; CP

Hélène de Fleury—Norman wife of friend of Montbryce brothers killed at Hastings. CP

Henry Dunkeld—son of heroine of FT

Hugh de Montbryce—Norman-virgin hero of ILDE; brother of Antoine and Ram CP, PIB

Hylda—Christian name of Mabelle's mother, purported to have been strangled by her husband, Mabelle's father.

Hylda Rhonwen de Montbryce (Rhoni)—Daughter of Ram and Mabelle born in captivity in Wales; CP, AMOV; heroine of DIK

Ingram Maknab—Scot; son of Neyll. STL

Isembart Jubert—Rat catcher from Montbryce; instrumental in saving the lives of Hugh and Devona; ILDE

Isolda verch Llewelyn—Welsh healer, heroine of WTH

Ivar Sigurdsen—Dane; captain in WVP

Jacquelle—Rhoni's maid DIK

Jean Venestre—husband of Marguerite de Montbryce FT

Jennet—Northumbrian peasant woman STL

Johann Dieter Marius von Wolfenberg—Dieter's son by his first marriage, CA

Johara—Arabic name given to María Catalina; means 'jewel' DOL

Joleyne—Norman mistress of Ram de Montbryce before he meets Mabelle; CP

Jolly—cook at Shelfhoc SP

Kirkthwaite—Surname of Agneta's family AMOV

Kjartan Eldarsen—Danish; comrade of Reider in WVP

La Cuisinière—Legendary Norman cook at Montbryce Castle; her name simply means 'The Cook' CP

Laurent de Montbryce—son of Robert; brother of Alexandre FT

Laurent Deschamps—military commander at Montbryce in Ram's absence CP

Leofric Deacon—Saxon friend of Caedmon AMOV; badly injured at Alnwick; marries Coventina Brightmore; appears in STL

Letyce Revandel—villainess HK

Lope Velasco—known as The Wolf; looks like a crow; henchman of Vermudo Díaz DOL

Lorcan MacFintain—villain DIK

Lucia—Grace's maidservant SP

Lucien Lallement—brother of heroines of HK

Mabelle de Montbryce—Norman heroine of CP; wife of Ram de Montbryce; Countess of Ellesmere and Comtesse de Montbryce; AMOV, PIB, DP

Mabelle de Valtesse—Maiden name of Mabelle de Montbryce; CP, AMOV, PIB, DP

Magnus Braunschweig—Dieter's comrade, CA

Malraux de Carnac—Breton, villain HK

Marc Lallement—father of heroines of HK

Margit Hansdatter—Dane; villain of WVP

Marguerite de Montbryce—Daughter of Robert and Dorianne; sister of Alexandre FT

María Catalina Tarazon—Aragonese mother of Farah; DOL

María Sancha Tarazona—Farah; DOL

Martin Bonhomme—Norman steward at Ellesmere; son of Mathieu

Mathieu Bonhomme—Son of Fernand; goes to England to be steward at Ellesmere, father of Martin Bonhomme

Mathieu de Montbryce—Son of Antoine and Sybilla. PIB; HK

Maudine Lallement—mother of heroines of HK

Melton Bernard de Montbryce—Eldest son of Hugh and Devona; named for Devona's family name and Hugh's father. PIB

Michel Cormant—Norman steward at Alensonne; father of Barat, Theo and Paul; CP

Micheline—maidservant at Montbryce FT

Montbryce—Noble Norman family at the heart of the Legacy

Morwenna verch Morgan—Welsh; betrothed to Rhodri; villain; mistress of Phillippe de Giroux; CP, DP

Moyra—maidservant DIK

Myfanwy Dda—Welsh mother of Rhonwen; healer; murdered by Phillippe de Giroux; CP, DP

Myfanwy Mabelle verch Rhodri—Eldest child of Rhodri and Rhonwen; becomes a Prioress. DP, DB

Neyll Maknab—villain of STL: stepfather of Nolana Kyncade

Nolana Kyncade—Scot; heroine of STL

Oda—maidservant to Sybilla ILDE

Olve—Danish thrall saves Ragna's life WVP

Orlaith MacLachlainn—Ronan's mother, reputed to be a selkie DIK

Padre Benito—Abbot of San Juan de la Peña DOL

Pascal Bonhomme—steward at Ellesmere; son of Martin. 4th generation to serve the Montbryces HC

Paul Cormant—Norman steward (Alensonne)

Paulina Lallement—heroine HK

Peridotte de Pontrouge—Angevin; marries Gallien de Montbryce; becomes Third Countess of Ellesmere HC; SP

Philippa de Grosmont—haughty lady-in-waiting; spy for Ermintrude HC

Phillippe de Giroux—Norman villain; CP, DP, PIB

Pierre de Fleury—Norman soldier; friend of the Montbryce brothers; killed at Hastings; CP

Pierre de Giroux—Norman villain PIB; brother of heroine, Dorianne

Quique Raúl—bandit leader DOL

Ragna FitzRam—English daughter of Caedmon and Agneta; holy terror; heroine of WVP STL

Rambaud (Ram) de Montbryce—Norman nobleman; hero of Hastings; confidant to William the Conqueror. First Earl of Ellesmere; Comte de Montbryce; eldest son of Bernard de Montbryce, brother to Antoine and Hugh. Hero of CP. AMOV, ILDE, PIB, DIK & DP

Reider Torfinnsen—Danish hero of Wild Viking Princess WVP

Renouf de Maubadon—Norman (Angevin) villain of PIB
Rhodri ap Owain—Welsh villain turned hero. CP, AMOV, DP
Rhonwen Dda—Welsh/Saxon heroine DP. Healer CP
Rhun ap Rhodri—Welsh patriot; son of Rhodri. Twin of Rhydderch.
Redhead. DB, hero of WTH
Rhydderch ap Rhodri—Welsh patriot; son of Rhodri & Rhonwen.
Redhead. Twin of Rhun. DB, hero of WTH
Rhys ap Rhodri—Eldest son of Rhodri; hero of DB. Appears in AMOV
Roar Knutsen—Dane; henchman of Gorm in WVP
Robert de Montbryce—Eldest son of Ram and Mabelle; born in England.
Becomes Comte de Montbryce. CP, AMOV, DP; hero of PIB; DOL;HK
Robert de Pontrouge—father of Peridotte HC
Rodrick Rambaud de Montbryce—son of Gallien and Peridotte; twin of
Grace HC; hero SP
Roget—Malraux's steward in HK
Romain de Montbryce—son of Robert; brother of Alexandre FT
Ronan MacLachlainn—Hero of Dark Irish Knight DIK
Rosamunda Lallement—mute heroine HK
Rosetta Venestre—Alexandre's niece FT
Roussel—Norman;first steward of Shelfhoc appointed by Ram
Simon Hugo—Norman serf at Alensonne who murders Arnulf de Valtesse
to avenge his daughter. CP
Stephen de Montbryce—Gallien's youngest son SP
Stephen Marquand—ILDE Norman neighbour of Meltons; grandfather
of heroines of HK
Suannoch Ascha FitzRam—(Swan) daughter of Aidan; heroine of SP
Sybilla de Taloche—ILDE; heroine; Angevin; widow of Denis de
Sancerre, mother of the dwarf, Denis de Sancerre. Marries Antoine de
Montbryce
Tandine Grisjaune (de Villiers)—lady-in-waiting to Empress Maud;
friend of heroine HC
The Wolf—nickname of Lope Velasco DOL
Théobald Cormant—Norman steward; brother of Barat
Titus—giant accomplice of Godefroy SP
Torfinn—father of Reider in WVP; murdered by Gorm
Torod—Norman villain; thug, henchman of Renouf ILDE
Trésor—Cook at Ellesmere. The French word means 'treasure'.CP
Tristan Bonhomme—Son of Honoré; steward at Montbryce
Tybaut—AMOV; steward at Shelfhoc Hall; Norman; his descendant in SP
Tyrel Venestre—Alexandre's nephew FT
Vangeline Bonhomme—Wife of Fernand; dies in 1066; CP
Vermudo Díaz—Aragonese; villain DOL
Victoire—Cook at Domfort Castle; ILDE
Victor de Cullène—first husband of heroine of SP

Vincent Lallement—brother of heroines of HK
William de Montbryce—Gallien's second son SP
Wilona Melton—Saxon mother of Devona, heroine of ILDE
Winrod Revandel—brother of Letyce HK
Woolgar—Married name of Ascha Bronson, widow of Sir Caedmon
Woolgar, a housecarl of King Harold who died at Hastings; CP, AMOV

Mythical/Religious

Aegir—Norse god of the sea DOL
Alban—first English martyr; the city of St. Albans grew around his shrine
HK;SP
Arianrhod—Celtic goddess
Belatucadros—Welsh god of war and vengeance on enemies HC
Freyja—Norse goddess of fertility;WVP
Hel—Norse word for Hell WVP
Hospitallers—Knights of the Order of St. John DOL
Màni—Norse god of the Moon
Order of Saint John—religious order founded to help the sick DOL
Valhalla—Norse 'heaven'
Vàr—Norse goddess of oaths

Locations

Alnwick—in Northumbria. Site of a battle in 1093 between Roger de
Mowbray, Earl of Northumbria, and Malcolm, King of Scotland. Malcolm
and his son were killed. Agneta rescues Caedmon from the battlefield and
tends his injuries. AMOV
Anjou—Geographic area of France south of Normandy. Its people are
called Angevins. Normans and Angevins were traditional enemies. ILDE;
HC;FT
Aragón—Medieval kingdom in northeastern Spain DOL
Arundel Castle—famous Norman castle in Sussex HK
Aure—river in Bayeux
Badajoz—city in Spain DOL
Bayeux—cathedral city in Normandy where historic tapestry of the
Conquest can be viewed
Beal—coastal village in Northumbria close to Holy Island STL
Belisle Castle—Antoine's castle in Normandie
Bolton—Village in Northumbria; location of Kirkthwaite Hall AMOV;STL

Cantabrian Sea—today known as the Bay of Biscay DOL
Carnac—village in Brittany; site of ancient monoliths HK
Capilla del Relicario—Reliquary chapel, Santiago de Compostella cathedral DOL
Chaca—Aragonese name for the ancient town of Jaca DOL
Civitote—site of the heroic rescue of thousands of crusaders by Caedmon and Amadour AMOV
Coll de Lladrones—Hill of Thieves DOL
Commote—A Welsh area of administration, similar to a county.
Dubh Linn (or Dyflin)—Dublin DIK
East Preston—Sussex village; sight of fictitious manor deeded to Antoine HK
Ellesmere—Location of castle given to Ram as a reward by William the Conqueror. Ram and Mabelle eventually turn a derelict Anglo-Saxon earthwork into a vibrant, thriving castle.
Flandres—medieval county of Flanders HC
Galicia—kingdom/region in the west of Spain DOL
Hastings—Site of a historic battle in 1066 that changed the history of England and Normandy CP
Hrolla-landriht—Hrolla's land; now known as Rollright famous for standing stones in England SP
Husembro—hidden cove on Danish coast WVP
King Stone—monolith at Rollright SP
King's Men—standing stones at Rollright SP
Kingston Gorse—Sussex village, site of fictitious manor deeded to Antoine ILDE;HK
Kirkthwaite Hall—Ancestral home of Agneta's family, destroyed in a raid by the Scots AMOV
Kolbrand's Path—fictitious seat of the MakNab clan on the coast of Scotland STL
Köln—German (Saxon) town, known as Cologne in English; CA
Lande Pourri—A wooded area outside Caen PIB
Le Manio—ancient giant monolith in Carnac HK
León—kingdom/region in central Spain DOL
Lindisfarne Abbey—historic Benedictine monastery on Holy Island STL
Llansanfraid—site of Myfanwy Mabelle's priory DIK
Malmesbury—English town site of many battles SP
Massilia—now known as Marseilles, France DOL
Mont St. Michel—Abbey church of Carolingian origin built on an island off the French coast.
Navarra—kingdom/region of Spain DOL
Northumbria—North east part of England; site of constant conflict between Scots and Normans.
Offa's Dyke—ancient earthwork built by kings of Mercia DIK

Oiasso—today known as Irún, Spain DOL
Ouistreham—village on the French coast HK
Pamplona—city in Spain; capital of Navarra; famous today for the running of the bulls DOL
Palazzo Laterano—medieval residence of the Pope in Rome SP
Poling—Sussex village; sight of fictitious manor deeded to Antoine HK
Prestetone—hamlet on Welsh seacoast (present day Prestatyn) DIK
Pyrenees (Perinés)—mountain range between France and Spain DOL
Rhydycroesau—Welsh border village CP;DP;DIK
Rosko—port in Brittany HK
Ruyton—Location of Shelfhoc Hall
Sagrajas—site of famous medieval battle in Spain between Christians and Moors DOL
St. Winefride's Well—historical place of pilgrimage DIK
San Juan de la Peña—monastery near Jaca; St. John of the Rock DOL
Santa Cristina—priory hospital in the Pyrenees DOL
Santiago de Compostela—Holy site to which thousands of pilgrims still flock; reputed resting places of bones of St. James DOL
Shelfhoc Hall—Ancestral home of the Woolgars in Ruyton, Shropshire, England.
Sord Colmcille—St. Columba's Well, near Dublin DIK
Strand—Danish island principality WVP
Tamworth Castle—historical building, seat of the Marmion family HC
Túr MacLachlainn—Ronan's estate in Ireland DIK
Via Francigena—medieval pilgrimage route from Canterbury to Rome SP
Wallingford—strategic town on the River Thames CP; SP
Whispering Knights—standing stones at Rollright SP
Ynys Môn—Holy Island, Wales DIK

Animals

Apollo—Izzy de Montbryce's horse DOL
Ariel—Rhodri's Welsh pony DP
Becca—hovawart dog at Shelfhoc SP
Bendik—hovawart dog at Shelfhoc SP
Boden—English mastiff in ILDE
Brevis—Denis' horse HK
Brigantia—English mastiff in ILDE
Brindis—Ram de Montbryce's horse in CP
Cob—Swan's palfrey SP
Espérance—Cat who brings solace to Robert during his imprisonment. The word means 'hope'. PIB;FT

Faol—Irish wolfhound; hero of FT
Fortis—Black stallion; Ram's favourite mount; saves his life at Hastings CP
Fortissima—Rhoni's mare, descended from Fortis DIK
Löwe—Dieter's Rottweiler, CA
Lux—Rosamunda's palfrey HK
Nox—Adam's black stallion HK
Regis—Antoine's stallion ILDE
Schnell—Dieter's greyhound, CA
Sibell—Mabelle's mare in CP
Souflette—donkey in HK
Thor—alaunt gentil hound belonging to Ragna FitzRam, named after Norse god of thunder WVP
Topaz—kitten HK
Velox—Hugh's stallion in ILDE
Vormund—Hovawart breed dog; saves Dieter's life CA
Wyvern—Caedmon's horse; saves his life at Alnwick. AMOV

Historical figures

Adelaide—daughter of Henry I; married Holy Roman Emperor and later Geoffrey of Anjou; became known as Matilda, then Maud.
Alfonso Sánchez—King of Aragón DOL
al-Kindi—born in Basra; medieval Islamic physician; DOL
Álvar Fáñez—Spanish hero of the Reconquista, cousin of El Cid
Boadicea—warrior queen in ancient Briton; also Boudicca HK
Clito—see William Clito
Curthose—see Robert Curthose
Earl of Chester—Hugh d'Avranches. Historical figure. Known by the Welsh as Hugh Vras (the Fat) PIB, DIK
Edgar the Aetheling—Saxon; Claimant to throne of England taken by William the Conqueror. Aetheling is a Saxon term for "next in line"; appears in CP and AMOV
El Batallador—nickname given to King Alfonso, means "The Battler" earned because he fought the Moors DOL
El Cid—Spanish hero of the Reconquista DOL
Empress Maud (see Adelaide)
Felicia de Roucy—mother of King Alfonso of Aragón DOL
Frangipane—influential family in medieval Rome AMOV; SP
Fulk—Count of Anjou; father of Geoffrey HC
Geoffrey of Anjou (the Handsome)—Angevin betrothed to Maud, Henry's daughter.HC; FT
Heinrich—Holy Roman Emperor; CA

Henry Beaumont—Earl of Warwick; DB
Iftikhar ad-Daula—governor of Jerusalem DOL
King David of Scotland(Dabíd mac Choluim)—FT
King Harald Hardråda of Norway—pretender to the English throne; killed by King Harold's army at Stamford Bridge; CP
King Harold II of England—Saxon brother-in-law of Edward the Confessor. Claimed the throne on Edward's death; slain at Hastings by the Conqueror's army; CP
King Henry I—Norman king of England; son of William the Conqueror; known as Henry Beauclerc; succeeded his brother William Rufus on the throne. PIB;HK;HC
King Henry II—Henry FitzEmpress Plantagenet SP
King Malcolm Canmore of Scotland—CP & AMOV
King William I of England—William the Conqueror, Duke of Normandie. CP, ILDE
King William Rufus—William II of England; son of the Conqueror; AMOV;
Lothar von Süpplingenburg—Saxon Duke who became Holy Roman Emperor CA
Margaret, Queen of Scotland (Saint Margaret)—AMOV, CP; known for her piety; Saxon; second wife of King Malcolm Canmore; sister of Edgar Aetheling.
Matilda (see Adelaide)
Nicolas Breakspear—Pope Adrian IV; only Englishman ever to become Pope; SP
Raymond de St. Gilles—Raymond of Toulouse; Crusader who took Jerusalem in 1099 DOL
Robert Curthose—Son of William the Conqueror; became Duke of Normandie on his father's death; coveted his brother Henry's throne; captured by Henry at Tinchebray and imprisoned for the remainder of his life. PIB
Robert de Bellême—son of Roger de Montgomery
Robert of Leicester—English earl SP
Roger de Montgomery—cousin of the Conqueror, notorious for his cruelty HK
Sancho Ramírez—king of Aragón and Navarra DOL
Sigeric—Archbishop of Canterbury who established the Via Francigena pilgrimage route SP
Stephen of Blois—grandson of the Conqueror; became king after Henry I; HC; FT;SP
Theobald du Bec—Archbishop of Canterbury SP
Waleran—twin brother of Robert of Leicester SP
William Adelin—Crown Prince of England, son of Henry I, drowned in 1120 STL; HC

William Clito—son of Robert Curthose, Duke of Normandy; killed at Aalst; HC
Yusuf ibn Tashfin—Arabic warrior DOL

Other

Cairdis—Ronan's sword, a gift from Rhodri, means Friendship DIK
Curia regis—Latin for King's Court ILDE
Encaustum—ink
La Blanche Nef—Infamous White Ship that sank in 1120 taking with it hundreds of sons and daughters of the English nobility, including the Crown Prince, William, son of Henry I STL
Les oreillons—mumps HK
Llys (plural Llysoed)—A building that served as a royal court for a commote in Wales. Stone castles were virtually unknown in England and Wales before the Conquest
Moors—peoples of Arabic origin who conquered most of Spain in medieval times DOL
Motte—raised central bastion of a Norman castle
Nakers—medieval drums -set of two worn by drummer
Neuadd—The communal great hall in Welsh buildings
Peridot—a greenish gemstone HC
Rebec—medieval stringed instrument
Reconquista—Reconquest of Spain from the Moors DOL
Shawm—medieval wind instrument
White Ship—see La Blanche Nef

LEXICON

Ab L. by
Abaya -Arabic garment
Abbesse Fr. Abbess
A bientôt Fr. See you soon
Adelante Sp. Onwards
A demain Fr. Until tomorrow
Adieu Fr. Goodbye
Af Odin! D. By Odin!
Afon Dyfrdwy W. River Dee
Ahora Sp. Now
Aingeal IG Angel
Alaunt gentil Fr. Breed of hound
À l'Irelande! Fr. To Ireland!
Allons-y! Fr. Let's go!
Alto! Sp. Stop!
Amici I. friends
Amour Fr. Love
Ange Fr. Angel
Anoche Sp. Last night
Ap (or Ab) W. Son of
Arrête Fr. Stop!
Arthrite Fr. Arthritis
Auf Weidersehen G. Goodbye
Au revoir Fr. Goodbye
Au secours! Fr. help!

Aux armes! Fr. To arms!
Ave Maria, gratia plena L. Hail Mary, full of grace
Barm OE. Yeast
Basta Sp. Enough!
Bella I. Beautiful one
Bébé Fr. Baby
Benedicat vos omnipotens Deus L. Blessed be Almighty God
Benedicti L. Blessed
Bien Fr. Good
Bienvenidos Sp. Welcome
Bienvenu(e) Fr. Welcome
Bliaut Fr. Medieval long sleeved dress
Brychan W. Woven blanket
Cairdis IG Friendship
Camilla Sp. Litter, stretcher
Camino Sp. Road, way
Céard sa diabhal IG What the devil!
Ceilliau W. Testicles,
C'est moi Fr. It's me.
Chansons courtoises Fr. Courtly love songs

Cisoires Fr. scissors

Codex L. journal

Cog -type of ship

Colonus, pl. Coloni L. Bondservants, later known as serfs

Commote W. area of administration in Wales

Comte Fr. Count

Comtesse Fr. Countess

Corre! Sp. Run!

Couilles Fr. Testicles

Críost IG Christ!

Croeso-i W. Welcome

Cuirass(e) Fr. Breastplate armour

Currach IG coracle

Cú G.Dog

Cymru W. Wales

Cymraeg W. Welsh language

Da Dad, father

Dadaidh S. Daddy

Dañjer! Breton word for danger

Demesne Fr. Estate

Demoiselle Fr. Miss, unmarried woman

De rien Fr. You are welcome

Derrière Fr. Bottom, backside

Dewch yn W. Come in

Dia IG God!

Dieu Fr. God

Dios Sp. God

Ddoe W. Yesterday

Dormitorio Sp. Dormitory

Dors bien Fr. Sleep well

Draugr D. Revenant, lost soul

Droit de seigneur Fr. right of a nobleman to take a virgin before her husband on their wedding night

Dros Cymru W. For Wales

Duw W. God

Duwiau W. Gods!

Dwale OE medieval drug for pain

Eke OE. Extra chamber added to the bottom of a beehive

El Diablo Sp. The Devil

Enceinte Fr. Pregnant

Enchanté Fr. Enchanted; delighted

Enfant Fr. Child. Mes enfants=my children

En route Fr. On the way

Entrez! Fr. Come in!

Epiphany Revelation; showing;

Esches Fr. Chess

Et L. And

Exactement Fr. Exactly

Excusez-moi Fr. Excuse me, I am sorry

Fág an bealach! IG Clear the way

Faol G. Wolf

Fardeles Sp. Pigs' livers

Fils Fr. Son

Fortæl mig D. Tell me

Foutaise Fr. Shit

Fromage cremeux Fr. Cream cheese

Fy Nuw W. My God

Gaeilge Gaelic

Garderobe Fr. Latrines, privy

Ghiniúna IG male genitalia

Godemite OE. Saxon expletive, God Almighty

God hund D. Good dog

Godisgood OE. Yeast

Go hÉirinn IG To Ireland!
Gottes segen G. Godspeed
Gott sei Dank G. Thanks be to God
Gracias Sp. Thank you
Gräfin G. Countess
Grandmaman Fr. Grandma
Grandpère—Fr. Grandfather
Gut! G. Good!
Hackle OE. Conical shaped protection for beehives
Hallowmas Triduum Three day celebration of Hallowe'en, All Saints' & All Souls'
Hermano Sp. Brother
Hore OE whore
Ich bin es G. It's me.
Ich liebe dich G. I love you
Il Papa I. Pope
Ja G. Yes
Jardin Fr. Garden
Je m'excuse Fr. I am sorry
Je t'aime Fr. I love you
Je vous demande pardonne Fr. I beg your forgiveness
Jongleur Fr. Minstrel, juggler, medieval entertainer
Kitgut OE catgut
Kommen G. Come!
Knarr D. Merchant ship used by Vikings
Labhandair IG Lavender
Laks D. Smoked salmon
Lamellar Armour made of leather plates
Là Fr. There
Le Bon Dieu Fr. The good Lord
Lentement Fr. Slowly
Le roi est mort Fr. The king is dead

Léine S. Shirt worn by men and women (Gaelic)
Liebling G. Sweetheart, darling
Livre Fr. Old French currency unit
Lladrones Sp. Thieves
Llys W. (plural Llysoed) A building that served as a royal court for a commote in Wales.
Ma chère Fr. My dear
Majestad Sp. Majesty
Majesté Fr. Majesty
Mal de mer Fr. seasickness
Mamá Sp. Mother (affectionate)
Maman Fr. Mother (affectionate)
Mantilla Sp. Lacy head covering
Ma petite Fr. My little one
Mea culpa L. My fault; I take the blame
Méchant Fr. Naughty
Meine damen und herren G. Ladies and gentlemen
Mein Gott G. My God!
Mein Schatz G. My darling, my sweetheart
Meine Tochter G. My daughter
Merci Fr. Thank you
Merde Fr. Swear word; shit;crap;damn it
Mère Fr. Mother
Meth OE. ordinary mead
Metheglin OE. Spiced mead (for nobility)
Mi amor Sp. My love
Mignonne Fr. Little one
Milagro Sp. Miracle
Milord Fr. My lord

Minnesinger G. Minstrel

Misericord L. Chamber where monks received their punishment for misdeeds

Mistiltan OE mistletoe

Mo croí IG My heart

Mo mhac S. My son

Mo nighean S. My daughter

Mon capitaine a tombé Fr. My captain has fallen

Mon petit Fr. little one

Mon seigneur Fr. My lord

Mo stór IG my darling

Motte Fr. Raised part of early Norman fortifications

Muette Fr. Feminine version of muet=mute

Nein G. No

Nej D. No

Noblesse Fr. Nobility

Oes W. Yes

Oncle Fr. Uncle

Oreillons Fr. Mumps

Oubliette Fr. a small cell where prisoners were forgotten Fr. Oublier=to forget

Oui Fr. Yes

Pacharán Sp. Sloe liqueur

Padre I. Priest

Parbleu Fr. Good heavens

Parler Fr. To speak, discuss

Pauvre Fr. Poor

Pax L. Peace

Perdóname Sp. Forgive me

Père Fr. Father

Peregrinati L. Pilgrims

Petit baiser Fr. a little kiss

Phoques Fr. Seals

Pik D. Shaft, manhood

Plantagenista L. Broom plant

Playd S. Woven garment, not tartan (came much later); often brown

Potel OE medieval stoppered container

Porquería Sp. Filth

Por supuesto Sp. Of course

Prie-Dieu Fr. Kneeler, prayer stool

Que diable! Fr. What the devil!

Rebec medieval stringed instrument

Refugio Sp. Place of refuge, shelter

Regarde Fr. Look!

Reina Madre Sp. Queen Mother

Rex L. King

Rien Fr. Nothing

Rundlet OE. small barrel or cask

Rute G. Shaft, manhood

Rwy'n Cymraes W. I am a Welshwoman

Rwy'n dy garu di W. I love you

Salaud Fr. Bastard

Schwarze ritter G. Black Knight

Sea IG You are right

Seigneur Fr. Lord

Selkie Seal that has become human

Seneschal Fr. Senior officer, seneschal

Shamshir -curved Arabic sword

Sieg G. Victory

S'il te plaît Fr. If you please

Siwrne dda W. Good journey

Sí Sp. Yes

Sjaund D. Ritualistic funeral ale

in Norse inheritance traditions

Skep OE. Man made beehive made of straw

Soeur Fr. Sister

Soule Fr. Medieval game involving kicking and hitting balls

Soyez les bienvenues Fr. Welcome, ladies

Sølje D. Traditional Norse silver brooch

Stridsøkse D. battle axe

Sunt L. They are

Sûrement Fr. surely.

Tá grá agam duit IG I love you

Tais-toi Fr. Be quiet, silence.

Tante Fr. Aunt

Tant pis! Fr. Too bad

Tarse OE. Male genitals

Tendresse Fr. Tenderness; "soft spot"

Tiarna IG Lord

Trouzes breeches, trousers

Truite Fr. Trout

Turaid S. Tower (Gaelic)

Tutto bene I. All is well

Ty bach W. Latrines

Uisce beatha IG whiskey

Verch W. Daughter of

Vite Fr. Quickly

Vive la reine Fr. Long live the Queen

Vous parlez francais? Fr. Do you speak French?

Walhaz- derogatory Saxon term meaning foreign; the word Welsh derived from it

Willkommen G. Welcome

Windlass hoisting mechanism

with a crank handle, e.g. to hoist a bucket from a well

Yr Arglwydd W. My lord

Zut Fr. Expletive. Darn it.

About the Author

I was born and educated in England, but I've lived most of my life in Canada. I was an educator for 25 years. It was a rewarding career, financially, spiritually and emotionally.

After that I worked with my husband in the management of his businesses. He's a born entrepreneur who likes to boast he's never had a job!

My final "career" was as Director of Administration of a global disaster relief organization.

Anyway, not content to fade away into retirement gracefully, I embarked upon writing a romance, essentially for my own satisfaction. I chose the medieval period mainly because that genre of historical romance is one I enjoy reading.

I have a keen interest in genealogy. This hobby has had a tremendous influence on my stories. My medieval romances are about family honor, ancestry, and roots. As an amateur genealogist, I cherished a dream (as do many) of tracing my own English roots back to the Norman Conquest—an impossibility since I am not descended from nobility! So I made up a family and my stories follow its members through successive generations.

One of the things I enjoy most about writing historical romance is the in-depth research necessary to provide readers with an authentic medieval experience. I based the plot of my first novel, *Conquering Passion*, on an incident that actually happened to a Norman noblewoman.

I hope you come to know and love my Montbryce family as passionately as I do.

I would like to acknowledge the invaluable assistance of my critique partners, Sylvia Blenkin, Reggi Allder, Jacquie Biggar and Helena Korin. Thank you for your help in polishing this manuscript.

Facebook~Anna Markland Novels
Twitter @annamarkland
www.annamarkland.com

If only my heroes and heroines had revealed their stories to me in chronological order, it would have made life much easier for you! If you prefer to read sagas in chronological order, here's a handy list.

Conquering Passion—Ram and Mabelle, Rhodri and Rhonwen
If Love Dares Enough—Hugh and Devona, Antoine and Sybilla
Defiant Passion-Rhodri and Rhonwen
A Man of Value—Caedmon and Agneta
Dark Irish Knight—Ronan and Rhoni
Haunted Knights—Adam and Rosamunda, Denis and Paulina
Passion in the Blood—Robert and Dorianne, Baudoin and Carys
Dark and Bright—Rhys and Annalise
The Winds of the Heavens—Rhun and Glain, Rhydderch and Isolda
Dance of Love—Izzy and Farah
Carried Away—Blythe and Dieter
Sweet Taste of Love—Aidan and Nolana
Wild Viking Princess—Ragna and Reider
Hearts and Crowns—Gallien and Peridotte
Fatal Truths—Alexandre and Elayne
Sinful Passions—Rodrick and Swan, Bronson and Grace

If you like stories with medieval breeds of dogs, you'll enjoy **If Love Dares Enough, Carried Away, Fatal Truths** and **Wild Viking Princess**. If you have a soft spot for cats, read **Passion in the Blood** and **Haunted Knights**.

Looking for historical fiction centred on a certain region?
English History—all books
Norman French History—all books
Crusades—**A Man of Value**
Welsh History—**Conquering Passion, Defiant Passion, Dark and Bright, The Winds of the Heavens**
Scottish History—**Conquering Passion, A Man of Value, Sweet Taste of Love**
European History (Holy Roman Empire)—**Carried Away**
Danish History—**Wild Viking Princess**
Spanish History—**Dance of Love**
Ireland—**Dark Irish Knight**

If you like to read about historical characters:
William the Conqueror—**Conquering Passion, If Love Dares Enough, Defiant Passion**

William Rufus—**A Man of Value**
Robert Curthose, Duke of Normandy—**Passion in the Blood**
Henry I of England—**Passion in the Blood, Sweet Taste of Love, Haunted Knights**
Heinrich V, Holy Roman Emperor—**Carried Away**
Vikings—**Wild Viking Princess**
Kings of Aragon (Spain)—**Dance of Love**
The Anarchy (England) Stephen vs. Maud—**Hearts and Crowns, Fatal Truths, Sinful Passions**

www.ingramcontent.com/pod-product-compliance
Lightning Source LLC
Chambersburg PA
CBHW031330170626
46807CB00002B/632